COWBOY SURPRISE

THE TRIPLE C RANCH SERIES
BOOK TWO

JILL DOWNEY

Cowboy Surprise

The Triple C Ranch Series

Book 2

by
Jill Downey

Published by Jill Downey

Interior book design by Julie Hopkins
Editor April Bennett @ TheEditingSoprano.com

BOOKS BY JILL DOWNEY

The Heartland Series:

More Than A Boss

More Than A Memory

More Than A Fling

The Carolina Series:

Seduced by a Billionaire

Secret Billionaire

Playboy Billionaire

A Billionaire's Christmas

The Triple C Series

Cowboy Magic

Cowboy Surprise

DEDICATION

Thank you Sandy for your endless support!

PROLOGUE

TWENTY YEARS AGO

Nicole was startled awake by scratching at the door of her motel room that she'd rented for the month. Terror gripped her for an instant, almost swallowing her whole until she felt the breath of her sleeping child tickling her neck. Survival instinct kicked in and the adrenalin propelled her into action. She gently jiggled her daughter, rousing her before pressing her finger to her lips. The security light from the parking lot slipped through a gap in the curtains, allowing a sliver of light to penetrate an otherwise dark room. *Just enough.*

"Shh," she whispered quietly. "Mama needs you to be her brave girl. Can you do that for me?"

Her child stared up at her wide-eyed, so trusting that Nicole thought her heart would explode right then and there. *My baby*. She forced a calm into her voice and said softly into the tiny shell-like ear, "No talking, okay? Don't make a sound. Remember how we play hide-and-seek?"

She nodded.

"Mama needs you to hide real quiet. You might hear talking and loud voices but don't come out no matter what. Not for anyone. Not until you hear the safe word. Promise me?" The child nodded again. Nicole held up her little finger. "Pinky swear?" The sleepy child's lips tilted up and she hooked her small chubby finger through Nicole's.

Nicole crawled out of bed, cradling the small bundle against her trembling body. She opened the closet door and set her down long enough to pull dirty clothes out of the tall hamper. She stood on her tip-toes, reaching for the princess backpack that she'd already prepared, just in case they needed to get away quickly.

She choked back a sob. When she'd packed it, she prayed they'd never need it. She glanced nervously over her shoulder; the chain on the flimsy motel door wouldn't be any match against a hard kick. She looked down at her daughter, wanting to scoop her up and never let go. Except that wasn't an option. So sweet...so innocent standing there in her Dora the Explorer jammies. "Baby, hold out your arms for me. Let's put this backpack on. That's a good girl. You're going to hide here in this hamper." Her daughter's lips quivered, her eyes enormous pools of green in her tiny face.

Nicole kicked herself because she knew she was exuding fear, her eyes stinging with tears, her voice shaking. "Here's Benny. You hold on tight to him." She wrapped her daughter's arms around the favorite stuffed dog she stubbornly insisted on taking everywhere. She couldn't sleep unless the tattered friend was tucked in her chubby arms with her thumb in her mouth.

"Remember to keep this backpack on no matter what, okay? And you don't get out for nobody. Not until someone says the magic word. Remember the magic word?"

Again, she nodded.

"Whisper to Mama what that is."

"Wodeo?" she whispered.

"That's right baby. If they say rodeo, you know it's your safe person." She picked her up and lifted her into the hamper then leaned down to kiss her cheek. "Mama loves you baby girl. You be brave for me." She covered her with some clothes before putting the lid back on, then closed the closet door.

By now they'd managed to pick the lock and the door was cracked as far as the chain allowed. The only thing between them and the bad guys was the flimsy security chain. She jumped back in bed and huddled beneath the covers pretending to be asleep. Cupping her hand over the phone to hide the glow from her flip phone, she punched in the number engraved in her memory. Nicole urgently whispered her location along with Cassie's safe word to her handler before the door splintered.

The overhead light was flipped on and Nicole slipped her phone between the wall and the mattress and waited. Suddenly the covers were ripped away and she stared up at two hulking goons looming over her. They both sported close-shaved heads and looked like they could be linebackers for the NFL. She sat up, feigning confusion and willed herself to calm, knowing this had to be the best performance of her life.

A menacing voice, smooth as silk, said, "Hello Nicky."

Fear slipped down her spine and she shivered. Her voice was a strangled whisper. "What do you want with me?"

The larger of the two men with glittering black eyes growled, "Cut the bullshit Ms. Valentine. You know exactly why we're here. Mr. Petrov misses you and understandably wants what's his. You've been a very bad girl. Time for you to come home, back where you belong."

Her body trembled so hard that her teeth chattered as she replied. "He can't keep me against my will."

"We both know that he can and will do anything he wants. Who's gonna stop him? You belong to him."

The second guy snickered.

In a low growl, he demanded, "Where's the fucking kid?"

This snapped her out of terror and into survival mode; strangely enough the mention of her baby centered her. "I left her with a friend."

He smirked, looking like a cat who had cornered its prey. "A friend, yeah right. You don't have any friends." His dead eyes studied her. "Where is she?" He grabbed her upper arm, squeezing her flesh hard as he yanked her up from the bed. "Roy, look for the kid."

Nicole heard the blessed sound of sirens in the distance and almost collapsed with relief. The men exchanged glances, then the one who had her arm in a death grip nodded. He pulled her roughly towards him sticking his face so close to hers that she could smell his rancid breath. "You're going to pay for this bitch. Let's get outta here, Roy. No time to look for the kid."

The cool air hit Nicole's bare skin, left exposed by her short lightweight nightgown. The gravel dug painfully into her bare feet as she was hauled across the parking lot and shoved into a cargo van. They pulled out as the police roared by. Only then did Nicole breathe a sigh of relief.

1

PRESENT

Cassie Morgan tucked her thick dark hair behind her ears and adjusted her stirrups, taking a deep calming breath. Silas looked up and clapped her on the thigh. "Don't ya worry Tater, I reckon this is yours for the takin'," he said.

Cassie glanced down from her mount at her grandfather Silas's weathered face, lined from hard living and baking in the sun. Seeing the worry in his faded silver eyes erased her own pre-performance jitters and she jumped into protective mode to reassure him.

"Gramps, you know Kiss and I are going to whip their asses." She grinned confidently, patting her chestnut mare, her wide gleaming smile a study in charm. "I got my lucky boots on; how could we go wrong?"

Silas's shoulders relaxed and his lips tugged up at the corners. "You and them old boots. You'd still be wearin' em if the soles was wore through."

"They'll be bringing it home today. We're going for the barrel racing jackpot, nothin' less," she said.

"Boots or no boots, Kiss is in tiptop shape. She hain't no crowbait, prit near perfect that mare is," Silas said. "Tween the two of ya, hain't no one in this competition that can beat ya."

Cassie winked. "Aww, ya think you might be a tad biased?"

"Nope. I call 'em as I see 'em. Anyhoo, y'already won the jackpot when ya landed that big endorsement. The rodeo's darlin' that's what ya are." Silas grinned, his pride evident.

"I'd give that accolade to Kiss. See how pretty she looks with her new turquoise reins? They match the plaid in my shirt." Cassie glanced down and straightened her shirt collar before adjusting the large silver belt buckle settled low on her belly, securing her Wrangler jeans. Lastly, she tamped down her white cowboy hat so it wouldn't fly off during her race.

Silas stepped aside as she prepared to enter the huge indoor arena. The three barrels were set up in a cloverleaf pattern. Running the course in the fastest time not only took skill, but a great horse that was agile, strong and intelligent as well. The rider needed the same. She heard the announcer introduce her and focused her thoughts. Huffing out a breath, she whispered, "Kiss, it's you and me girl. Let's do this."

They entered the arena through the alley at top speed, greeted by an enthusiastic crowd of fans in the bleachers cheering them on. Cassie leaned forward, her athletic body at one with her mare, her long dark hair flying behind her. The timer began when they crossed the starting line and Cassie felt it in her bones...They were in the zone today and they were going to win.

Adrenalin coursed through her as she felt the power of her horse under her seat. There was no thought now, only sensation. Speed, agility, and hugging the barrels, as they liked to say. They circled the first barrel, leaning in so far her boot was mere inches from the ground. As she approached the second barrel it was imperative that she timed the lead change perfectly. *Yes! Number three coming up.* The crowd and noise had completely faded from Cassie's awareness. The hooves pounded the ground, matching her beating heart as they made the third loop and headed for the finish line. Crossing, Cassie knew they had nailed it and she whooped with joy.

Only now did she hear all the clamoring from the crowd. They were chanting 'Kiss and Cass, Kiss and Cass.' She rode over to Silas, who had left his observation perch to wait for her. He was gesturing enthusiastically in an animated conversation with a cowboy whose back was to her. Even so, she knew exactly who it was. Broad shoulders tapering down to slim hips, coal black hair peeking out from under his cowboy hat, perfect butt...Yet today, even the arrogant Elijah Cane couldn't steal her joy.

Silas pumped both thumbs in the air when she rode up. "Tater! You did it!"

Elijah's piercing hazel eyes, with striking shards of amber, caught her attention as she stopped next to them. His gaze raked across her face, then traveled slowly down her body and back up again. "Congratula-

6

:r a short pause, he drawled out her nick-
ιer."

catching her breath, she retorted, "The name's
:, but thanks."

'You hugged them barrels like they was magnets," ˎ ɩlas crowed, his gray eyes sparkling with pride.

Cassie leaned down and patted Kiss on the neck. "It was Kiss that did all the work."

"Aww now, don't be modest, doesn't suit you. It takes an athlete in top shape to do what you just did. And I'd say you're in mighty fine shape," Eli said, flashing a wicked grin.

She straightened. Ignoring the comment, Cassie tilted her head and squinted. "When do you ride?"

"Not till this afternoon. Why? Ya gonna come and cheer me on?" His eyes crinkled at the corners when he smiled. "How about if I win, you buy me a drink, if you win, I buy you two. We can celebrate together."

She flipped her long thick hair over her shoulder and shrugged. "I'll pass. Besides, I might not be celebrating. How do you know I won't be in my trailer crying my eyes out?"

He shook his head. "Not a chance."

Her eyes narrowed suspiciously. "Thanks for the vote of confidence, but why you being so nice all of a sudden? I thought you were a charter member of the Charmaine Fan Club," she said, referring to her biggest rival.

His eyes widened innocently. "Can't I be a fan of both? Besides, when haven't I been nice to you? I didn't know you even knew I existed, let alone that you were hankering for my attention." He winked.

Cassie snorted. "Oh brother."

"I'm partial to beautiful women and you definitely fall under that category."

She rolled her eyes. "Save it for Charmaine."

He slung an arm over the fence rail and hooked his heel on the bottom rung. "Membership to my personal fan club is free. Would you like to join?"

She ignored the flutter of her pulse. She wasn't about to let this silver-tongued cowboy get under her skin. He was way too good-looking for his own good. He had a reputation around the rodeo circuit as a player and she'd always made a point of keeping a wide berth between them. As if on cue, a gorgeous blonde in western attire approached and slipped her hand through the crook of Eli's elbow, looking up at him through her lashes. "Are you ready to get that lunch that you promised me?" she asked.

Cassie looked heavenward holding back a sneer. Not Charmaine, but another buckle bunny. The rodeo was full of groupies whose biggest thrill was to follow the cowboys around like they were God or something. No pride what...so...ever.

"Sugar, I was born ready."

Cassie snorted and nudged Kiss forward. Looking at Silas she said, "Gramps, I'm going to hose Kiss down. I'll meet you at the barn." Without a backward glance, she clicked her tongue and trotted off.

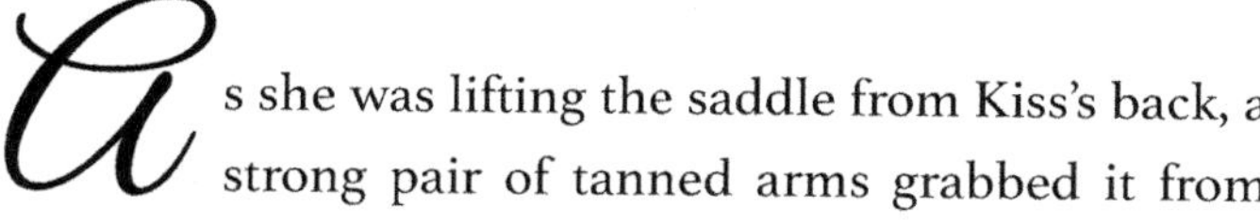

As she was lifting the saddle from Kiss's back, a strong pair of tanned arms grabbed it from her. Cassie glanced up. "Oh, hi Nash. Thanks. Did ya catch our race?"

"What do you think? Course I watched. Nobody's gonna beat your time."

"Hope you're right about that."

"I heard there's going to be a big party at The Dew Drop Inn tonight. Karaoke, dancing and lots of cold beer."

"Sounds good to me," Cassie replied.

"Maybe I can coax ya to sing a song."

Cassie laughed. "That will depend entirely upon how drunk I get."

His dark blue eyes sparkled. "Sure it does. Last time I had to practically haul ya off the stage."

Cassie looked up, grinning sheepishly. "It was the tequila."

He flashed his pearly whites, which made most women drool. She and Nash Gentry were best friends and had been since she was four. The rodeo circuit had been the backdrop of their childhood. They'd learned everything there was to know about horses, riding and roping together. They'd never been bored, finding plenty of ways to keep themselves entertained, getting into loads of mischief along the way. Nash, being two years older, had taken on the role of her protector from the git-go and that had never changed. She'd have to admit, her daredevil nature had landed them both in hot water more times than she could shake a stick at, but he'd always followed along. He never could say no to her.

She studied him as he deftly used the soft brush on Kiss, his movements natural and practiced having spent a lifetime tending to horses. He really was a beautiful man. He wore his blond curls a bit long and they fell across his eyes as he leaned down. Tall, with cobalt blue eyes that were warm and kind, he was a rodeo favorite with the women.

He competed in calf roping and was damn good at it. Even with the adoring females throwing themselves at him, he never seemed to get a big head. Partly because he was a little shy, except with her. She probably took him for granted, but she counted his friendship as one of her biggest blessings. Too bad she couldn't see him as anything but a friend, since he was the perfect guy. A sudden thought of Elijah Cane flashed across her vision...*too bad he was so full of himself.*

She sighed. "Let's get Kiss cooled down and head back to the arena. I don't want to miss Charmaine's ride." Charmaine was the only rider that could beat today's time.

"Sounds like a plan."

They finished taking care of Kiss and put her back in the stall, then headed to watch the rest of the barrel races.

2

Eli looked around as he pushed through the bar entrance. Seemed like half of the rodeo competitors were at the watering hole, either celebrating or drowning their sorrows. The bar was a noisy cacophony of excited voices and loud music. He'd won his bronco riding competition handily on a horse named Lonestar and was high from his win.

He glanced casually around the dimly lit dive, trying not to be Captain Obvious as he searched for one woman in particular. His boots stuck to the scarred wooden floors, slightly sticky in places from spilt beer. The air smelled musty and sour, with an overlay of cheap cloying perfume. *There she is. Cassie Morgan.* Damn but if she wasn't a sight for sore eyes. Built like every guy's fantasy...soft swell of rounded breasts, slim hips, great ass and long legs to die for.

His lips twisted. Only problem was her mouth didn't match that feminine package. She had a temperament that'd try a saint. She was a handful and notorious for her sharp tongue and fiery temper. A man would have to be half crazy to have a go with her. Even so, he felt like there were a thousand moths beating their wings inside his chest and she was the flame.

He watched several guys competing for her attention, one of which decided at that moment to pick her up and throw Cassie over his shoulder and carry her to the small stage at the back of the bar.

Her dark hair swung in thick waves as she hung upside down, her perfect butt in cutoff shorts high in the air, cowboy boots dangling. He could hear her shrieks and laughter cut through the bar noise. He watched as her ever present sidekick, Nash Gentry, plunked her down on the stage. Looking embarrassed, she laughingly waved her hands while shaking her head emphatically.

Nash said something to the DJ, who then grabbed a microphone and handed it to Cassie. She playfully glared at Nash, while reluctantly reaching for the mic. Cassie closed her eyes and stood stock still, as if to gather her courage. Cassie sang the first couple of lines, and the whole house stilled. All the chatter ceased as the smooth-as-whiskey voice seduced the entire audience. Eli's gut clenched. It was a song he'd heard a time or two, and thought it might be a Miranda Lambert tune, some words about a house that had built her.

He was mesmerized, couldn't take his eyes off of Cassie. He swallowed...hard. *Holy mother of God!* The top buttons of her sleeveless blouse were undone, offering subtle glimpses of the gentle swell of her breasts as she moved. She was so beautiful.

He was so fucking drawn to her, despite—no, if he were being completely honest with himself—*because* of being on the receiving end of her glowering emerald green eyes spitting fire. *Call me crazy.* But right about now, she sounded like an angel. A broken angel at that. There was no mistaking the emotion behind each note she sang. A song, far as he could tell, that was about childhood memories and searching for something. He squinted, suddenly realizing he knew nothing personal about Cassie Morgan. Her singing like that, well, it made him want to know a whole lot more.

He grabbed his beer and made his way to the crowded dance floor. He jostled through the swaying bodies to the front and stood right in front of Cassie. A jolt went through him when she met his gaze. For a long moment their eyes locked. *Shit!* He could swear he saw tears shimmering in hers. Gripping the microphone tight she looked away, breaking the spell.

He took a long swallow of his beer and shook it off. The beer hit the back of his throat; it was cold and slightly bitter. Satisfying, but he needed something stronger, like a shot of Jack.

She handed the mic back to the DJ as she finished the song. Eli narrowed his eyes as he watched Nash grab Cassie's hand, helping her down from the stage. He felt a stab of jealousy rip through his gut at their familiarity and wondered what their deal was. *No business of mine.* He shook his head and turned, heading back to the bar.

"Eli!"

He groaned inwardly, recognizing Charmaine's voice. "Did you just get here? I've been looking everywhere for you."

"Yeah. First beer."

"Let me buy your next one."

"No need. Next round's on me."

"Congratulations on your big win today. You had some stiff competition," Charmaine said.

"Thanks. You weren't too far behind Cassie's time today. You did pretty good yourself."

"Close only counts in horseshoes and hand grenades. I'm going to whip her butt one of these days, even if it's the last thing I do."

He chuckled. "Good luck with that."

Eli spied Cassie, who'd made her way to the end of the bar, and said, "I'll go grab us a beer." He left Charmaine to wedge himself in next to Cassie. Their shoulders and hips touched and his whole body lit up. He caught a whiff of something floral and feminine. "You sounded pretty good up there...Tater."

She cocked her head and looked up glaring. "Only my nearest and dearest get to call me Tater."

"Would you prefer Dragon Lady?"

She had just taken a swig of her beer and her laughter caused the beer to slip down the wrong pipe. She bent over coughing and laughing at the same time as he patted her on the back. "You okay?"

She nodded then wiped her forearm across her mouth.

"At least I got a chuckle out of you for a change of pace," Eli said.

"At my expense," she managed to say between coughs.

"Can I buy you a beer, or maybe something a little stronger?"

Eyes still watering, she nodded. "You'd better. You owe me two, if I recall. I'll have a shot of tequila and a beer."

"By the way, we both won today," he drawled. He signaled to the bartender and ordered beers for Charmaine, Cassie and himself, a shot of Cuervo, and a Jack for himself. He jerked his head towards Nash who was on her other side. "What's your boyfriend drinking?"

Her eye's widened in surprise. "Boyfriend? Oh, Nash. He's drinking Bud draft."

"I guess it wouldn't hurt to buy my competition a drink."

She arched a brow. "Competition?"

He grinned rakishly as his eyes lingered on her lips suggestively. He signaled to the bartender to refill Nash's beer.

"Dream on," she said, rolling her eyes.

He chuckled, enjoying the verbal sparring. He leaned his elbows on the bar, noticing how thick her lashes were, before returning his gaze to her lush pouty mouth. "I reckon I've got as much of a chance as the next guy."

"Think again." She chewed on her bottom lip, the only tell that she wasn't as sure of herself as she'd have him believe.

"If you knew me better, you'd know you're only stoking my fire. I never back away from a challenge."

"I'll keep that in mind. And cowboy, you'd be doing

yourself a big favor if you memorize these words. *Never in a million years.*" She licked the salt off her hand and threw back her shot.

He laughed out loud. "You're a feisty one, aren't you? Fires up my alpha male cowboy something fierce. Makes me want to discover what it is you're guarding." He winked and threw back his own shot.

She rolled her eyes again and turned her back to him, giving Nash her full attention and him a delectable view of her ass. Charmaine tugged on his arm, pulling him away from the bar as he grabbed his beer. "Let's dance," she said.

Eli smiled. "After I finish this beer."

"Promise?"

He took one last look at Cassie who was flirting with Nash and a couple of guys who had stopped to congratulate her on her win. Slinging his arm across Charmaine's shoulders he said, "Why not?"

3

Despite herself, Cassie's gaze kept drifting back to Elijah Cane. He was something, that was for sure. And he was getting under her skin big time. Her pulse fluttered erratically, thinking about the desire she'd seen burning in his eyes. Him in that V-neck white tee-shirt hugging his bulging biceps and muscular chest like a second skin. Sakes alive, *he was smokin' hot*. His arm muscles flexed every time he raised that bottle to his sexy lips. His mouth...full, with a deep cleft above his upper lip, chiseled cheeks, silky, thick coal black hair and the longest, darkest eyelashes she'd ever seen on a man...*Gaah! Stop it!*

"Earth to Cassie." Nash waved his hand in front of Cassie's eyes before following her gaze. His lips tightened when they landed on Eli.

He frowned. "You aren't getting any ideas about Elijah Cane I hope."

"Do I look stupid? You don't need to worry none

about me falling under Elijah Cane's spell. He can't be fenced in no-how. I guess we're the same that way. I don't know why he's being nice all of a sudden. He never even knew I existed. It's like he suddenly noticed me after all this time."

"I don't know why either, except he's not blind. I've seen him in action; stay away from him, Cass."

"I'm a big girl, Nash. I'll forget you even said that. Oh, listen to what's playing. I love this song!" She stood and grabbed Nash's hand, tugging him along behind her. "Dance with me," she coaxed, as a Kacey Musgraves tune filled the room.

They stepped onto the crowded dance floor and he slipped his arms comfortably around her waist. They'd been friends so long it was natural. Neither of them minded that a lot of folks assumed they were a couple. It was a great shield from unwanted attention for them both. She rested her cheek against his chest and let the music carry her away. He led her expertly, large hands resting at the small of her back, their steps matching perfectly. He propped his chin on top of her head and sighed. "Promise me you'll stay away from Eli. He is nothing but trouble."

"You don't have to worry. It's me, remember?" She squeezed him. "Thanks for caring." They swayed to the music, both quiet until a voice broke into her thoughts.

"My turn," Elijah interrupted.

Nash's hold tightened. "Don't think so. We just got here."

"Now I'm here. New song, new partner."

Scowling, Nash replied, "Get lost."

Eli smirked as he arched his thick dark brows at Cassie. "You afraid?"

"Afraid of what—you? Don't flatter yourself."

"Then you won't mind a dance."

He tugged on her arm, pulling her away from Nash and she fell against his solid chest. He smelled heavenly. All man. Old Spice did her in every time. It's what all the old-time cowboys used to wear when she was growing up. She looked over at Nash and shrugged. He glared at Eli, but acquiesced.

Eli led her around the dance floor, holding her tightly against him. Cassie wedged her hands between them and pushed. "You don't have to suffocate me."

His chuckle was a slow sexy rumble in his chest. "I'm getting to ya already? That was quick."

Intentionally exaggerating her Texan drawl, she arched her brows and said, "Where in your past did someone mistakenly tell you how great you were?"

He grinned. "Are you saying they got it wrong?"

Cassie looked away, trying to ignore her fluttering pulse and his intense gaze.

"Aren't you even a little bit tempted by my charm?" he asked, his face mere inches from hers, voice like liquid heat.

"I'd sooner wrestle a snake."

"Mm. That pulse beating in your throat says otherwise." To prove his point, he cupped her neck and let his thumb rest on her traitorous thudding heartbeat.

"I'm a real quick learner and I learned a long time ago to avoid temptations such as yourself," she said.

"I like the sound of that."

"The sound of what?"

"That I'm tempting you."

She guffawed. "Oh brother. I hope no one ever pricks that hot air balloon you live in, because it's going to be a long way down."

"I love it when you talk dirty to me." He dipped her and she couldn't help but laugh. He certainly did have his fair share of charm, not that she'd ever tell him.

"By the way, your boyfriend looks like he'd like to murder me right about now."

She glanced over and saw Nash, arms folded across his chest, staring angrily at Eli. "Nash thinks you're a player and he's protective of me. He watched me go through hell after a breakup. He's understandably defensive. Besides that, he's like my brother. We go way back, like all the way back to when I first showed up on my daddy's doorstep. I was only four, he was six."

Eli opened his mouth to speak, but then closed it. If he was curious about her and Nash he didn't say so.

After several beats, veering towards an easier topic, he asked, "How old are you now?"

"Twenty-six."

"Ahh, you're still just a youngin," he said. The song ended and Eli released her. "I'll return you to your bodyguard." He placed his palm in the small of her back and walked her over to Nash. Her skin was scorched from the heat of his hand through her thin shirt. When they reached Nash, Eli smiled kindly and said, "Thanks for letting me cut in."

Nash glared, but nodded his head in acknowledgment. When she met Eli's gaze, she felt her cheeks heat. He winked knowingly and said, "See ya round, Tater."

"Not if I see you first."

He barked out a laugh, a low sexy sound that sent tingles down her spine.

"Let's do a shot," she said, quickly grabbing Nash's hand and leading him back to the bar.

"Won't hear me arguing none."

She saw Silas hunched over the bar, his gray hair curling around the nape of his wrinkled neck, and ran over. "Grandpa, you made it!" He pushed his cowboy hat back from his brow as Cassie threw her arms around him from behind, hugging him tightly.

"Can't let my champion drink alone. A course I knew your trusted sidekick would be here." Silas grinned at Nash.

"Bout time ya got here," Nash grumbled. "Elijah Cane's been putting the moves on our girl. That guy is as slick as a whistle."

"Datin' that wild one would be like uncorking a wild Bronc," Silas said. "Just 'cause trouble comes visiting don't mean you have to offer it a place to sit down." His eyes bored holes into Cassie to emphasize his point.

Cassie could talk cowboy with the best of them. "You two ain't learning nothin' when your mouth's a jawin'. As I told Nash before, I'm smart enough to steer clear from Elijah. You're both caterwauling over nothing."

"That's my girl," Silas said.

Nash smiled and ruffled Cassie's hair. "Now about that shot, what'll it be?"

"*He don't love me like Tequila does*," Cassie sang a line from one of her favorite Miranda drinkin' songs.

Nash waved his arms like an orchestra conductor

grinning and sang the next line off tune. "*And nobody can.* Two shots of Jose Cuervo," Nash said to the bartender.

"You got it."

"Lick, salt, shoot," Nash said.

Cassie sprinkled salt onto the back of her hand, licked it, then threw back the shot, quickly sucking on her lime wedge. Her nose crinkled. "That never gets any easier."

"Lightweight. Mm, I love it."

She grimaced. "You're a masochist."

"One more dance, then I'm turning in," Nash said.

"Yepper, this old cowboy is gonna finish his beer, then head for our trailer," Silas said.

Nash took a slug of beer, then set his mug on the bar counter. "Come on Tater, let's cut the rug."

One dance turned into two when a new hit song came on. Cassie jumped up and down to convince Nash to stay for one more dance. "Pretty please!" Cassie beamed at him when he caved...as he always did. His arms were slung loosely around her body and she wound hers around his neck. She was laughing up at something Nash had just said, when she happened to glance up into pair of brooding eyes. Her heart thudded and heat licked her cheeks. She diverted her gaze, bringing her attention back to Nash.

Nash looked down at her flushed cheeks then quickly searched the crowd, his eyes landing on Elijah standing alone in the shadows, watching Cassie with an intensity that could be felt across the room. Elijah abruptly turned away.

"Let's get out of here before you decide to do something stupid," Nash said.

Cassie stayed quiet and let Nash take her hand as he led her out into the balmy summer night. The bar was a short walk from their camp. Cassie sighed as she looked up at the night sky, a full painted canvas of brilliant stars against the black backdrop. They crossed the road and entered the gate to the campgrounds. Most everyone was already in bed and most of the trailers were dark and quiet. As they passed a small run-down trailer that had seen better days, they heard voices raised in anger coming from inside. She knew the trailer belonged to Cody Wells, who lived with his young girlfriend Cissy and their four-year-old daughter, Lily.

Casey's body stiffened. She met Nash's eyes and he wrapped his arm across her shoulders and squeezed. "You alright? You look like you've seen a ghost or something."

She nodded, smiling weakly. He got her. He always did. His concern grounded her, but when the child began wailing for her mama, it cut right through Cassie like a knife. They paused beside the trailer and waited it out, neither wanting to butt in between a private domestic matter. It was none of their business unless it escalated beyond an argument.

The yelling stopped and soon after the child quieted too. Relieved, they continued on to Cassie and Silas's trailer. Nash scooted her to the front door and shot Cassie a worried glance. "Want me to stay for a bit?"

"No! I'm fine. Go home a get some sleep. I'm doing the same. Now git! And quit your worrying."

"If you say so. I'm a phone call away."

"I know you are. Thanks."

Concern still clouded his eyes but along with that she saw resignation. Cassie wasn't one to wallow in her pain or let anyone see her vulnerability if she could help it. She smiled at him reassuringly and went inside.

She awoke with a start, her face streaked with tears. Sitting up, she switched on her bedside lamp with unsteady hands. Her whole body was trembling and she took a few slow deep breaths. As often happened after her nightmares, she couldn't recall many details, just the feeling of terror they evoked. She hated the way the dreams tickled the edge of her consciousness. It'd been months since she'd had any nightmares. They were always the same...her mom's soft skin against her cheek...the scent of her, the comfort. Then huddled in a dark place, alone and terrified that the angry men outside her hiding place would find her.

There was a quiet knock at her door. "Cassie? You alright? Can I come in?"

"Yeah, but I'm okay Si."

He opened the door, concern etched across his face. He sat on the edge of her bed, his large wrinkled hand reached for hers and held it. "Bad dream?" he asked. She nodded.

He brushed her hair back from her damp forehead,

his bushy gray brows knitted. "Want to tell ole Silas about it?"

"Same ole dream. Alone in the dark, terrified the bad men are going to find me."

He looked so worried that it made Cassie's heart ache. Sniffling, she said, "I don't get it. I haven't had a nightmare in forever."

She began to softly cry. Silas gathered her up in his arms and held her tight. He rocked her, murmuring quietly, "Let it all out, ole Si's got ya."

"I don't know what's wrong with me. I feel so messed up in the head when I get like this. So weak. I'm just a ball of nerves." She held out her hands, which were trembling.

"Now Cassie, you know that hain't true. You're strong and good. You got a bad hand dealt ya that's all. Yer luck, ya ended up with a couple of clueless cowboys ta raise ya."

She pressed her face against his chest, her tears dampening his tee-shirt. "I'm the luckiest girl ever for that." She sniffled.

"Your ma loved you so much. You was her precious baby girl. You know that right? And me and Reed the same."

She bit her bottom lip. "Why can't I remember? These dreams seem so real, like it really happened."

"Reckon it's from the trauma of losin' yer mama so young."

Cassie nodded. "Yeah, I suppose. I miss her."

He nodded solemnly. "There's no replacin' a mother. Reed and I did our best but..."

"Oh Si, what would I do without you? You and Daddy were the best!"

"We tried. You're strong and brave and far as I kin tell, you've already survived whatever goblins are chasin' ya in your dreams."

Her lips quivered. "I miss Dad."

A deep sadness passed over Silas's face. "I do too, Tater. We lost him too soon. But we got each other and Reed wouldn't want us wallowing around like pigs in mud now, would he?"

She sniffled, her lips tugging up at the corners. Straightening, she studied the familiar, dear face of the man who had been her rock since she could remember. Her heart clutched seeing how much he'd aged. "You always know what to say. I guess you're right about that. When I have those dreams though, it makes me feel like I'm all alone again. It all feels so real."

"Dreams are like that, but that's all they is...just dreams. They can't hurt ya none."

She squeezed him in a bear hug. "I'm all better now. You can go back to bed Silas."

He tilted her chin up, staring deeply into her eyes. "You better getcha some sleep too." He stood and walked to the door. "I'll leave the door open case in ya need me." She nodded. Keeping her lamp on, she lay back down thinking about her next race. Finally, her body calmed down. Right before she drifted off a pair of smoldering amber flecked eyes danced across her mind. She rolled onto her side and fell into a deep sleep.

4

Cassie slipped her earbuds in and leaned back against the hay bales stacked six high, listening to Miranda Lambert ...again. One of her favorite bad girls of country music. Reed had surprised her with her first guitar on her ninth birthday and she'd been playing ever since. She wrapped her arms around her bent knees and rested her head there. Her cowboy boots tapped out the beat on the dusty hard ground.

The last couple of weeks had flown by. Today was their last show day in Oklahoma, then they'd be hauling ass to get to Fort Worth, Texas, where the next rodeo event would be held for ten consecutive days. In many ways, the rodeo life was like having one big dysfunctional family. They all depended on each other and helped haul horses, carpooled from state to state, whatever was needed. Set up, tear down. The up-side was that you could make some damn good money if you had talent. Some of the purses paid out tens of thousands.

Everyone was passionate about it, otherwise no sane person would put themselves through the grueling schedule, the travel, the expense with no safety net, benefits or retirement. Not to mention the toll it took on their bodies. Especially the bull riders.

She was startled when someone plopped down beside her and tugged her left earpiece out. Her head shot up and she stared wide-eyed into a pair of mischievous hazel eyes that somehow managed to be a different color every damn time she locked onto them. *Elijah Cane.* Today they were a chocolate brown with flecks of amber and green. A shiver ran down her spine.

He grinned, flashing his ridiculously white teeth and stuck the nub into his right ear. She watched Elijah's body relax as he listened. With his shoulder pressed against her bare arm, she felt his body sway in time with the music. He smelled of leather and Old Spice and her breath hitched. *Way too close.*

His thick, silky black hair was slicked back today, curling around his ears and brushing the nape of his neck. Her fingers itched to rake through it. She watched his large hands drum the beat against his muscular thighs and gulped. He was trouble with a capital T.

When the song ended, he pulled out the earbud and said, "Great song. I like it."

"Miranda Lambert. It's like a big joke amongst anyone who knows me that she's the only one I'll listen to or play lately. Kacey Musgraves is a close second, though."

"I probably shouldn't admit this since my brother opened for her tour last spring, but I didn't know how good Miranda was until now. I dig Kacey, though."

Cassie shoved him hard. "Your brother played with Miranda Lambert? Get out! You're messing with me, right?"

He regained his balance and chuckled holding up his right palm. "Nope. Cross my heart, it's the truth, I swear. My brother is Gunner Cane. You may have heard of him. He's trying to make a name for himself out in Nashville."

"Nope, but I'll look him up."

"He's pretty good. You weren't too bad yourself the other night. You could have yourself a second career if you ever decide to leave the rodeo life."

She rested her cheek on her folded arms and looked up at him. This was a different Elijah than the one she was used to. Softer somehow. He'd dropped his swag and his eyes were warm and engaged, his body relaxed and open. She studied him intently. Her heart did funny things in her chest and warning bells went off in her head. This Elijah was downright dangerous. *And real.*

"Tell me about that song you sang the other night," he said.

Cassie shrugged, suddenly feeling shy. "Tell you what, exactly?"

"Seemed like it meant something to you."

"I suppose you could say that. Um...well...it kind of hits close to my heart. I don't remember having a place to call home, maybe I did, I just don't recollect. My mama died when I was four. I can hardly recall her, mostly it comes in flashes." Cassie hugged herself before continuing. "I remember how she felt...warm and safe and she was pretty and smelled good. I have a photograph of her though." Cassie smiled wistfully.

"I'm sorry Cass," he said quietly. "Must be hard."

She glanced at him and the look of tenderness in his hazel eyes made her belly flip-flop.

"I think back to the day I landed on Reed and Silas's doorstep; I reckon that's all I know about a home is what they gave me. A course you know as well as I do that rodeo life is like, um, well, living like a nomad. Not that I'm complaining, mind you." She shrugged a shoulder. "Hardest part was knowing I had no real family of my own. Reed was Mama's best friend and childhood sweetheart; she had no family, that's why she picked him to raise me."

"What about your real dad?"

Cassie shrugged. "Don't know. I reckon I was out of wedlock. It was just Mama and me."

"It's lucky she had someone like Reed then," Eli said.

"I can vaguely remember crying for her and missing her like crazy in the beginning. But now, honestly, I'm mostly grateful...to Reed and Silas, lucky they took me in and raised me." She chewed on her bottom lip. *Now why did I just go and tell Elijah all that?* Cassie sighed. "I don't know why I'm going on like this."

"I'm sure it was quite a shock for a four-year-old... not to mention a couple of bachelor cowboys."

She chuckled, but it was devoid of humor. "Yeah. Can you imagine? Surprise, you've been awarded a four-year-old child. I suppose if I hadn't had Mama's green eyes, he might not have taken me in, but he'd loved my mama since forever. Wasted no time in adopting me and making me his own."

His intense gaze made her squirmy, the way he was staring at her with his penetrating eyes, as if he could read her thoughts. Almost like he was seeing her for the first time. He shook his head, then nodded toward her phone, "Hey, I'd like to hear that song from the other night again. Would you mind playing it for me now?"

"I suppose I could." She scrolled through the screen on her phone and swiped when she found the song. "It's called 'The House That Built Me,'" she said. She held out her palm, returning the earbud, and he stuck it back in his ear. He slumped against the hay bales and closed his eyes.

She watched him as he listened intently, his insanely long lashes fanning across his cheeks. She could tell by the stillness of his body that he was completely immersed in the song, paying close attention to the words. *I thought if I could touch this place or feel it, the brokenness inside me might start healin'.*

There was something so intimate about sharing earbuds and listening together like this. It was a first for Cassie. It felt like they were the only two people on the planet. Her chest ached with something akin to longing. A bottomless pit of yearning that threatened to pull her under. Tears stung her eyes and she blinked them away. She'd blame it on the song. After all, no matter how many thousands of times she'd played it, it always evoked some elusive emotion deep inside of her.

She'd always figured it was because it sounded like

the idealistic childhood of her dreams, the one that had passed her by. She jerked when Eli brushed a lock of her hair behind her ear.

"You okay?" he asked gently.

She flashed an embarrassed smile. "Yes, I was just lost in the song. I'm sorry." When she met Eli's eyes, she felt regret. She was damaged goods. No matter how fast she ran, or how deep she thought she'd buried it, eventually the pain of loss always caught up with her...in her dreams or through her music or anytime someone tried to get too close.

He tilted his head, dipping it near her face. She could feel his breath, smell the mint, his eyes all warm and gentle doing a number on her senses. His voice husky, he said, "Don't be, Cass. We all have our soft places. I'm really sorry you ever had to feel all alone. I'm sorry about your mom."

She straightened and tilted her chin up, shaking off her melancholy. "All in the past now. I'm all grown up. How about you? Does Elijah Cane have his soft places?"

His lips tugged up. "Yep, even me, the rough and tumble obnoxious me."

"Hm. Who'd a'thunk?" she teased.

He grinned and pulled up his shirt to wipe off her earbud before handing it back. She caught a glimpse of ripped abs and a trail of soft dark hair disappearing into the waistband of his low-slung faded blue jeans. She gulped. He stood and brushed the dust and hay off his butt.

"Thanks for the music. Company wasn't too bad either," he said.

"Anytime."

"I've got to get my trailer ready for the big haul tomorrow."

"Yeah, I was taking a little break myself. I need to get back to it."

He arched a brow in question and held out his palm to help her up. She smiled and nodded, holding out her hand. Grasping it, he tugged her to her feet. His fingers brushed through her tangled hair, dislodging some hay. She flushed and looked down, suddenly feeling uncomfortably exposed.

"See ya around," she mumbled.

"Count on it."

Cassie practically ran from the barn. *Not if I see you first.* She felt discombobulated, almost like her emotions had been thrown in a blender and pulverized. Up was down and down was up. She didn't let many people in—as a matter of fact she could count them on one hand with fingers left over. *So why did I just spill my most vulnerable feelings to a man I hardly know?*

She thought she'd had Eli's number, but it seemed as if she may have missed a digit or two. She'd never really been alone with him before, not like that anyway. She was shocked by the feelings he'd triggered. Cassie preferred to skim the surface; her past seemed too dark. Introspection led to hurt and was way too painful. Except sometimes on those tequila nights, she'd let herself cry on Nash's shoulder. But it wasn't Nash she'd just spilled her secrets to and she hadn't been drinking tequila. Sharing herself like that and then playing that dang song for Elijah just now was a mistake, one she had no intention of repeating. She got to the trailer she shared with Silas and slammed the door behind her, leaning against it. *Breathe.*

A familiar gravelly voice came from the dimly lit kitchen galley. "Hey Tater. Looks like ya seen a ghost."

She startled, letting out a squeal. "Silas. I didn't know you were here." She straightened her shoulders and plastered a smile on her face. He was holding his tiny Chihuahua/Rat terrier mix, Dios, his bottom lip balled up from the chewing tobacco lodged there. He put the mongrel on the ground, who immediately ran to Cassie. She scooped him up and giggled when he covered her cheeks with tiny kisses. "Dios, you wouldn't bite a biscuit."

Silas stared at her with his all-knowing, penetrating gaze. *Darn it anyway! He didn't miss a thing.* "Everything alright?" he asked.

"Course it is. Why wouldn't it be?" She padded towards the kitchenette and plopped down across from him in the small booth tucked in the corner of the trailer. Meeting his knowing eyes, she acquiesced. "I'm fine really, it's like, well...just feeling, I don't know, a little melancholy today for some reason."

"There are days like that fer sure. Probably why you're havin' them dreams again. Or maybe it's the other way round. You sure it hain't nothing more?"

"I'm sure. Quit worrying. I swear, you're worse than Nash. You both treat me like I just emerged from the cocoon or something. I always get a twinge of sadness when we pull up stakes and hit the road again."

"You know I'm here for ya iffin ya ever need a shoulder. You fancy yerself tough as old shoe leather, but when I look at ya, I still see little Tater Tot, clutching that stuffed animal like it was yer lifeline. Those green eyes was too big fer that tiny face, and staring up at us like we was aliens or something." He chuckled. "I loved ya the minute I set eyes on ya. Same with Reed. He loved ya like you was his own. Don't ever forget it."

She smiled softly, "You're just an old softie. You know I couldn't get by without you."

"I don't have no plans of leavin' anytime soon."

"So quit that tobacca, ya hear me?" she said, wagging a finger at him.

He grinned sheepishly. "I reckon."

She balled her fist at him, shaking it, "I'll reckon you one. If you can't do it for yourself, do it for me."

He stood up stiffly, rolling his shoulders while grimacing. "Today I'm feeling every single time I got thrown off a gol' darn horse. We'd better git er done while I still have some giddy up."

"Sounds like a plan," Cassie replied, setting Dios down. "We have a long day of driving tomorrow."

"Yeah, least we have a few days to settle in before the rodeo starts."

She stuck her thumb up, grinning. "Thank God!"

5

After watching Cassie run away like the devil was on her tail, Elijah walked thoughtfully back to his trailer scratching his head. *Cassie Morgan.* Damn those eyes! He could drown in them. They'd widened in surprise when he'd snatched her ear bud and he'd had a crazy need to feel the softness of her full lips against his.

When she'd told him about her childhood, it'd been like taking a knife to his heart. It'd taken everything he had not to gather her up in his arms when she'd looked so vulnerable back there. It woke up a protectiveness he didn't even know he had. He also knew that would have gone over like a lead balloon. She'd have coldcocked him from here to Sunday.

There was something feral about her. She was skittish with him. Untamed, restless and now he knew... wounded. He'd glimpsed it the other night when she was singing. Now he knew why, at least part of the story. Rather than satisfy his curiosity, he wanted to know more. She was a contradiction for sure.

Used to the confident prickly woman he'd come to know, he'd been caught off guard by her vulnerability. Cassie came off bold and sassy, fearless in the saddle, and truth be told she could give most cowboys a run for their money. She could be one of the guys, while simultaneously being the sexiest woman he'd ever laid eyes on. Now, she'd gone and surprised him by being all soft and irresistible on the inside.

It's not like he hadn't noticed her way before this; he definitely had. How could he not? He'd taken note the first time he'd laid eyes on her a couple of seasons ago. But besides the obvious, her delectable body and ripe lips, she wasn't his type. He preferred the soft feminine version. The kind that liked to flirt and cuddle, not the prickly sarcastic kind. He'd have to admit though, he'd always been curious about what it'd be like to have his hands all over that killer body. But being with someone like Cassie Morgan, well that would be like ten rounds in the bull ridin' ring. No thanks. One long headache. At least that's what he'd thought up till now.

He had the feeling she wouldn't be interested in a casual hookup and he liked his freedom too much. He only wanted as much as it took to load up in the back of his Silverado. *Right?* As tempted as he might be to discover what made her tick, and to see her naked body writhing under his, he'd have to take a hard pass. That woman had trouble written all over her. A vision of her sad puppy dog eyes flashed through his mind and gave him pause.

Drop it dude! She's too young and besides that, she has that blond barnacle Nash attached at the hip...it's all good.

He stopped to pat Howdy's head, the Australian Cattle dog that roamed freely around the grounds but always stuck pretty close to his person. Sure enough, he was right behind. "Hey Otis. How's it going?" Howdy sat at Elijah's feet and barked, tail wagging, his expression expectant.

"Sorry buddy. I'm fresh out a treats."

Otis chuckled. "He's hit up prit near everyone today. He's gonna hafta go on a diet pretty soon."

"No doubt. Do ya need any help getting things together for the long haul?"

"Just might. I'll let ya know."

"I'll be around. Just text me if ya need anything. Don't be shy."

"Thanks Eli. Come on Howdy, lets gitcha yer supper." Howdy barked and happily followed Otis.

Eli flipped the light switch as the screen of his trailer banged shut behind him. He toed out of his cowboy boots and flung himself on the couch, draping an arm over his eyes.

His mind wandered as he tried to fall asleep. All he could see were a pair of glittering green eyes and full lush lips made for kissing. He briefly fantasized about what it would be like to trace the softness of those lips with his tongue. Feeling his dick harden, he slammed on the brakes. *Fuck!*

He huffed out a breath. Any hope of a nap was now a pipedream. He got up and brewed himself a pot of coffee. He could have used the shut-eye, but what the hell. Yawning, he mentally went over what he needed to do before he could call it a day. He'd have to round up someone to help hitch his truck to the trailer. Thankful to have distractions, he downed a cup of strong black coffee then left to line up some help.

He passed Nash on his way to the barn and ignored the daggers aimed his way. Cassie said he was like a brother, but he wondered. Nash was a good-lookin' guy and he supposed most women would find him appealing. He shook his head. *Focus! None of my damn business what their relationship is.*

6

"Cassie, wake up," Nash said shaking her shoulder, his voice gripped with panic.

She sat up and yawned. "What time is it?"

"Midnight. Cody and Cissy are having another whopper of a fight. The kid is crying and I thought I heard furniture crashing."

Cassie immediately sprang out of bed and threw a flannel shirt over her tee-shirt and pulled on a pair of jeans. She slipped into a pair of flip-flops lying by the door. "Let's go."

They ran to the mobile home and arrived just as Cody was flying out the door. His eyes were wild and unfocused, the panic unmistakable, and he reeked of alcohol. Nash grabbed his arm to stop him from leaving. In a calm low tone Nash asked, "Cody, what's going on here? Everything alright?"

He choked back a sob. "Fuck my life!"

Nash faced Cody and put his hands on his shoulders, bracketing him. "Where's Cissy and Lily?"

Cody jerked his head toward the trailer. "It was an accident that she fell, I swear."

"I'm going inside to check on them," Cassie said. She could hear Cissy crying from inside.

Cassie flew up the steps and pushed the door open. Her eyes landed on Cissy who was curled up in a ball on the floor in the cluttered living room, blood trickling from her forehead and looking completely checked out.

"Cissy, it's me, Cassie." Cassie approached slowly, alarmed by Cissy's blank stare. "Where's your little girl?"

She looked up at Cassie and then scanned the room as if waking up from a deep sleep. She whispered, "I don't know."

"You're bleeding. Are you hurt bad?"

She shook her head, touching her fingers to her forehead; her eyes showed her surprise when she felt the blood.

"I tripped and hit my head on the coffee table, not hard."

"Okay then. Stay put. I'm going to go look for Lily. I'll be right back."

Entering the back bedroom, she heard muffled sobs coming from the closet. She could see Lily's unicorn pajama bottoms and a little blonde head buried against her crossed arms and bent knees. Cassie's hands went clammy and she broke out in a cold sweat. Swallowing the bile rising in her throat, she forced herself to step forward. *Get a grip Cassie. You're safe. This isn't about you.* She slowed her breath.

In a soothing voice that was about as far as one could get from how she was really feeling, she murmured, "Lily. It's Cassie. Everything's gonna be alright. Your mama is fine." Her little body heaved. Cassie's knees felt weak, like they could give out on her any second.

"Lily, alright if I join ya in there?" Without waiting for confirmation, she crawled in beside the terrified little girl. Cassie wrapped her arm across the tiny shoulders, holding Lily's trembling body close to hers. "I spect you saw your mama and daddy fighting." A pair of large corn-flower blue eyes looked up at her. Lily's head bobbed.

Cassie's heart clutched. She'd always shied away from kids. She figured it had something to do with her own childhood, but hadn't overanalyzed it, except to acknowledge that she never wanted to bring a child into this mess of a world. She wouldn't pass on her screwed-up self to another innocent human being.

"Believe me, I know how scary that is. But nobody hurt you, did they?" Lily shook her head. Cassie let out a sigh of relief.

Lily's breath hitched then she said, "Mama fell."

"I know she told me. I talked to your mama right before I came here to check on you and she isn't hurt."

"Daddy was yelling." She turned and buried her face against Cassie's chest wrapping her tiny arms around Cassie's middle. Cassie pulled her onto her lap and sat cross-legged, rocking her, murmuring comforting sounds.

"Shh, you're safe little one. Your mama's fine." Cassie squeezed her eyes shut. Her heart ached so bad she was a second away from breaking down in sobs herself. She did the only thing that came natural to her in that moment and began to quietly sing.

"*Somewhere over the rainbow, way up high.*" Her voice faltered. The song had surfaced out of nowhere. A misty memory that had been locked tightly away now teased the edge of her consciousness. *Mama sang this to me.* She could almost latch onto the tendrils of her remembrance...it skittered around the periphery of her mind and she was desperate to grab onto the thread.

Lily's tremors penetrated through her wall of emotion and she forced herself back to the present, continuing to rock her and sing. Cassie fought against the waves of pain, wanting to sob as her reverie rolled away like the fog at dawn. *Funny, I'm soothing myself as much as I am this child.*

"Cassie? You in here?"

Cassie frowned.

"Over here in the closet."

Eli crouched down in front of them. Cassie met his gaze and the worry she saw in his eyes was almost her undoing. It was worry for her. She had the strongest urge to bury her face against his neck and sob while he held her.

He reached out and cupped her face with his palm, stroking her cheek with his thumb. "You need anything?" At Cassie's shake of the head, he turned his attention to Lily.

"Hey Lilykins."

Her lips tilted up in a shy smile.

Geesh, even four-year-olds can't resist this man.

"I was walking by. Nash is still outside with Cody," he explained. Turning to Lily, voice soothing, he said, "You ready to come out and see your mama or should we sweettalk Cassie into another song?"

Lip trembling, she said, "Song."

"I was hoping you'd say that," Elijah ruffled Lily's hair and winked at Cassie. He sat down in front of them cross-legged and waited expectantly for Cassie to sing.

Without any thought, she picked up an old song she hadn't heard for years. "Let Your Love Flow" by The Bellamy Brothers. Her head swam as memories assailed her. *Mama. Singin' this song.* It had been one of her favorites and until this second, it'd been locked up tight in the vault of her childhood. She'd forgotten until now. Her world tilted on its axis for a moment. It'd been buried so deep that she wondered if it was even true. But it was. She could hear her mama's beautiful voice.

Eli smiled at her as she finished the song, the intimacy almost too much for her. His gaze was so warm and full of admiration it made her toes curl. He looked down at Lily, "Well Miss Lily, you ready to go see your ma?"

Lily nodded shyly. Eli stood effortlessly and bent down, lifting her from Cassie's lap. She wrapped her little legs around his waist and her skinny arms circled his neck. Cassie stretched out her legs and bounced them against the floor, her left foot half asleep. Eli offered a hand, hauling her up. She grimaced shaking out her leg. "My foot fell asleep," she explained.

"Better now?" he asked.

"Yeah. I'm fine. Don't worry about me none," Cassie said, avoiding his gaze.

Softly, he said, "I wouldn't dare."

Cassie felt the blush creep up her cheeks. *Damn. What in the Sam Hill had I been thinking when I shared my mixed-up childhood with him?*

After Eli extracted her promise to call if she needed him and was satisfied Cassie was all right, he left the trailer and headed home. It was decided that Cody would sleep over at Nash's place and Cassie would stay with Cissy and Lily. Apparently, the fall really had been an accident. Cissy had turned away from Cody and tripped over a rug, hitting her head on the corner of the coffee table. Cody admitted he'd been red-hot mad, but he'd never hit Cissy before and wasn't about to start.

Later as Cassie listened to Cissy's side of the story, one thing was for certain—they needed help. It couldn't go on like this for Lily's sake. The first step was Cody getting sober. Cissy said the fights always started after Cody got home from the bar or playing poker and drinking with his friends.

"You've got to stand firm on this Cissy. If he won't quit, you need to leave."

Cissy ran her hand through her fine dishwater blonde hair. She seemed listless, beaten down by life.

Cissy let out a humorless laugh. "Sounds simple, don't it? I'm here to tell ya it's not. Where am I supposed to go? We have no money. Cody hasn't won a good purse in forever. Besides, I love him. And he loves us. He'd die if we was to up and leave him."

"Then he'll quit."

Cissy covered her face with her hands. "You know the worst of it? I'm reliving my parent's life. Dad would go out drinkin' and come home itching to fight." Cassie took that in. Proof. The very thing that had ruled kids out for herself. She was terrified she'd never be able to mother anyone. *Can't be what I've never known.*

"We'd better get some sleep. It's past three and we're heading out tomorrow."

"You can go home and sleep in your own bed. We'll be fine."

"You sure?"

"I'm positive. I'm sure Cody is passed out on Nash's couch and I'll be asleep before my head hits the pillow."

"If you're sure...um...I guess I'll do that. I'm dead tired."

"Night. And Cassie? Thank you for not judging us."

Cassie shrugged. "Who am I to judge anyone? You got nothing to feel ashamed of. Life hands us lemons we make lemonade, right?"

Cissy lifted her lips but the smile didn't reach her eyes. "Right."

7

Eli sprawled out on the couch, tired after pulling up stakes the day before. This'd be home for the next two weeks. He mulled over the scene at Cody's the other night. Cassie had looked like a scared rabbit when he'd found her huddled in the closet next to Lily, but she'd still managed to be there for the kid. Singing that song, her eyes unfocused, like she was reliving something in her past. He'd felt her. The soft knock at his door startled him.

"Come on in," he called out, frowning when he saw Charmaine standing at the threshold.

"Full moon tonight. Want to go for a walk?"

She seemed hesitant, a contrast to her normally overconfident demeanor. He was tired after driving all day yesterday then setting up, but he was restless at the same time.

"Why not?" He tugged on his boots and they headed out the door. Charmaine slipped her arm through his as they strolled around the campgrounds. There was everything from rusted run-down campers to luxurious motorhomes on wheels; some people greeted them as they passed, hanging out, drinking beer. It was comforting in its familiarity.

"They've got a campfire going over by the shelter house. Let's check it out," Charmaine suggested. Eli nodded and let her lead the way.

He heard them before he saw them. A banjo and guitar accompanying a smoky unmistakable voice. *Shit.* He saw the glow of flames and a small group of about a dozen or so folks sitting round the large campfire. He stopped at the edge of the shadows and observed. Otis was relaxed, sitting in his canvas chair drinking a beer with Howdy at his feet. A few women he knew from the barrel racing clique were there. Most of them he recognized to look at, but didn't really know them.

Cassie was lit up. Beautiful, confident, her voice felt like a warm bath of Epsom salt washing over his soul. No sign of the inner turmoil he'd seen dance across her face the other night. She cradled her guitar, Silas sitting on one side with Dios stretched out under his chair and Nash flanking the other side of her. Silas picked his banjo strings with a huge grin plastered across his face. Nash slapped musical spoons across his knee to keep the beat. The spoons almost sounded like horses' hooves. Nash wore a wide smile, showing off his pearly whites, all directed at Cassie. Everyone looked happy, like they were having fun, laughing and drinking, carrying on.

Eli's jaw tightened. He hated the feeling of being on the outside looking in. It settled somewhere in his chest and he tried to shake it off. Overlooked, never good enough, trying to fit in with a family of talented over-achievers. A misfit. As a teen, he'd learned to cover up his insecurities behind daredevil stunts, a wide smile and easy banter, but sometimes they'd sneak up on him at the most unexpected of times. *Like now. But holy hell, what do I have to complain about? Compared to the cards Cassie was dealt, I pretty much had the idyllic childhood.*

Cassie took that moment to look up and captured his gaze. Something flickered in her eyes, before her lips curved up in greeting. Her brief flash of warmth left him wanting more. She knew. She had read him. Eyes still locked, he felt his pulse thud when she sang as if they were the only two there. *"Coming through the melody when the night bird sings...Love is a wild thing,"* she crooned softly in that husky voice of hers. Cassie's eyes drifted over to Charmaine and her expression became shuttered. Like that, the moment was gone, leaving him to wonder if he'd been imagining things. *Damn!*

Charmaine hugged his arm tighter against her curves and pulled him towards the circle. The song ended and Charmaine drawled, "Can we join in on the fun, or is this a closed set?"

"The more the merrier," Silas said.

Nash got up and threw more wood onto the fire. Eli, spying an open space on a log, took Charmaine's hand and led her over to it. Charmaine made sure she was snuggled up as close as she could get, her attitude territorial. As much as Eli wanted to discourage her, this wasn't the time or place, plus why should he care what anyone thought anyhow? Except, he did care, about one person's opinion in particular. The green-eyed goddess who held the entire group in the palm of her hand at the present moment. Damn, she had a voice alright. He hadn't been kidding when he'd told her she could sing professionally. She was that good.

"Silas, you're kicking some ass on that banjo," Eli said, when they took a break from playing. He was painfully aware of Cassie's curious gaze and of Charmaine glued to his side.

Silas tipped his cowboy hat and grinned. "Thank ya."

"That was a Musgraves tune, right?" Eli asked him.

"Love is a wild thang or somethin' like that. Ask Cassie."

Cassie smiled fondly at Silas and touched his arm. "You got it right Si and you're right Eli, he is a master on the banjo."

Silas bowed his head shyly. "Aw, now there ya go, butterin' me up again."

"You know I never tell a lie," Cassie said.

The close bond between the two of them was obvious and Eli felt that ache in his chest again. He'd never had someone like Silas in his life...someone older to guide him and take him under their wing. The sweetness of it stirred him. Also made Cassie that much more desirable. *What would it be like to have her look at me like that all the time...all soft and warm and trusting?* Charmaine bumped against him interrupting his thoughts.

Her voice was sulky as she said, "What ya thinking about?"

He met her narrowed blue eyes and smiled. "Nothing. Tired I guess, zoning out a little."

"Past your bedtime already?" Charmaine said. "Maybe I should take you home and tuck you in." She batted her lashes at him playfully and he inwardly cringed. He liked her just fine, she was cute and fun, but he wasn't interested in more than a friendship; he'd told her so more than once. They'd had a one-night stand over a year ago and she still had her sights set on him, despite his honesty.

He happened to catch Cassie watching them, but she hurriedly looked away when their gazes clashed. His heart thumped. *Hm, maybe she isn't as immune as she'd like me to believe.* He stretched his arms overhead to get away from Charmaine's clinging fingers.

Leaning forward, he rested his elbows across his knees. "Cassie?" He deliberately kept his voice low and seductive.

She looked up, arching a brow in question.

"You going to play that song you and me shared yesterday in the hay mound?" Her cheeks flushed.

Nash narrowed his eyes and sat up taller, looking suspiciously between Eli and Cassie, at the same time Eli felt Charmaine stiffen beside him. He smiled to himself. Mission accomplished. He'd managed to get a blush from Cassie and a message to Nash and Charmaine with one line.

Cassie's eyes flashed with fire before the veil dropped again. With a fake smile and eyes narrowed she said, "You're too late, I already played that one before you got here."

Eli felt a rush. He was getting under her skin. This made him happy and even happier that she was trying not to let it show. He clutched at his heart and said, "Aw,

I'm bummed. And here I thought that was 'our song' now."

Cassie snorted. "You've got quite the imagination cowboy. With your oversized opinion of yourself, I'm surprised you can find a hat big enough to cover that head of yours." Everyone hooted with laughter.

Silas cackled the loudest. "Well Elijah, I guess she just tole you."

"Truth hurts," Nash muttered.

Elijah laughed along with everyone else. "Yeah, I guess she did." He shrugged, wearing his most charming grin. "Win some, lose some. On that note." He stood and pulled Charmaine to her feet. "Night y'all. Thanks for the hospitality."

8

Cassie watched Elijah walk away and tried to ignore her sudden mood shift. Noticing Nash's eyes on her, she forced a smile and strummed her guitar deciding on what to play next. "Any requests?" she asked.

"How about White Liar?" her friend Adeline said.

Cassie strummed her guitar and smiled. "Perfect. Nothing better than a cheatin' song." She'd been there done that, falling for a rodeo hotshot and it had not ended well for her. A young and naïve seventeen-year-old virgin, she'd fallen fast and hard for a champion bull rider. Gorgeous to boot. All the girls had wanted him and he'd picked her. Deke had swept her off her feet then drug her through hell and back. She'd trusted him, believing his smooth lies over the rumors, until he'd been caught outright with his fingers in the cookie jar.

If it hadn't been for Nash and Silas, she'd have gone

off the deep end. As it was, she'd been pretty darn close. That breakup had brought up all her old abandonment issues. She'd channeled that heartbreak into barrel racing, determined to be the best, and she'd succeeded. Now she was the one to beat. After that, she'd put a solid wall around her heart and kept her relationships light. She'd bedded a few guys here and there, always leaving before the sun came up. If they didn't like it, too bad, that was their problem. As far as she was concerned, she was taking a page out of the cowboy handbook.

Most of the group were making noises about turning in for the night. The booze had been flowing and everyone was tired from traveling. Cassie put her guitar in its case, snapping it shut. Nash handed her a beer and clicked his bottle against it before guzzling his down in two swallows.

Wiping his forearm across his mouth, he said, "Cassie, I'm warning ya, Elijah Cane is up to no good. He has his sights set on you."

She waved her hand at him. "Nash, I'm a big girl now. You know I'm not the same innocent that fell for the likes of Deke Rivers. You don't have a thing to worry about." She knew she was spitting in the wind, because Nash was nothing if not fiercely loyal to her. She sighed. *Damn Pit Bull is what he is.*

"Easy for you to say. Me and Silas had to stand by and watch after you and Deke split. Never felt so useless in my life. I could a killed that bastard."

Adeline piped in, "Eli is a nice guy. I've gotten to know him a bit this summer and far as I can tell, he doesn't live up to his reputation. He can't help it he's hot as hell."

Silas piped in, "He's not a bad guy I reckon, but he's got too many of them buckle bunnies fawning all over him. That spells trouble."

"It's a good thing I'm not interested now, isn't it?' Cassie said. "I swear Nash, you're like a dog with a bone. Can we please change the subject?"

Nash looked sheepish and the corner of his mouth turned up. "Sorry."

"I know you mean well," Cassie said, throwing her arm across his shoulders and giving him a squeeze. She yawned loudly. "I don't know about y'all but I'm tuckered out."

"If you want to head on to bed, I'll see to putting out the fire and taking care of the trash. You guys can all head on back to your trailers," Nash offered.

"I'll stay and help you, Nash," Adeline offered.

Cassie stood and reached down for her guitar. "Silas, ya ready?"

"Yepper. Night kids." He grabbed his banjo and whistled to Dios, who stretched out and groggily followed them as they headed for home.

Cassie hooked her free arm through Silas's. "I had fun tonight, how about you?"

"Yep. Good people." He blew out a breath and Cassie waited. She knew he had something on his mind and you couldn't rush Silas.

"Don't be too hard on Nash. He's always looked out fer ya. Old habits don't go easy."

Cassie sighed. "I know. I don't hate it. It makes me

feel cared for...it's just sometimes it feels like everyone still sees me as a child. I'm twenty-six now."

Silas chuckled. "I know you think you're all grown up, but when you get to be my age you'll realize, you didn't know shit from Shinola. The more ya know the less ya know... all those old sayin's are true. But you have a good head on yer shoulders."

"I know I got a lot to learn, that's what I depend on you for."

He chuckled, then his expression grew serious. "You have any more nightmares?"

She shook her head. "Nope. I'm cured."

"If ya need to talk I'm always here fer ya, but I reckon you already know that."

"I love you, Si."

"I love ya too, Tater."

Cassie couldn't get to sleep. She blew out her breath and turned onto her left side, plumping her pillow again. *I'm beginning to feel like a rotisserie chicken on the spit.* She might have convinced her friends that Eli wasn't on her radar, but lying here in the dark, all by her lonesome, was an entirely different story. When he'd stood watching her with his intense gaze, tendrils of fire had licked her skin. His coal black hair...the firelight flickering in his dark eyes...those lashes... those lips. She groaned. *Why did he have to be so damn sexy?*

They'd managed to avoid each other for the last two seasons, why now? It's like a light switch had been flipped on and she couldn't find the off button. A flash of him stretching his arms overhead, his shirt riding up to expose those ripped abs... *Mm. Stop it!*

As the sun was coming up, Cassie finally drifted off to sleep. She didn't even rouse when Dios jumped onto the bed and curled around her feet.

9

Cassie removed Kiss's saddle and threw it over the top fence rail. She glanced at her watch, making sure she still had time to bathe Kiss and catch Elijah's ride. Today was opening day of the rodeo and she was glad that she didn't have to compete until tomorrow. She slipped on the halter and held out a treat. The feel of Kiss's soft velvet lips nuzzling Cassie's palm made her smile. "Tomorrow is showtime girl. I think we're ready."

She led her mare down the barn aisle to the back where the bathing area was. There were several other riders already there with the same idea. It was hot and the horses were sweaty after exertion. She aimed the nozzle at Kiss's hind quarters and hosed her down, starting from the rear and working forward. Kiss stood patiently, enjoying the refreshingly cold soak. After the final rinse Cassie used her plastic scraper to remove any excess water and returned her to the stall. She threw in a flake of hay and turned on the fan before leaving.

She wasn't sure why she was so nervous. She'd watched Elijah compete before. *Oh yeah...* Last time she'd watched him ride, he'd been violently thrown from his horse and didn't get up. He lay unconscious in the ring until the paramedics could get him to safety. Her heart had been in her throat as he was hauled away on a stretcher to the local hospital. He'd ended up taking time off to recuperate at home.

It had scared everyone and was a grim reminder that rodeo competitions were a high-risk sport. Although bull riding and bare bronc riding was wilder and harder on the body, saddle bronc riding was still no joke. Barrel racing seemed tame in comparison. Especially when you had a horse as good as Kiss. She was one in a million.

Even after all these years, Cassie still watched these cowboys ride it out with a certain measure of awe. The rules state that a rider could only use one hand; if the other touched they were disqualified. Their score depended on how much the horse bucked and the rider's control during the eight second ride. Eli was one of the best.

She weaved her way to the front of the stands and caught the last of Wyatt Smith's ride. Eli was next. She saw him in the chute, wrapping the thick rein tightly around his gloved hand, his face a study in concentration. He'd drawn a good horse named Silver Bullet, the one everyone wanted.

Cassie trembled with nerves, her heart in her throat as Eli burst from the chute. He made his mark, keeping both heels touching above the horse's shoulders as they burst into the ring. His chaps flapped as the powerful horse kicked his back legs forcefully in the air. Elijah rode with lots of style, smooth and graceful as the horse bucked wildly. The buzzer went off signaling the end of the ride and as far as Cassie could tell and by what the announcers were saying, he'd had a near-perfect run. Cassie held her breath waiting for his score. She cheered loudly from her perch when his high score placed him well into the lead.

She made a split-second decision to go find Eli and congratulate him. She'd never done that before and didn't give herself time to second guess the reason why. She found him covered in dust and sweat, standing close to the action perched on the rail, watching a rival preparing to mount his horse as a stable hand led Silver Bullet away.

She climbed up next to him and touched his arm. "You were amazing. You make it look so easy."

His surprised face creased in a smile; his white teeth bright against his olive skin. "Hey Cass! Thanks. So, I guess you watched?"

"Yeah. I'll admit, it's hard to imagine what those eight seconds must feel like."

He laughed, his eyes crinkling. "Like you're going to die."

"Oh my God! That's what I thought! Why do you do it?"

"Only thing I'm good at."

Cassie elbowed him hard in his side. "Stop it."

He shrugged. "What can I say, I love it." He slung his arm casually across her shoulders and pointed to the chute. "Now watch this guy up next very closely. He's my biggest competition and he drew a pretty good mare."

Her nose crinkled. "What am I watching for?"

"Rhythm. Is he in-tune with the horse, how much does he control the horse? Look for a smooth ride, and of course staying on for those eight seconds." Cassie had to admit, bronco riding was exciting to watch. She was completely swallowed up with awareness of his arm draped over her shoulder and his body pressed against her side. She swallowed hard. *How had this happened?*

Once again, Cassie found herself holding her breath waiting for the score, only this time her fingers were crossed that it'd be a low one. When they announced the score and Elijah had beat him, Cassie whooped with joy and threw her arm around Eli's waist, hugging him tight. "Congratulations!"

He jumped down from the rail and reached for her. Hauling her into his arms, he lifted her up and twirled around full circle as she pealed with laughter. He gave her one more squeeze before setting her back on her feet. She could feel her cheeks heat, whether from excitement for his win or something else, she wasn't entirely sure, but her fluttering pulse could be a clue.

He reached out and tugged on one of her pigtails. "You sure do look cute with your hair braided like this."

Her breath caught at his fiery gaze. "I do?"

"Yeah, and you look like you're about fifteen years old." He grinned, lifting his cowboy hat and swiping the sweat from his brow with his forearm, before plunking it back down.

There was a pause, then he asked, "Your race is tomorrow?"

"Yep. Kiss is on fire. Just exercised her right before your ride, barely made it here in time to see you." Cassie stuck her hands in her back pockets to keep herself from fidgeting.

His eyes half closed and smoldering, he studied her face. "Thanks for making the effort."

A loud voice boomed behind them. "Elijah, you rode that bronc like a real champion!" Wes Hancock, a large and burly announcer, came over and slapped Eli on the back. "I'm proud of ya, son. Last year about this time you were getting hauled away on a stretcher."

Eli grimaced. "Don't remind me."

Wes turned to Cassie. "Good to see ya, Cassie. Haven't run in to Silas yet. How's he been?"

"Ornery as ever."

"Good to hear. Wouldn't have it any other way."

Cassie smiled warmly. "It's great to see you Wes, but I need to get going." Glancing up at Eli she said, "Congratulations." She turned on her heel and took a step, until a warm hand wrapped around her wrist stopping her. Surprised, she looked over her shoulder. Arching a brow, she waited.

"Are ya hungry?" Eli asked.

"I was born hungry."

"I need to grab a quick bite, how about we go together. My treat."

"There's a pretty good food truck with killer knockwurst and brats."

A smile lit up his face. "Sold. Let's go. I want to get back in time to see Darrel King ride." They bid Wes goodbye and walked in step with one another, gravel crunching under their boots as they made their way to the food court.

Cassie slathered mustard onto her knockwurst while Eli settled up the bill. She grabbed a wad of napkins then, juggling her food and drink, found an empty picnic table and slid onto the bench to wait for Eli. He plopped down across from her and spread his fries out on a napkin. Gesturing towards them he said, "Help yourself."

Cassie grabbed one and bit into it. Chewing she moaned, "Mm. Good fries. Nice and crisp, the way I like them."

"Me too." He took a big bite out of his knockwurst and ketchup oozed out and down his chin. Without thinking Cassie took her napkin and reached over to wipe it off. He startled and their eyes locked. Her cheeks flamed.

"Um, sorry," she mumbled.

He stifled a laugh at her embarrassment, his eyes sparkling with humor. "Not a problem. By the way, where's your bodyguard?"

Recovering, she sucked on her straw without bothering to pretend she didn't know who he was referring to. "He's helping Silas fix something or other."

"Ah, so he let you off your leash for a bit."

"You're a fine one to talk. Charmaine never seems to be too far from your side."

"I can't help it if I'm irresistible."

Cassie snorted. "Like an itch." He chuckled. She

was relieved that they were back to their easy banter and on familiar ground.

They wolfed down their food in friendly silence. Cassie was in her happy place. She loved the atmosphere of the rodeo. The sun was warm on their backs and she could hear the announcer from a distance, along with cheering spectators. She breathed in the smell of it all...horse and cow manure mingled with burgers grilling, leather and liniment. Rodeos provided some of the best people-watching and she noticed a family with twin boys who looked to be around five. The kids carried big puffs of pink cotton candy swirled around sticks. They wore hats and cowboy boots. Adorable. Cassie smiled wistfully.

Eli turned to see what had caught her eye. "Pretty cute," he said.

"Right? I love the little boots."

She licked some mustard from her lip, the tangy flavor a perfect match with her spicy dog. Polishing off the last bite, she said, "That was awesome."

Eli's eyes twinkled as he tapped his own cheek, indicating she still wore some of the condiments.

She scrubbed at her cheek. "Did I get it all?"

He nodded and frowned when his cell phone buzzed, but after glancing at the screen, his features softened and he answered. "Hey, Ma." She watched as Eli smiled into the phone before responding. "I'm fine. Nothing broken, not even a scratch...I swear, here, ask Cassie. I'll put ya on speaker phone." He thrust the phone at her as Cassie waved her hands, laughing and shaking her head in consternation. "Cassie meet my mom, Abby. Ma this is Cassie

Morgan. The prettiest barrel racer I've ever laid eyes on."

Glaring at Eli, she leaned in close to the phone. "Hi Mrs. Cane, nice to meet you."

A warm voice with a definite twang greeted her. "Cassie, is it? I can't remember the last time Elijah introduced me to a lady friend. You must be special."

Cassie cleared her throat, momentarily speechless. "I'm not...um...I'm..."

Eli interrupted, "Cassie you can vouch for me, that I'm all in one piece, right?"

"Yes, Mrs. Cane, it's true. I watched his ride. He was amazing. Had the best ride and highest score with zero injuries."

"Thank you, dear. I swear I'll never get used to him risking his life and limb to make a damn living!"

"I'm sure it's hard. I saw his ride last year when he got hurt. I'll admit my heart was in my throat today watching. I think I held my breath for the entire ride."

"I'm pleased as punch he has someone watching over him. Thank you, Cassie. He's my problem child. The one I worry about the most. Got a wild streak a mile long, that one does."

Cassie laughed. "Common knowledge to us here in the rodeo world."

"You take good care of my boy. I can't wait to meet you."

Cassie sputtered and began to deny any sort of relationship, but Eli switched off the speaker and took over the conversation. He squinted as he watched Cassie while listening. "Yes, Ma. I will. I'll be sure to tell her.

I'll take a selfie of us and send it to you. Give Freak a kiss for me. Love you too."

When he'd disconnected, he got up and crouched behind her, holding his cell phone above their heads. "Smile real pretty now," he said. He checked out the first one and snorted, showing it to her.

She tried to grab his phone. "No way are you sending *that*. It's hideous! Erase it now," Cassie demanded, then asked, "Who's Freak?"

"My horse. Why can't I send this one? You look kind of cute with your mouth wide open like that, catchin' flies."

She glared.

He erased the offending photo, then said, "Take two." This time Cassie was ready and smiled sweetly into the camera as he slung his arm across her shoulders, pressing his face next to hers. He aimed the camera at them and snapped several pictures, then angled it so they could both see the photos. "This one is a keeper. What do you think? Does it pass your inspection?"

She looked at the screen and said grudgingly, "I'll go with the second one, I reckon."

He winked as he pressed send. "Mom's sure to love those pigtails and freckles." They both jerked when a voice called from behind them.

"There you are. You were supposed to wait for me! You're a very bad boy," Charmaine said, sliding onto the bench. Cassie and he exchanged a look and she smirked at Eli, as if to say "Told ya."

"Hey Charmaine," he said. "I don't recall saying we were meeting anywhere."

"You disappeared after your ride. I'm not gonna lie; you were so damn sexy I was ready to jump your bones. That may have been your best ride ever," she said, resting her palm possessively on his corded forearm.

"I had a good horse. Got lucky on that draw."

Cassie cleared her throat and stood, gathering up her trash. "Gotta go. Thanks for the grub."

"You're welcome. Thanks for the company. If I don't run into you before, good luck on your race tomorrow." Charmaine shot daggers at Cassie. She knew this wouldn't be the end of it for Eli. He was sure to get an earful. She smiled to herself when she saw Charmaine glaring at Eli as she left. If looks could kill. He had just wished Charmaine's biggest competitor good luck. Cassie snickered. It normally wasn't like Cassie to be that way. She liked to win and was a good sport in general, but she just didn't like Charmaine.

She checked in on Kiss, then headed to her trailer to cool off in the AC for a bit. Maybe even catch a nap. Then she'd take in a little more of the rodeo. She planned on retiring early tonight so she'd be fresh for tomorrow.

Kicking off her boots at the door, she lay down on the couch, enjoying the cold draft of the air conditioning blowing right on her. She was asleep within minutes.

10

Eli watched Cassie walk away, her long shapely thighs and perfect ass in those tight cut-off jeans making him half hard. Strange. He should be flying high since he'd just hit pay dirt with that last ride, but he felt deflated with Cassie gone.

"Well?" Charmaine said huffily.

He scowled. "Well, what?"

"You didn't hear a word I just said, did you?"

"Sorry. That would be a no."

Annoyed, she repeated herself, talking slowly as if to a child, "I said, do you want to go watch the rest of the bronco riding?"

"Yeah, I was planning on it. I hope I'm not too late to catch Darrell King ride."

He threw his trash out and they headed back to the arena. Charmaine clung to his arm and chattered about nothing the entire walk back. He tuned her out, his thoughts drifting back to Cassie, thinking about how her eyes sparkled with humor, the light brush of freckles across her nose, those dimples when she smiled full-on, her toned arms and that smooth creamy skin. *Shit.*

When she wasn't being her usual thorny self, she was quite charming. Easy to be with and *very* easy on the eye. He hadn't missed that she'd buried their intimate conversation about her past like it'd never happened. He had already figured that'd be the case, but it still rankled that they weren't moving forward as fast as he wanted. He liked her...wanted to know her.

Eli was greeted by well-wishers and pats on the back as he made his way to the stands. He arrived just in time to see Darrell climbing onto the snorting wild-eyed mare he'd drawn. They burst out of the chute, the horse bucking high and doing complete one-eighties in the air.

"That horse is crazy," he muttered to himself. Darrell was thrown after several seconds and disqualified. Eli sympathized. He liked Darrell, he was one of the good guys.

"You're so much better than he is," Charmaine said.

"Darrell is an excellent rider," Eli snapped. "He just got a bad break with the mare he drew."

"Well e-x-c-u-s-e me," she replied, tossing her long blonde hair over her shoulder. "What are you so pissy about?"

"I don't like hearing ya talk smack about a friend of mine is all."

"All I said was that you were better than him."

They were interrupted by a couple of teenage girls holding the event schedule booklet and pens. The older of the two stepped forward and thrust hers towards Eli. "Um excuse me but can we have your autograph?"

"It'd be my honor," he replied graciously. Pen poised he looked at her and asked, "Who do I make it out to?"

She blushed, "To me, I mean, um, my name is Amy, with one m and a y, I mean instead of an ie, or two m's." She nervously wrung her hands.

"Got it," he smiled and winked.

He scrawled 'Warmest wishes Amy,' and signed his name before handing it back to her and reaching for the other booklet. He raised both eyebrows at the second girl and she said, "I'm Jenny, with a y."

"I appreciate you coming out," he said, sending both girls into a fit of nervous giggles.

"Amy has your poster on her wall," Jenny said. Amy's cheeks turned beet red and she glared at her friend.

"Well, that's the best compliment I heard all day," he said. "None of us would be here without fans like you." They backed away thanking him and he waved.

"You're such a flirt," Charmaine said, rolling her eyes.

"Being kind to fans isn't flirting, it's part of the job. Now you're going to complain about autographs?" Eli shook his head. Why had he never realized how negative Charmaine was until now?

"I was teasing you. I don't know why you're so sensitive lately. I can't say anything right."

He pinched the bridge of his nose. "No, you're right. I'm sorry. Listen Charmaine, maybe this isn't the best time or place but let's find somewhere we can go and have a conversation in private. I've been meaning to talk to ya for a while now."

She narrowed her eyes and looked at her watch. "I can't right now." Eli knew it was more about the fact that she didn't want to hear what he had to say.

"You sure 'bout that?" he asked.

She wouldn't meet his eyes. "Eli, you already told me you're not ready to settle down or anything. I get all that. I can handle it. So, if you're worried about hurtin' me, don't be. I'm a big girl."

Eli blew out his breath. "Charmaine, you say that, all the while being all possessive and shit...treatin' me like I'm your boyfriend."

She grabbed his arm. "Why can't we keep things the way they are now? Casual companions...friends. I wouldn't mind an occasional roll in the hay, you're single, I'm single. Why not? It gets lonely sometimes."

"You know, Char, it's easy to say those things but in real life it generally doesn't work that way. You're right, I don't want to see you get hurt. I like ya just fine...but as a friend."

"I'll admit I don't get it. We were great in bed together. Am I wrong about that?"

"No. It's just that I know you want more. Don't settle for less. You deserve to have someone that will appreciate you and give themselves to you one hundred percent. I'm not that guy."

"Elijah Cane, you're sounding like you think a woman can't enjoy a casual relationship. Isn't that old-fashioned?"

"I can tell I'd have better luck talking to a wall right now. To be continued."

"Now you're speaking my language. Life's too short to be so dang serious," Charmaine said smiling.

Eli rolled his eyes heavenward and shook his head. He knew he'd lost this round and he'd let it go for now. Why make a bigger deal out of it than it needed to be? Charmaine knew where he stood with it all and she was a great buffer between him and the unwanted attention of certain groupies. His own personal Pit Bull. Only problem would be if he found someone that he wanted to get close to...like Cassie Morgan.

11

Cassie pulled at the tee-shirt that was plastered to her sweaty body like a second skin. She felt sticky and gross. Perspiration beaded at the nape of her neck and rolled down her back in rivulets after mucking stalls all morning. The summer was flying by. They'd been touring non-stop for the last six weeks and she was dead tired. And, it was hot. Texas hot. July heat. *Nuff said.*

They'd been in San Antonio for a couple of days now. Tonight, the campground was hosting outdoor movie night followed by fireworks for the fourth of July celebration. She'd heard it was a doubleheader, *True Grit* and *City Slickers*. She could use a laugh. They all could.

After San Antonio, they'd have a short but much-needed break. Two whole weeks off. *Two weeks without Elijah Cane popping up everywhere.* She, Silas and Nash would head back to their home base in Austin where they'd park their trailers and chill. Elijah would head back to his ranch in Wyoming. Instead of relief, she felt depressed.

She stood in front of a fan and leaned her face in close. The breeze helped some but it was still freakin' hot.

"Mind if I join ya?" Elijah said, sneaking up behind her.

She stifled a scream and shot daggers at him. "One of these days you're gonna get decked sneakin' up on people like that."

He leaned in next to her and let the breeze from the fan cool his skin. "It's hotter than hell."

"Ya think?"

"Going to the movies tonight?"

"For sure. Looking forward to Wyoming?"

"Yep. Triple C Ranch, here I come."

Cassie looked at him from the corner of her eye. "I checked it out on the internet. Looks beautiful. Do you miss it?" She noticed that she was a little too eager for his answer. The last several weeks Eli had been slowly wearing her resistance down and they had entered into new territory. What that was, she hadn't a clue, she only knew that he no longer irritated her and she looked forward to her encounters with him.

"I'm always glad to leave the ranch, but I'm just as happy to return home. Mountains, rivers, horses, views for miles. I get a little homesick sometimes."

"I wonder why you ever leave."

"Meet my daddy and you'll wonder no longer."

Not what she expected to hear. "That bad?" she asked.

He shrugged one shoulder. "He's probably not that bad, unless you're the black sheep of the family. My mom's great though. You could probably tell that by talking to her."

"She sounded lovely. She said you were her problem child, but the black sheep? I'm shocked," she said sarcastically.

He bumped against her, throwing her off balance. "Sure, ya are." He shrugged. "She'd never call me that, even though it's the truth. She always took my side over Dad's. She'd stand between me and him like a mother bear protecting her cub. Helped that she's the only one my dad listens to."

"I kind of pictured you as the hero of the family."

He scoffed. "Yeah right. That'd be my oldest brother, Luke. He's a saint far as my dad's concerned."

"How many sibs do you have?"

"I have a sister, Becca, and two brothers, Luke and Gunner. He's the singer I told you about awhile back."

"I remember."

"Since Luke's the oldest I think he carries most of the pressure. I don't envy him none. He manages the finances for the ranch. He majored in business. Fell right in step with our father's wishes. Married his high school sweetheart and returned straight home after college. Me and Gunner wanted something different for ourselves. Me, I just wanted to get away and out from under Dad's thumb. Becca joined the rodeo for one season then went back to work at the ranch. She's happy to be there. She's got the personality for dealing with the guests. Got a nephew Clayton, Luke's son. He's five now. His mom, Lauren, died of cancer a few years back."

Cassie covered her mouth in shock. "Good Lord! I'm sorry. That must have been hard on everyone."

He nodded. "Yeah, Luke took it real hard. Clay's doing alright except he's on the spoiled side. Between my mom and sister and Gunner's fiancée Sophia, he gets his way all the time. They dote on him. I know it's not the same as having his mama though."

"At least he has the feminine touch. Although Reed and Silas didn't do too bad a job raising me."

"I'd say that was true except for that foul mouth and sharp tongue of yours."

She sputtered her eyes alight with humor. "Foul mouth? Who you calling foul-mouthed? I have half a mind to give you an earful right this minute."

"Nothing I haven't had the pleasure of hearing before. You've got all the cowboys tip-toeing round ya like they're afraid of your wicked tongue."

"Now I know you're lying."

He laughed, the sound low and husky, sending shivers along her spine. He held up his hands, "It's the honest truth."

"How's come you're here hanging around then, if I'm so scary?"

"I'm immune to it."

She crossed her arms over her chest and playfully glared, "A-huh."

He reached over and tweaked her nose and suddenly the air became charged between them. They both froze, eyes locked onto each other. Eli's smoldered, no other word for it. Cassie was the first to break away, but Eli's fingers under her chin nudged her gaze back and she fell into his pools of warmth and desire.

"Sit with me tonight?"

She blinked. "What?"

"Tonight, the movies, remember?"

Licking her lips, she nodded. "Movies, right. Okay. I'm sure Nash and Silas will be there too."

"I'll bring a cooler. Anything special you'd like me to pack?"

"If you grab me a bottle of Chardonnay, I'll pay you back."

"I can do that."

"Thanks. I'll bring the blanket, um, unless you're bringing a chair."

"Nope blanket sounds good. Please tell me I don't have to snuggle with Nash all night."

Cassie laughed out loud. "No promises."

He brushed his thumb over her bottom lip and she shuddered. "Looking forward to it," he said. Then he was gone and she was left feeling like her cage had been rattled something good.

12

Cassie spread the oversized blanket out before setting up a camping chair for Silas. Her stomach was doing flip-flops.

"Si, go ahead and sit. Nash will be here with the beverages soon." Silas sunk into the canvas chair and patted his lap. Dios didn't need to be prompted twice. He jumped up, curling into a ball as Silas scratched behind his ears. As if on cue, Nash appeared carrying a cooler and a couple of sleeves containing more chairs slung over one shoulder. Adeline was following right behind him. *Interesting...progress perhaps?*

"I brought the popcorn," Adeline said.

"Can't watch a movie without it," Cassie responded. Feigning a nonchalance she was far from feeling she said, "Eli's going to join us tonight."

Nash stiffened and barked, "Say what?"

"You heard me."

"I'm hoping I heard wrong." He glared down at Cassie, making her squirm.

"Since when do I need your permission to hang out with someone?"

He ignored her as he set up two chairs, for himself and Adeline.

"Nash?" *Silence.* "Really? Is this how you're going to be?"

"You know how I feel about him. That's all I got to say about it."

Silas who'd been watching them both, piped in, "Now Nash, this rodeo, well we're like one big family. Cassie can invite anyone she wants."

Nash ignored the comment as he opened the cooler, pulling out a beer for himself and Adeline. "What'll you have Si?"

"Give me a bottle of that sweet tea."

"Here ya go. Cass?"

She cleared her throat uncomfortably. "Um, Eli is bringing me some wine."

His lips twisted. "Course he is."

"You're being ridiculous."

"Don't expect me to be around to pick up the pieces this time."

Cassie sucked in her breath, her hand flying to her chest. "Ouch." His words hit their mark.

Nash's expression softened and he mumbled, "I'm sorry. That was below the belt."

"No, you have a say. You're the one that had to pick up the pieces. It couldn't have been easy on you and Silas."

"It's just that ya need to use your head," Nash said.

Silas grumbled, "Hain't we here to have some fun? Will you two quit yer bickering?"

"I second that," Adeline piped in.

Cassie and Nash exchanged a glance. Cassie still felt hurt but she knew Nash didn't really mean it. Smiling she murmured, "Truce?"

"Yeah, I spect."

Cassie plunked down on the blanket and propped back on her elbows, surveying the scene. There were quite a few people gathered. The atmosphere was relaxed and it felt like they'd stepped back in time. She had a prickly sensation at the back of her neck, sensing him before she saw him. Then there he was, sitting down next to her. Adrenalin surged as he caressed her with his eyes.

"Hey," he said softly. "Sorry I'm late."

She tilted her head up and smiled at him. "Wine please."

"Howdy Silas, hope you don't mind me crashing your party," Eli said.

"Naw, glad ya could make it," Silas said, his eyes darting to Nash, issuing a stern warning.

Eli nodded at Nash and Adeline. "How's it going?" he asked.

"Hey Eli," Adeline said, her expression open and friendly.

Nash nodded his head grudgingly.

Eli opened his soft cooler and pulled out the wine. "I bought two bottles for ya Cass, just in case." She held out her red solo cup and he filled it halfway.

"How'd you go and read my mind like that. Feels like a two-bottle kind of night." She heard a faint snort coming from Nash's direction and ignored it. The movie couldn't start soon enough.

Eli stretched out and turned on his side, elbow bent, head braced on his palm. "Congrats on your win today, Nash. I didn't get to see it but I sure heard plenty about it."

Nash blew out his breath and mumbled a thank you. Cassie felt hopeful that she'd detected a slight thaw. She reached into her tote and pulled out two cushions, bopping Eli on the head with one. "Here. For your head or your ass, your pick."

"Hey," he said laughing, blocking her next blow with his forearm. He rolled up yanking it out of her hand then sat on it. Cassie followed suit. He pulled a metal flask from his bag and took a long swallow.

"What're you drinking?" she asked.

"Jack."

Cassie wrinkled her nose. "Can't stand the stuff."

He grinned and took another long swig. She watched his throat as he swallowed, the movement of his Adam's apple making her mouth water. Nash was shooting daggers at Eli and you could cut the tension with a knife. The movie began and Cassie murmured, "Thank God."

Eli whispered, "Ya got that right, if looks could kill." She elbowed him in his side and they shared a moment of comradery.

Cassie thought she'd feel relief once the film started but she was wrong. It just shifted. The knots in her neck caused by Nash's attitude were now replaced with a thundering pulse and tingling nerves. She couldn't focus on the movie. All she was aware of was the heat of Elijah's body next to hers, where his thigh pressed against her, searing her skin. She took another large slug of her wine and knew it was hitting her hard; the fact that she'd been too excited to eat supper was doing her no favors now. That peanut butter and jelly sandwich at noon was long gone.

Forcing herself to focus on the movie, she was soon relaxing, even laughing out loud. It'd been a long time since she'd seen this comedy classic. Billy Crystal was a great comedic actor. She let the sound of Eli's laughter wash over her. It was so sexy. *But everything about Elijah Cane is sexy.*

He leaned in close to her ear and she could feel his breath stirring her hair as he whispered, "You smell great."

His breath smelled of whiskey and she caught a hint of Old Spice. It wreaked havoc with her jumbled senses. She swallowed. "Um, thanks."

Pouting, she held her empty glass upside down right under his nose and he chuckled. "You'd better slow down, you have another movie to get through."

The alcohol emboldened her and she ran her tongue over her lips as she stared at him. "Do we have to?"

His pupils dilated and he took in a sharp breath. "Cassie Morgan, you're playing with fire," he growled softly.

She let her eyes linger on his lips. "That's the point."

He reached over and tucked a stray tendril of hair behind her ear. His eyes blazed a path across her face. "You better not open that cage door unless you're ready for the consequences." His fingers trailed down her bare arm before clasping hers in his. She turned her palm up and held his hand.

He leaned close to her ear and whispered, "You know, I'm kind of hating to say goodbye to some green-eyed barrel racer."

"Is that so?" she answered as the warmth of the wine coursed through her body, lowering her inhibitions and stripping her defenses. The desire for Eli consumed her. It was everything. She couldn't remember why she was even fighting it. It'd been so long since she'd been with a man. *Just a few kisses tonight, then I'll go back to resisting him tomorrow. What harm could that do?*

Her tongue suddenly had a mind of its own and she was surprised when she put her mouth against his ear and whispered, "I'm fine if we just skip the second movie altogether. We could go to your place and hang out." She heard his sharp intake of breath and smiled.

"Not sure that'd go over very well with your Pit Bull over there," he said, jerking his head towards Nash.

She shrugged a shoulder then ran her tongue over her lips, holding her empty cup for a refill. "He's not my keeper."

Eli chuckled as he drained the last of the first bottle into her glass. "I don't think he got that memo. You are in some kind of mood tonight Ms. Morgan. One down," he said.

She grinned, her eyes flashing wickedly. "I'm celebrating."

From that point on the movie dragged on and on. She was itching to get her hands on Eli. When the first movie ended, Cassie made a decision. She whispered into Eli's ear, "Follow my lead." She carefully stood, a bit unsteady but not wanting anyone else to know it. "I'm going to skip the second show." Eli kept his gaze lowered.

Nash complained, "You can't miss the next one. *True Grit* is one of the best westerns ever made. And what about the fireworks?"

"I know, but I'm done." She looked down at Eli and winked. "I can leave the blanket for you Eli."

"No, I think I'll call it a night as well. Can I walk you home?"

"Sure." The wine was really starting to hit her and she lost her balance when she bent down to grab the blanket.

"Here let me do that," Eli said. He shook it out before folding it neatly and tucking it under the strap of his cooler. Crooking his elbow, he grabbed her hand and slipped it through his arm, holding her tight up against his body. She tripped, missing a step, and would have fallen if it hadn't been for Elijah's hold on her. She was still sober enough to know she was drunk.

"Your place?" she asked. "I still have a bottle to finish."

His eyes were hooded as they scanned her face. "Between the whiskey and wine, I'm not so sure that's the best idea."

"Don't be a stick in the mud. I'm a grown-ass woman."

His voice came out in a growl. "No doubt about that. Let's go."

13

Cassie was startled awake by a hairy leg brushing against her thigh. Her eyes flew open and she quickly squeezed them shut again. *Shit shit shit shit! Oh my God!* She peered under the covers and suppressed a groan. Buck-ass naked. Both of them. Flashes of the previous night teased the edges of her foggy brain, a bit disjointed, but enough to have her insides squirming uncomfortably.

No! Please no! Nausea gripped her. *Did I really stand on his bed in my bra and underwear and sing a Dolly Parton song? "Jolene," I think it was. Oh no! Did we even use protection?*

Still asleep and snoring softly, Eli's arm draped across her waist and the weight of his muscular leg on top of hers pinned her to the bed. She was tucked up close against him. His breath fanned against her skin, the stubble on his chin rough on her forehead, his muscles hard, skin soft, the coarse hair tickling her, all made her hunger for a repeat of the previous evening's madness.

When they'd made it back to his place last night, they'd continued drinking. She even had a hazy recollection of doing a shot or two of some peppermint Schnapps of all things. On top of the wine. After that, things got even more hazy. Except not hazy enough. *A total blackout would be preferable right about now.* His kisses had been like putting out a fire with gasoline. The slow burn of seduction had finally erupted into a barn-burning blaze of passion.

It would be so damn easy to let herself go back to sleep in his arms...to sink into him again. Forget about common sense. Be the free spirit she'd been last night... the person she used to be before her heart had been shattered. *Run! Get the hell out of here! But how without waking him up?*

Her head throbbed and it felt like a dozen contractors were jack hammering in her skull. She suppressed a groan as she gingerly slid one leg out from under Eli's, touching the rough shag carpeting with her toes. Inching her way slowly out from underneath him, she held her breath when he mumbled in his sleep and his arm squeezed her tighter. Alarmed that she'd disturbed him, she fought the full-blown anxiety attack threatening to take over. *Shit!*

Gently clasping his arm, she tucked it against his chest, then contorted her body as she slithered out of the bed like she was doing the Limbo dance. Finding purchase with her other foot, she grabbed the side table for balance before tumbling out of bed and landing in a heap. She froze and held her breath, waiting to see if she'd disturbed him. When his steady breath continued, she sent up a prayer of thanks and gathered her clothes before scurrying to the bathroom to dress. One look in the mirror said it all. Hair a wild mess, bloodshot eyes, lips swollen, she wanted to die right then and there. *First things first Cassie, get the hell out of here, then crawl off and die somewhere.*

She tip-toed past the sleeping hunk who was now face down, head buried in the pillow, his gorgeous ass on full display. She paused to gape for a moment before catching herself, then skedaddled to the front door. Spying one of Eli's baseball caps hanging on a coat rack, she grabbed it, stuffing her hair up inside on her way out.

She breathed a sigh of relief as the door clicked shut behind her. The sun was just coming up and the familiar sound of birdsong at the break of dawn reminded her the world was still turning despite the mess she'd just gone and made of hers. Keeping her head down, she briskly headed for home. She made it past the first trailer when Nash called out to her. "Cassie." Her stomach roiled and she thought she might be sick.

She pretended not to hear, but he called again, this time louder. "Cassie! Where are you heading from so early in the morning?"

She slowly turned around to face Nash. She knew she was fifty shades of red and kept her head down and her eyes lowered.

"Oh, hey Nash," she mumbled.

"Tell me you didn't just leave that asshole's trailer," he demanded.

This actually made Cassie's alcohol-laced blood boil over and she pierced him with her eyes. "Breaking news: you don't own me Nash Gentry."

He scoffed. "I thought you were smarter than this, but I guess not."

"Not that it's any of your business, but nothing happened. I passed out on his couch." Cassie couldn't look him in the eye. She was a terrible liar and Nash knew her far too well. Plus, this was Nash, her best friend. She'd never lied to him before and didn't want to start. But, right now, she was way too hungover and vulnerable to have a discussion about her sex life anyhow.

"You expect me to believe that? I've seen you both circling around each other. He can barely take his eyes off ya. I saw this coming from a mile away. I was hoping that you'd come to your senses before you went and got hurt again." Cassie's shoulders slumped for a moment. She knew Nash wasn't saying anything she hadn't already said to herself. He was right. However, that didn't give him the right to think he could lord it over her and tell her how to live her life.

She straightened to her full height of five foot seven and waved her index finger under his nose. "I'm done talkin' about it ya hear? I swear Nash Gentry, if you breathe a word of this to Silas or anyone else, I will strangle you with my bare hands."

Cassie wished she could eat those words as she watched the hurt flicker across Nash's face. "You're going to go there? Geesh Cass, you know I've always had your back. It's just...it's like watching a train wreck,

I know you're gonna get your heart broken all over again. You're way too good for him."

She warily glanced back towards Eli's trailer. "I've got to get out of here, now. We'll have plenty of time to talk on our break. Don't worry about me, Nash. I'm all grown up. Now let me get back home, before Silas wakes up."

"Go on, who's stopping ya?"

Cassie turned on her heel and ran the rest of the way back home. She slipped between her sheets to the muffled sound of snoring coming from Silas's bedroom.

14

Eli felt like his head was about to explode, his mouth so dry he couldn't work up enough spit to swallow. And he was alone. He tried to shake off his disappointment. *What'd I expect, anyhow? Damn her. Guess she told me what last night meant to her.*

It was as if they'd been possessed. The weeks of pent-up sexual tension building between them had ignited with the first touch of their lips. Her passion was unparalleled and he knew he'd never be satisfied with one night. If he thought he'd craved her before, he knew that his imagination hadn't come close to the reality of Cassie Morgan. Even hungover, he got half hard thinking of her head thrown back, her rounded breasts with their plump pink nipples bouncing in his face as she rode him. Hard.

He sat up and groaned, scrubbing his face with his calloused hands. When the room stopped spinning, he tentatively stood up. *Aspirin, shower and coffee. In that order. Wonder how Cassie's feeling?*

He stepped out of the shower and was towel-drying his hair when he heard someone knocking on the front door. "Give me a sec," he called. Wrapping a towel around his waist, he opened the front door and was shocked to see Cassie standing there.

His heart thudded in his chest. "Cassie."

She gaped at him wide eyed, with barely veiled hunger as her eyes raked his body.

"Did you happen to find my cell phone anywhere?" she asked, avoiding his stare.

"No. Come on in. You're welcome to look for it. I'll go check the bedroom."

"Thanks." She stepped inside.

Eli touched her arm surprised when she jerked like a startled deer. "Hey it's okay. It's just me."

She nodded and surveyed the room. He watched emotions play across her face as she looked over the evidence from their wild night. The pillows from the couch were on the floor, an empty wine bottle and red Solo cup were still resting on the coffee table and an empty Schnapps bottle lay on its side. He wanted to pull her into his arms so bad when he saw her shrink with embarrassment.

"Cassie, last night was nothing short of amazing. Thank you."

Her cheeks turned a fiery red. "Can we not talk about it please and thank you."

"Why?"

"It was a mistake, that's why."

"That's some kind of bullshit and you know it. It was long overdue."

"Eli, it was one night. Period. That's all I signed up for. I know you're not the settling kind either. We knew it going into it. Let's not complicate things and make it more than it was."

"Don't speak for me, Cassie. I'm not going to lie, I like you. A lot. I want more than one night. I'd like to see where this takes us."

He saw something flicker in her eyes before she shut it down. "Not going to happen. Been there done that. Eli let's be honest here. We're both adults with needs. Last night we got those needs met. It was...shall we say combustible? However, one and done. We're two of a kind. Neither of us want any commitment."

"There you go again, thinking you can read my mind. Come on, Cass."

"Eli, please, I'm hung over and I can't deal right now. Okay? Just let me get my phone and leave."

"I'll go put some clothes on and help look for your phone." Eli could see that her walls were up a mile high and it was pointless to try to convince her of anything at the moment. If she was half as hungover as he was, he couldn't really blame her. But still...it wasn't in his nature to give up without a fight.

"Don't you dare go anywhere until I get back," he commanded, watching her kneel to peer underneath the couch.

Her muffled, "I won't," was enough reassurance for him to leave her for a minute. He threw on a pair of gray sweatpants that hung low on his hips and returned to the living room bare-chested.

"Any luck?"

"No." She glanced up and swallowed, her eyes large in her pale face.

Eli knelt beside her and ran his hands in the cracks of the couch and pulled out her cell. "Score," he said, holding it in the air out of her reach.

Her lips tightened and she held out a palm. "Gimmee."

"Not until you hear me out. Sit with me for a minute." He patted the couch in front of them.

"I'll stand."

Eli shrugged. "Suit yourself." They both stood and she crossed her arms defiantly in front of her. The mutinous expression she wore, meant to intimidate, had little impact with the vulnerability he saw behind it. It only made him want to throw her over his shoulder, carry her to his bed and erase any traces of doubt.

"Well?" she prompted, risking a glance before quickly looking away.

He stretched his hand out and cupped her jaw, running his thumb across her lips. "Look at me." She looked at him through her lashes. "Can you honestly say that wasn't the best, most mind-blowing sex you've ever had?"

Her lips twitched. *Progress.* He bravely pressed forward. "I know you have cold feet and lump all us cowboys in the same pen, but dammit Cass this feels different, you and me."

"Different how? It's always intense in the beginning.

Guys like you are into the chase. Look, I grew up around cowboys. I learned my lesson. I'm not going to get burned twice."

"You're willing to ignore what you really want? Your body knows, even if you won't admit it. You want me as bad as I want you. Why deny it?"

"I don't trust my response to you. The devil on my left shoulder could convince me of most anything. I've learned to shut her down quick."

Mule-headed woman. Eli tamped down his irritation. "Doesn't that voice have a say in anything? If it weren't for her, you'd still be lusting after me and would have missed the best sex of your life."

She scoffed, brushing off his attempt at humor. "Now who's speaking for who?"

"I recall you using the adjective 'combustible'. Or have you forgotten?"

Cassie cupped her hand over her eyes, rubbing her temples. "You're making my head pound."

He gripped both her shoulders and pulled her against his chest. Wrapping his arms around her he held on tight. She stiffened, then he felt her melt against him. Her hot cheek resting against his bare chest, he buried his nose in her thick hair that smelled of shampoo and breathed in her heady scent. "Lay with me. I missed waking up next to you. I feel cheated."

He felt her take in a ragged breath then her arms slipped around his naked waist. Her lips brushed against him. In a whisper she said, "I'm sorry, Eli. I know you believe what you're saying. I've gotten to know you this summer and I think you're a good guy.

It's not you, it's me. I'm much better at keeping things short and sweet. I can't do commitment."

He rolled his eyes. "You're fucking twenty-six years old. How in the hell do you know that? Look, I get it. You're scared. You've been hurt. We're all broken in some way, Cass."

"I won't lie to you and say last night wasn't amazing, but it doesn't change anything. We both head in different directions tomorrow."

"All the more reason to come to my bed now. Give me this time. I'm just asking for a couple hours. We both need to sleep off this hangover anyway. Pretty please." Her body softened and he knew she was weakening.

"Just to sleep," she said. "I'll admit I wouldn't mind feeling your arms around me. I'm kind of a mess this morning."

"Come on." Without giving her time to think about it he scooped her up into his arms, cradling her against him and carried her to his bed.

After laying her down, he removed her sneakers and jeans, tossed them aside, and crawled in next to her. She rolled onto her side facing away from him and he gathered her up, tugging her tightly against his chest. She sighed and nestled into him. He kissed her hair just behind her ear and said softly, "Babe, you feel so good. There is nowhere on God's green earth I'd rather be right now."

"Eli you best quit sweettalking me."

"Not going to happen."

He heard a smile in her voice. "Go to sleep, cowboy."

"Yes, darlin'."

Half asleep, she said, "Do you always get your way?"

"No, but I always give it my best shot. You've been warned." Soon he felt the steady rise and fall of her breath and drifted off himself.

15

Cassie groggily snuggled against the warm body enveloping her from behind and sighed contentedly. Her eyes popped open when she felt something large and hard pressing into her bottom. *Eli.* She held her breath.

"You awake?' he murmured into her ear, his breath fanning her cheek.

"Yeah, barely."

"How's your head?"

"Better. Yours?"

"Better."

He moved her hair aside and brushed his lips across her neck, that tender skin just below her ear. Shivers rippled down her spine.

"Babe, how can you feel so damn good? Did you know you have the cutest constellation of tiny moles on your butt?" His fingers traced along the curve of her hip before inching down to kiss her there. His voice was all gravelly and seductive and despite herself she was aroused again. All she could think about was his lips and hands roaming over her body. Tomorrow would come soon enough, but for today she wasn't going to overthink everything. She wanted him, he wanted her.

Rolling over, she turned to face him and met his hooded gaze. He lazily leaned down and pressed his soft lips against hers, his kiss slow and sweet. She parted her lips and he groaned. He licked into her mouth and leisurely explored, sucking on her tongue, her bottom lip, then nibbled on her upper lip. He circled the pad of his thumb over her nipple and her body thrummed.

She rocked her hips and the sweet friction of his erection pressing against her belly made her gasp. His hand coasted to the small of her back pulling her tightly against his stiff cock as he rutted against her. Cradling the back of her head with his free hand, he buried his fingers in her hair, peppering her face with tiny kisses...her forehead, then each eyelid, her nose, her cheeks, before landing on her lips again. "Babe, you have no idea what you do to me," he said against her mouth.

His hand slipped under her tee-shirt, the roughness chafing against her soft skin as it skimmed over her waist and rib cage. She moaned when he found her breast and cupped it, gently squeezing as his thumb rolled slowly over her silk-clad nipple. She reached down and rubbed his cock through his sweats and he panted.

His voice was gruff when he murmured, "Cass, I want you so bad right now. You're so damn hot you make me crazy."

She responded by pulling his sweatpants down over his hips. His shaft sprang free, jutting up straight and hard against his stomach. "My, my, cowboy," she said, her voice breathy. She fisted him and rubbed her thumb across the slit, which was already wet from his arousal. He took in a sharp breath. She released him long enough to slip out of her tee-shirt. She needed to feel his skin against hers. He unclasped her bra and her breasts spilled out.

His breath ragged, he bent down to suck her nipple into his mouth. The gentleness was gone, replaced with desperation as he tugged and tongued her sensitive nub. She framed his head between her palms, holding him to her breast. "Yes, yes! Do that. Don't stop!" she said, voice thick with passion.

Still suckling her nipple, he slipped his hand under the elastic of her panties then plunged a finger inside. He thrust until he was buried up to his knuckles. He circled his finger and she moaned. He withdrew then inserted a second finger inside, stretching her, while his thumb pressed against her clit. As he continued his practiced torture, her body bucked against his fingers, demanding more. He continued thrusting in and out, almost withdrawing only to bury himself again and again. She used him to pleasure herself while he enjoyed his cock nestled in her tight fist. He thrust up, pumping into her soft firm grip.

"I don't know how much longer I can hold out. I'm about to come," he rumbled.

"Mm," she moaned. "Please Eli, I need you inside of me," she said, breathless and panting. She craved him, needed him to take her. He pulled down her skimpy lace panties, then reached across her body to open the drawer of the bedside table. He ripped the foil packet open with his teeth. Cassie took it from him and pulled out the condom, then rolled it over his shaft.

He pushed her back onto the mattress and used his knees to spread her thighs wide. Bracing his forearms on either side, he devoured her with his smoldering eyes, the flecks of amber blazing with desire. He stroked her sweet spot, driving her into a frenzy. When she began to writhe against his fingers again, he poised himself at her entry. "You're so wet," he ground out.

"Please...Eli...I..."

With one hard thrust, he pushed inside and growled, "Is this what you want?" With his throbbing cock deep inside her tightness, he stilled. Sucking and nibbling her neck at the curve of her shoulder, his lips grazed the delicate skin as she rocked her pelvis impatiently against him.

"Please...Eli...please," she said, her voice somewhere between a purr and a growl.

Her words seemed to ignite his storm of desire. He pistoned his pelvis, greedily riding her, his muscles bunched, sweat dampening his chest and torso. He shoved her legs wider, needing to be even closer. The slapping sound as their bodies coupled sent her to the edge of climaxing. Her fingers gripped the sheets, the sight of her pale thighs against his dark skin arousing her further. His face was engulfed by hunger and Cassie knew she was about to come.

"Eli...I'm going to..."

He buried himself until he was seated inside, his mouth covering hers, licking, tasting, taking. He pressed his face in her neck as his body shuddered. She climaxed right behind him and they rode the waves of their orgasm together. She could feel him pulsating inside her. His soft wet mouth against her skin made her nerve endings tingle as her body trembled with the aftershocks of release. The smell of musky sex assailed her senses.

As they lay spent, the length of his body melting into hers, their breathing slowly returned to normal. Cassie loved the feel of him on top of her. The coarse hair on his thighs chafing hers, his hard muscular body and damp skin branding her memory. She didn't want to move.

He nuzzled her ear. "That was amazing."

She stroked his back, letting her fingers trail down his spine and across his rounded buttocks. The hair was soft and felt good against her palms. His muscles bunched when she teased his crease and she giggled softly. He rolled onto his side taking her with him so that they were facing each other. His tousled hair and sexy stubble made her mush inside.

Gently brushing her hair away from her brow, he caressed her cheek. "Now what?" he asked.

"As in...?"

"Can I call you while I'm in Wyoming and you're in Austin?"

She felt herself stiffen and hated that her walls were going back up so soon.

"Eli, I don't know. Can we not talk about it? We've

already gone over this. Can we keep it light for now? Maybe since we're not going to see each other for a couple of weeks it'd be a good time to take a break. Who knows what will happen between now and then? You may meet your soul mate."

"Maybe I already have," he said it quietly, a challenge in his intense gaze.

Her heart lurched in her chest. "Cowboy, you best not be saying things you don't know nothing about."

"Cass, don't shut me out. This was more than sex and you know it."

Cassie felt her insides melting and cursed under her breath.

"We can agree on one thing. It was great sex," she said.

"Babe, I don't believe you're near as tough as you want me and everyone else to believe. I'd say we have a lot in common in that way, were ya to ask me."

"I'm not asking."

He leaned close, so close she could feel his breath fan across her cheeks. Her stomach fluttered. "I want you, Cassie Morgan. And I can't say I'll ever have my fill of you. Even more than that, I like you. A whole lot. I don't want any other cowboys sniffin' around. I'm greedy like that." He closed the distance and grazed her lips with his own. "When we meet back up in two weeks, I want to spend time with you. Just the two of us. Date. What do you say?"

Her pulse raced and she floundered momentarily. "I…I'm not sure it's a good idea. I like my life the way it is right now. No commitments, no complications."

He looked into her eyes with such intensity that she

felt like he could see into all her dark secret places. He brushed his lips against the corner of her mouth. "You're scared. I can see it. It's all right there, in your gorgeous green eyes, the ones that make me half-crazy every time I look into them."

"Who's scared? I'm being sensible is all." Her voice sounded strained to her own ears.

He gathered her close, burrowing his nose in her hair, then his lips skimmed a path along her throat making her desire flare up all over again.

"Whatever you say darlin'." He ran his hands down her back and cupped her bottom. "We'll take it at your pace. So long as you know, I'm coming for ya. And I *will* be calling ya while we're apart."

She gulped, relieved that by tomorrow evening there'd be hundreds of miles between them.

16

Eli let Freak have his head and they galloped through the meadow heading towards his favorite spot, where the mountains met the stream. He was shirtless and the hot sun beat down on his back. It was good to be home, but he had to admit that he had Cassie Morgan on the brain. He could picture her here, mingling with his family and fitting right in. Galloping right along beside him.

Now that was a scary thought. He'd never been one to get serious enough to let anyone inside his private domain. He'd never needed anyone...never let himself need anyone. Until now, he'd kept his sex life fairly compartmentalized. Casual hook-ups, some for one night, some for several, never serious. He wasn't going to lie about it, he loved women...their softness, their bodies...sex.

When did I start getting bored with it? He had to admit, somewhere along the line, he'd grown weary of the superficiality of one-nighters and buckle bunnies. In his whole life, the only girl he'd ever invited into his personal world was his high school sweetheart Rose. They'd lost their virginity together. First love. That relationship had ended when she went off to college and he to the rodeo. He'd never looked back.

The women he'd bedded since then were mostly interested in the package anyhow. The rodeo star, the cowboy. His looks and his image.

Cassie was different. To her, his status was a detriment rather than an aphrodisiac. She was completely unimpressed by his resume. He liked that. He felt like she saw through his public persona and got him. She was complex; there was so much more to her than her beauty. She listened. She asked questions. She was smart as a whip. He grinned. *Who'd have known that could be such a turn-on?* He wasn't going to give her up without a fight. He might not be sure what he wanted, but he sure as hell knew he wanted—no, correction—*needed* more of her.

When they reached the stream, he jumped down from Freak, toed off his boots, rolled up his pant legs and led Freak into the water. The cold swirled around his calves as he carefully picked his way over the rock bed. Freak was a solid white beauty with a couple of black freckles on his nose.

He'd named him Freak because when Eli had first adopted him from the BLM, he'd been feral as all git out. He'd been one of many at the auction held for mustangs that had been rounded up early that spring. Eli had spotted him right away and picked him up for a hundred bucks. He'd worked with him slowly, preferring the evolved way of training a horse over the neanderthal old school way of 'breaking' them. Their relationship was about as solid as you could get, one based on mutual respect and trust.

Freak pawed the water before dipping his head down to drink. Eli cupped his hands and filled them, splashing his face, then his arms and torso. He let the ice-cold water trickle down his chest and back, cooling him off. Lifting his face to the sun to dry, he felt that deep connection to the earth that always cleared his head and made him feel whole.

"What do ya think, Freak?" He slung an arm across the horse's withers and Freak let out a sigh, blowing air through his nostrils. "Relaxed, aren't ya, buddy? Me too. Now, what should I do about this skittery filly I'm smitten with?"

There was a gentle stir of the air, offering some relief from the dry heat. Eli wasn't in any hurry, so they hung out in the water for a spell, taking in the mountains and jutting rock formations and the big azure blue sky. He filled his lungs with a long slow breath. The smell of pine, cedar and sage, as much as anything, told him he was home.

As he stepped onto the sandy bank, Freak's ears perked forward suddenly alert. He followed the horse's gaze as a herd of antelope thundered off in the distance. He watched until they disappeared over the horizon before mounting and heading for home.

. . .

Slipping quietly into the lodge kitchen, Eli held his finger to his lips to keep Sophia and Becca from giving him away. He snuck up on his mom, Abby, wrapping his arms around her waist from behind hugging her tight while she kneaded dough.

"You makin' my favorite welcome home supper?" he asked.

"You're a spoiled brat," she grumbled, but her smile gave her away.

"Now Mama, I've been dreaming of your gnocchi for two months. Those jokers get to eat your cooking every day. Tell me who's spoiled."

His sister Becca chimed in. "Yeah right. We all know you're her favorite."

Eli grinned wickedly. "Ya think?" He turned to Sophia. "What do you think Soph?"

She held up her hands. "Leave me out of it. I wouldn't touch that with a nine-foot pole. I don't think Abby plays favorites though."

"Chicken," he taunted.

"I have no experience with sibling rivalry. I'm an only child, remember?"

"Not anymore," Becca said. Obviously touched, Sophia's cheeks turned pink.

A small whirling dervish with black hair and sparkling brown eyes raced into the kitchen and threw himself at Elijah. "Uncle Eli! You're really here!"

"Hey, Clayton. How's my favorite kid on the planet?"

His answer was to hold his hands out, palms up, proudly showing off several large blisters.

"Holy cow dude. What happened? Did ya get drug by a wild bull?" Eli asked, eyes wide, feigning shock.

Clay let out a peal of laughter. "No."

"Spill it."

Eyes sparkling, he said, "I was in a tug of war contest at the county fair."

Eli grinned. "Looks like you held on tight."

"Yep. Our team won. And know what the best part was?"

"No, but I have a feeling you're going to tell me."

He snickered uncontrollably. "The losing team got pulled into a sloppy pit of mud."

"I'd have bust a gut on that," Eli said.

"Guess who was on the other team?"

"Um...Aunt Becca?"

He shook his head, eyes dancing. "Nope. Grandpa Cane!" He bent over laughing, while holding his stomach. "It was the funniest thing I ever saw."

"I so wish I had been there to see that." Eli said, glancing over at his sister Becca with raised brows. "How'd the old man take it?"

"Actually, he laughed as hard as the rest of us," Becca said.

"It was such a fun day," Abby shared. "Fortunately, it was towards the end of our day, so we left right after so your dad could come home and clean up."

"I'm so bummed that I missed it."

Becca went over to Eli and gave him a big hug. "I've missed you."

"It's good to be home. I'm going to take a quick shower then watch the rest of the game. The Diamondbacks are playing the Cubs. I'm surprised you aren't glued to the TV, Sophia. Surely you're a Chicago Cubs fan."

"Of course, I am. We're going to kick Arizona's butt."

"We'll see. Come catch a little of the game with us. I don't know about you but I'm ready for a couple of cold ones."

"I'll be there after I finish filling this pie. Save me a seat," Sophia said.

Eli crouched down eye level to Clay and said, "You staying here or going up to the house?"

"Dad said I had to come home and take a bath." His nose wrinkled. "I hate taking baths."

"I'm with ya on that bud. Hop on. I'll give you a ride." Eli squatted and Clay clambered onto his back and they headed for the main house. Clay chattered in Eli's ear about baseball, his favorite team and his dream of being a major league baseball player someday.

17

Silas pushed the grocery cart and Cassie checked off the items from their list as they went along. Adeline had decided at the last minute to come stay with them in Austin instead of heading back to her Arizona home. She and Nash were in charge of buying the beverages and picking up some wood for their campfire.

They'd invited some neighbors and friends from the trailer park to join them and to bring a side dish to go along with the pig shoulder they were barbecuing for the smoked pulled pork. It was a perfect night for it. Cassie's cell phone rang and her heart skipped a beat when she saw that it was Elijah calling.

"Hey," she said, slightly breathless.

His lazy drawl warmed her insides. "Whatcha up to, beautiful?"

"Me and Silas are buying us some groceries for a

gathering tonight. We're roasting a pig. How about you?"

"Watching a baseball game with my family. It's the seventh inning stretch, so I thought it'd be a good time to check in."

Cassie heard a child's voice in the background say in a sing-song teasing tone, "Uncle Eli has a girlfriend."

"That must be Clay I hear in the background."

He said dryly, "How'd ya guess?"

"Is your team winning?"

"Unfortunately, my future sister-in-law Sophia is busy gloating, because her hometown Chicago team is ahead by two runs."

Cassie laughed. "Well, you still have two innings to catch up."

"Who's that on the phone?" Silas grumbled. "I'm gittin tired of pushing this dang cart around."

"It's Eli. We're practically at the finish line, hang in there Silas."

Silas's bushy brows drew together for a moment. "Eli huh? Tell 'im I said hey."

"Silas says hello."

"Hi back." Eli's voice grew husky. "I guess I'll let you go. I needed to hear your voice." She heard Clayton's peal of laughter.

"Uncle Eli is in love!" He drew out the word in a long-exaggerated drawl and she could hear others laughing in the background at his shenanigans.

She heard a deep stern voice reprimand him...*must be his dad Luke*, but it didn't stop Clayton from giggling. He had to be practically on top of Eli, because she could hear him clear as a bell.

"Thanks for calling," she said softly.

"I'll check back in tomorrow. Enjoy your party."

"We will. Good luck with the game."

She hung up and stared into space until Silas cleared his throat noisily. "Things getting serious between the two of ya?"

"No! Nothing like that. We're just friends."

"Now Cassie, my mama didn't raise no fool and I've known ya since you was knee high to a grasshopper. You look like you like you're fixin to fly to the moon."

Her cheeks flushed. "I'm telling ya, we're friends. I'll admit, I had him pegged wrong. He's not bad, once you get to know him a little."

"I'm sure that's true. I got no beef with Elijah, but he better not go hurting my girl or there will be hell to pay. That's all I'll say about the subject."

"Thank you, Si. I'm a big girl and you don't have to worry about me none. We're just hanging out here and there."

He snorted. "Ah-huh. I spect that's why he's calling you after only being apart fer one dang day." He cleared his throat. "And after not coming home the other night."

Cassie averted her gaze and studied the canned baked bean selection like she'd be tested on it later. "Okay. Beans are the last thing on the list, we're good to go."

Her voice was bright and held way more enthusiasm than the statement called for. It made Silas smile. "Tater, I'm not here to judge. If he's the one, you know I'll dance at yer wedding."

She sputtered. "Whoa Nellie! Wedding? You're getting way ahead of yourself."

His eyes twinkled at her. "I was just yanking yer chain a little. I trust you to know what's in your own best interest. You don't have to hide nothing from me, ya hear?"

"I know that." She squeezed his bony shoulder. "Thanks Si."

"Let's get the hell outta here. My hip is killing me," he said.

They got in the checkout lane and soon they were loading the bags into the bed of their pick-up and heading home.

That evening everyone was happily settled around the campfire with full bellies. The sky was bursting with stars, barely space between them all. They'd put the food away and cleaned up and now it was time to relax.

Nash said, "Oh I almost forgot to tell ya Silas, some guy came by today when you were shopping, asking about your son Reed. Nice fancy car, he smelled like money."

Cassie frowned. "Wonder what they wanted?"

Nash shrugged. "Don't know."

Silas narrowed his eyes. "What'd he say, exactly?"

"Just wanted to know where Reed was or his family."

"Huh." Silas narrowed his eyes, rubbing his thumb across his unshaven chin. "What'd ya tell 'em?"

"Just that Reed had passed."

"Anything else? Did you say anything about me or Cass?"

"Naw. It was a little weird coming out a nowhere like that, so I clammed up. He just thanked me and left."

"Probably somebody wantin' to do a rodeo article or some damn thang. Reed was pretty big in his heyday. Set some records," Silas said.

"I'm sure that's it," Nash agreed.

"Is your food settled enough to play us some tunes?" Adeline asked.

Cass looked over at Si and he nodded. "I'll run in and get our instruments." She jumped up and jogged to the RV, returning with a banjo case and her guitar. They sat and tuned their instruments, with easy conversation flowing amongst old friends.

Playing some chords to check the tuning, she was satisfied and rested her arm on the body of her guitar, waiting for Silas to finish. He glanced up and nodded.

"You good?" Cassie asked.

"Yep."

They played anything and everything from Noah Cyrus, Miley's little sister, to campfire songs. When Nash stood up and reached into the cooler, pulling out graham crackers, marshmallows and dark chocolate, it was game over. She and Silas quickly stowed their instruments and grabbed sticks to skewer their marshmallows with.

Cassie looked at the familiar faces she'd grown up around, when they weren't on the road. Some were retired now and some even had grown grandchildren. *Time is so weird*. She looked at Silas as he tried to eat the gooey s'more without wearing it, Dios waiting at his feet for any fallout. She remembered a time when his face had less wrinkles and his body was hard and strong. She felt a fierce love rip through her and was so grateful to him for all that he'd been and all that he was in her life.

Nash laughed at something Adeline said and Cassie felt a pang, but only for a second. Even though it would certainly change things if and when he found his mate, she knew he'd always be her best friend. Life moved on and it was time for Nash to find that special someone to share his with.

That brought Eli to mind. She wondered. It seemed like there could be something if she could let herself trust again. And what if she did and she was wrong about him? What if it was all about the chase? She wasn't sure she could survive another heartbreak. But nothing was without risk really. She knew that. *Hells bells every time I race, I can get hurt, but I can handle about anything except being left again.*

She stood and stretched her arms over her head, yawning. "I'm hitting the hay y'all. Don't worry about cleaning up, ya hear? The foods put away and everything else can wait till morning."

A few others stood to leave and Cassie waved and went into the RV. She brushed her teeth, slipped into a fresh, oversized tee and crawled between the sheets. She'd left her phone by the bed on its charger and glanced at it, surprised to see a text message had come in from Eli.

Elijah: Hope you're having fun. Miss you. 

A heart emoji! Really? She figured he probably wouldn't see her message until tomorrow but with butterflies in her stomach she typed a reply anyway.

Cassie: Would have been even better if you'd been here. Good night cowboy. Sweet dreams.

She turned off her bedside lamp, plumped her pillow and was out like the light she'd just switched off.

18

Cassie sat on the toilet and counted the weeks backward for the umpteenth time...back to that first night they'd been together. The only night they hadn't used protection. Six weeks almost to the day. Since that first wild night, they'd been careful to have plenty of condoms on hand.

Cassie and Eli had drifted into an arrangement that had Cassie sleeping over at his place several nights a week. They didn't talk about it. So far anyway. Eli seemed to sense that topic was out of Cassie's comfort zone and hadn't pushed her, but he'd made it clear: if he had it his way she'd be in his bed more nights than not.

She'd started to feel nauseous in the mornings a few days ago. Probably a virus or something. Nothing sounded good to eat. She'd brushed it off, normal for her in the summer heat. No biggie, she'd told herself. It wasn't until she'd absently checked her calendar, counting the days since her last period, that she unburied her head from the sand. *Okay, calm down, it happens, I've been late before*...she'd reassured herself, unconvincingly. She couldn't ignore the sense of panic that took over her entire being.

Now here she was, clutching the wand that came with the pregnancy test kit she'd bought earlier that day, too terrified to pee on the stick. *Well here goes nothing*. She got the nerve up, positioned the absorbent end of the plastic stick under her stream and took the test. She washed her hands and placed that devil on the sink, then put the toilet lid down and sat. And waited. Five minutes the directions said.

Her hands trembled and she thought she might get sick. She was practically hyperventilating, so she stuck her head down between her thighs and gulped in air. She glanced at her watch. Three minutes had passed. *It's a fluke. A series of coincidences.* Four minutes. *Nobody is that unlucky. Are they?* Five minutes. *Times up. Thank God*...She sat frozen. Unable to move, filled with dread.

With shaking hands, she finally reached for the stick and dared a glance at the control panel. A red plus sign appeared in the display window. All the air left her lungs in a whoosh and she collapsed onto the bathroom floor and curled into herself. She had no sense of time or how long she lay there on the cold tile.

She was aware of some sounds coming from the kitchen. Silas was home. She pushed herself into a sitting position and then slowly stood. She placed her palms against her flat stomach. *Oh, dear Lord give me strength.*

"Cassie?" Silas called.

"I'm in the bathroom. I'll be out in a minute."

"I'm fixin' us some supper. Just ran into Elijah and invited him to join us."

Her eyes widened in horror and she stuck her fist in her mouth and bit down hard. Maybe she could pass it off as the flu or something, but she was a terrible liar. She needed time to wrap her own mind around it before they found out.

She splashed her face with cold water and stood staring at herself in the mirror. She was as pale as a ghost, her eyes huge in her face. She grabbed her makeup kit from the vanity drawer and smoothed on foundation, then added lipstick and mascara. *Better.* After taking a deep breath in and exhaling slowly, she went out to help with dinner. Silas was peeling potatoes so she put water in a pan and placed it on the stove.

"Did ya hear that they found drugs in Kelly's mare? They say she got permanently disbanded from professional barrel racing."

"How'd they know to look?" she said, trying to sound interested.

"Apparently the horse went down and when the vet did blood work, they found traces in her system."

"Huh."

"That's all ya got to say? I was spectin' you to go off the rails. '*That's horrible. How could you treat your horse like that just to win?*' Your usual rant," Silas commented, looking closely at her. He shrugged and shook his head. "It probably goes on more than we'd like to think."

"I'm sure." Cassie answered distractedly. "Silas, before Eli gets here, I need to tell you something, but I don't want it to worry you none."

He'd finished with the potatoes and was now chopping carrots. His knife stopped in mid-air and turned to look at her. "Spit it out, Tater."

"I'm dropping out of Monday's competition. It's getting near the end of the season for us anyways and I'm not at my best. I'm tired."

His forehead furrowed, concern etching his face. "That's not like you at all Cassie. What's going on?"

"Silas, don't press me about this right now. I have a lot on my mind. Give me a couple of days and we'll revisit this. For now, keep it between us. Don't even tell Nash."

"He'll know soon enough."

"I'm aware of that."

He stared at her with his penetrating eyes, as if he could see all the way to her soul. "I'll be here when yer ready to talk."

Cassie wrapped her arms around him, breathing in his comforting scent of laundry soap and tobacco and hugged him tight. She fought back tears, then was sidetracked by Eli's knock on the screen door. Plastering a smile on her face she let him in.

"Hey Cass." He did a double take. "Something wrong?"

She shook her head.

"You look awful pale babe," he said, studying her intently.

She smiled wanly. "I've got a slight headache is all."

"You sure?"

"Can you give it a rest already?" she snapped. His head whipped back like she'd slapped him. Immediately contrite, she said, "I'm sorry. I didn't mean for it to come out like that."

His eyes narrowed; she could tell he still wasn't convinced. "If you say so."

"Eli, after I git the taters going, could you fire up the grill fer me?" Silas requested.

"Be happy to."

"Cass if you'd sprinkle some salt, pepper and garlic powder on those steaks then cover 'em that'd be a help."

Cassie peeled back the plastic wrap from the meat and almost gagged when she smelled the blood pooling on the plate. "Excuse me for a minute." She ran to the bathroom and kneeled over the toilet. She dry-heaved a few times then her stomach finally settled.

"Cassie? Are you alright?" Eli said, right outside the door.

"I'm fine. I'll be right out. Could you go ahead and take care of seasoning them steaks?"

"Okay. But I can I come in first?"

She stood then cracked the door and he stepped into the bathroom. He touched her forehead. "You're clammy as hell. Do you think you have the flu?"

"Maybe that's it. It could be the heat."

He pulled her against his chest. "I'll take your place in the kitchen tonight. You can sit and relax. Silas and I can handle preparing supper."

"I won't argue."

"Now I know you're sick."

"Ha ha," she said, offering a weak smile.

He took her hand and weaved their fingers together. "Come on. Let's get you settled in on the couch."

She felt a lump in her throat the size of a golf ball. Eli was being so sweet and she hated that she had to lie to him. He wouldn't be so adoring when he found out what was really wrong. In fact, he'd probably go running and screaming all the way back to Wyoming.

He led her to the couch and lifted her legs up so that she was reclining, then propped up pillows behind her back. He left and grabbed a can of ginger ale from the fridge and poured her a glass with ice to settle her stomach. After handing her the drink, he directed the fan towards her and switched it to oscillate. Dios jumped up and curled beside her, belly up, legs splayed out already looking like he'd achieved nirvana.

"Dios you're making me jealous," Eli said, as Cassie absently rubbed his belly.

"Is there anything else you need before I go outside to fire up the grill?"

"No thank you." She watched him walk away, all broad shoulders and tight ass, moving like a panther. She leaned her head back and closed her eyes. Now that the panic had settled a bit, it was slowly dawning on her that she had a baby growing inside her, granted it was only about the size of a sweet pea...but still. It was her sweet pea. And Elijah's.

Suddenly, the semblance of calm she'd managed to latch onto vanished and she began shivering, paralyzed with fear. Instinctively she cupped her hands protectively around her belly. Her breathing was rapid and shallow and she forced herself to take a few deep slow breaths. She grabbed her phone from the end table. She needed to talk to someone or she'd lose her mind. Her best friend Nash, as always, answered her text immediately. He agreed to meet her after supper for a walk. Her breathing returned to normal.

Eli came back inside, the screen door slamming behind him. His eyes caressed her and it warmed her heart. *It would be okay. Wouldn't it?* She knew in that moment that she did love him. Probably had from the beginning. It didn't change anything and it didn't mean he loved her back. She'd never corral anyone against their will. Even with her fear of being abandoned, it'd be far worse to have a person stay because they felt trapped or obligated. That gate would always be left open. She valued freedom too much herself.

19

Cassie begged off Eli's invitation to spend the night at his place, telling him she'd already made plans to hang out with Nash after supper. Her stomach threatened to purge the small portion of her dinner she'd managed to choke down. Throughout the entire meal, she'd been acutely aware of Eli and Silas exchanging concerned glances. It had done nothing to soothe her nerves. She could hardly wait to excuse herself and get the hell out of there. She clung to the meet-up with Nash. He'd always been her rock.

He was waiting for her and opened the door wide. His platinum blond curls hung low across his brow, the wide smile disappearing when he took one look at her face. "Cass, come on in. What's wrong?"

"Oh Nash!" She threw herself at him and he enveloped her in his strong arms.

Holding her tight he said, "Shh, Tater, I've got ya. Come on in and have a seat. I'll pour ya some sweet tea." He led her over to a loveseat and sat her down then walked to his fridge to grab the pitcher of tea and pour a glass. He handed it to Cassie and sat down beside her.

"You were right. I've really gone and done it this time." The tears that had been threatening spilled down her cheeks as her body wracked with sobs. "I... I..." Her hands shook uncontrollably and she felt a soft handkerchief gently dab her cheeks.

"Shh." Nash slung his arm across her shoulders and pulled her against him.

He was so strong and solid, his scent as familiar as the smell of horses, barn and liniment. As he rocked her, she could feel herself relaxing into the warmth of his embrace.

Voice hitching, she said, "Nash, please promise me you won't be mad."

"Cass, I can't promise ya that, not without hearing what ya got to say, but I can promise I'm here for ya no matter what."

She looked up into his deep blue eyes and took in a ragged breath then blurted, "I'm pregnant." She sniffled then blew into the handkerchief, her hands trembling. "I'm shakin' like a leaf."

The color drained out of his face. "Oh, Cassie." He hugged her tight, patting her back like he would a child.

Her breath hitched. "Wha...wha...what am I going to do?" she whimpered.

"I reckon you're the only one that can answer that. But no matter what, it's going to be alright. You got to be scared out of your ever-lovin' mind."

She realized the minute she'd uttered that question to Nash, that she'd already made up her mind. She'd have this baby and raise it herself. She wouldn't ask for a dime from nobody. She had Silas and Nash and that was all the help she needed.

"Does Eli or Silas know?" he asked quietly.

She shook her head no. "Not yet. You're the first person I've told."

"How far along?"

"Around six weeks, far as I know, it happened the first night we were together." She glanced up at him through her thick lashes, swallowing hard. "That's the only time we didn't use protection. We were drunk out of our gourds."

His lips tightened and she could tell by the tick in his jaw that he was reining in his emotions. Through gritted teeth he said, "I knew it! It was movie night, wasn't it? I never should have let that scumbag walk you home. I knew he'd take advantage. You could hardly walk straight when you left. That's when it happened, isn't it? Movie night?"

She nodded. "It wasn't your place to stop us. I'm a big girl Nash. It was my decision. Plus, it was more the other way around. I'm the one that pushed for it that night. I practically jumped his bones. Nobody forced me and this isn't anybody's fault. Especially not yours."

Pinching his nose he said, "It *is* my fault. I'm supposed to protect you, keep you safe. I let you down. You know the worst part of it? I saw this coming from a mile away. He's a no-good, womanizing cock hound." His voice snarled out the last part, bitter and full of self-blame.

She placed her palm against his chest. "Nash, I know you mean well, but this isn't helping none. Right now, all I need is for you to tell me everything is gonna be alright."

She watched as an array of emotions danced across his face. He blew out a deep breath and said, "And all that is true. It will be. You got me and Silas. Whatever you decide to do, we'll be right beside ya."

In a small voice she said, "I'm keeping the baby."

He sighed. "I figured." He brushed her hair back from her damp forehead. "We'll figure it all out. When are ya gonna tell the asshole?"

"Nash, he's not an asshole. The more I'm with him, the more I know he's not the man everyone thinks he is. He's a good person. You should know that the gossip pipeline isn't reliable. They've had you and me linked as a couple for years. It's practically incestuous around here. And besides that, he's the father, and...I really like him."

Nash nodded and pinched the bridge of his nose. "I could see that, and you're right. He is the father. If I were a bettin' man, I'd say he'll do right by you and the baby. Do you want me to be there when you break it to him and Silas?"

"No, but thanks. I'll tell them myself. I'm going to wait till after I see a doctor to tell Si. No sense in riling him up until it's a hundred percent sure."

"If ya need me to go with ya to the appointment, you know I will."

"I know, thank you. I feel better. I needed to talk to someone to get my head cleared up. It's like a thousand pounds has been lifted." Cassie felt more tears welling up and swiped them away. Her lips curved up. "You're going to make the best uncle ever."

"That little tater tot won't want fer nothing," he replied, the smile returning to his eyes.

"I don't know what I ever did to deserve you, but Lord have mercy, am I ever thankful," Cass said, hugging him tightly.

"Must have been something pretty bad," he said, chuckling.

She lightly punched his chest. "Ya think?"

"I'm sure of it. You know I'm here for you, for anything, anytime."

She smiled softly. "I do know."

20

The following day Cassie was bent over the toilet again, praying her morning sickness would pass quickly. Eli had a ride today and she didn't want to miss it. It was an important competition and a win would pad his pockets very well indeed. It only slightly assuaged her guilty feelings about keeping her secret from him. He didn't need any distractions right before competing and this one was a whopper.

An hour later, feeling slightly better, she traded the bathroom for the kitchen and rummaged through the cupboard for some saltines. She pulled the box down from the top shelf, checked the expiration date, then ripped open a sleeve and sat down at the table to nibble on a cracker. Her phone pinged and she saw it was a text from Nash.

Nash: How ya feeling?

Cassie: ☹️ Sicker than a dog this mornin. Finally able to nibble on some saltines.

Nash: Anything I can do?

Cassie: No. Concentrate on your performance. Good luck!

Nash: 👍

Nash's ride was later this afternoon and she hoped to get there to watch him. But right now, she had to shower and get her butt moving if she wanted to make it in time to see Eli's ride. She was anxious, her nerves a jittery mess. Ever since she and Eli had slept together, she hated to watch him bronc ride, yet she couldn't not watch. It was a conundrum. Her heart stayed in her throat the entire time he rode. Eight seconds had never felt so long. She managed to get down a couple more crackers then headed for the shower.

Cassie stared at her face in the mirror, surprised that she looked the same as always. She felt so different on the inside that she couldn't believe it didn't show on the outside. She gathered her hair up into a high ponytail then swiped gloss across her lips. She pulled on an orange tank-top over a pair of jean cut-offs, noticing how golden her skin had become. She wrinkled her nose at the dusting of freckles across it.

Oh well. At least Eli likes them.

. . .

Eli was buckling his chaps when she found him. She watched as he wrapped the leather around his muscular thighs and secured them. She could tell he was already in the zone. So focused, so sexy. Sensing her, he turned and locked his gaze onto hers. He smiled. He took two steps towards her and she ran the rest of the way throwing herself into his arms.

"Wow, I'm beginning to think you might like me," he said, chuckling as she clung to him. "I could get used to this."

Her voice sounded muffled against his shirt. "Please be careful."

He tugged her ponytail. "I've had plenty of practice and I got a good draw. Midnight Storm."

"That's good. I just came by to wish you luck and to cheer you on."

He tilted her chin up and brushed her lips with his. "Thanks. I'll see you after the ride. Quit worrying."

She let go of him and backed away. Sticking her thumb up in the air she flashed him a grin she wasn't feeling on the inside. "You got this."

"And you've got me, Cassie Morgan." The emotion behind the softly spoken words made her breath catch.

She leaned against the rail that surrounded the arena and waited nervously as Eli climbed onto Midnight. The chute opened and they shot out like a canon. He was riding it perfectly far as she could tell. Six seconds in and the horse jumped to the side and Eli flew high into the air, landing flat on his back. The crowd gasped and Cassie had to fight not to climb into the ring and rush to his side. He wasn't moving. Clearly the wind had been knocked out of him but she couldn't tell if he was seriously hurt or not. *Please, please, let him be alright. He doesn't even know he's going to be a father yet. Oh God no!*

With the help of the medical staff on standby he sat up then slowly stood. He looked shaken but he waved his cowboy hat at the crowd and they cheered as he left the ring. Cassie was shaking in her boots and her teeth were chattering. She was frozen to the spot. Her eyes fixated on Eli. He scanned the arena until he spotted her. He waved but she didn't wave back. For some reason now that she knew he was okay, she was madder than a wet hen and wanted to wring his neck. Legs unsteady she weaved through the crowd and made her way to Eli.

His eyes lit up as she approached. He was covered in dust and dirt, his black cowboy hat worse for the wear. He looked puzzled as she marched up to him. Everything and everyone else faded, it was just the two of them in the sea of people and animals. Hands on hips she got in his face and hissed. "I hate you right now!"

She watched the confusion dance across his face as he absorbed her statement. "W-w-what?"

"You could have died out there!"

"Cassie I'm fine. Just had the wind knocked out of me is all."

She gritted her teeth and said, "What about last year? Huh? I saw you laying there and you didn't get up."

"Yeah, so what's your point? Is this something new? It's not like I'm a closet bronc rider. You're being ridiculous right now."

"Me ridiculous? Don't you think you're getting a little old to be testing fate like you are?"

Eli scratched his head, looking completely lost. "Who are you? Did some alien take over your body?"

Suddenly deflated, her eyes filled with tears. "I've never been so scared in my entire life." She turned to leave, but he gripped her arm and hauled her to his chest. He patted her head like she was a child and held on tight. "Shh, I'm fine Cass. I'm sorry you were scared. But this is nothing new. You've been around it your whole life. I'm kind of at a loss here."

She sniffled into his shirt and his arms tightened around her bringing her even closer against him. "My emotions are all over the place lately. Honestly when I knew you were okay, I could've killed you I was so stinkin' mad."

He laughed softly; his nose nestled in her hair. "I sort of picked up on that."

"I hate to break in here, but Eli you'd better stop by the medical tent and let them check you out. Just to be sure."

"I'm on my way," he said. "Thanks Jim. Want to come with me Cass?" She nodded her head. "Let's go then."

He interlaced their fingers and led her through the throngs of people, many calling out well-wishes to Eli as they passed. Cassie had gone from fear to anger and now plain pitiful. That little devil on her left shoulder was taunting her again. *Not gonna corral anyone huh?*

He's a bronc rider, what'd you expect? Now you gonna tell him he shouldn't be bronc riding?

They arrived and she watched as Eli sat on the exam table and unbuttoned his shirt, revealing his six-pack abs. They listened to his heart and lungs, his hazel eyes crinkling as he laughed and joked with the paramedics. They looked into his eyes and then had him follow the light. After skillfully palpating his body, they released him with advice to use ice and have a good long soak in an Epsom salt bath and take ibuprofen as needed. He winked at Cassie, promising to do so.

"Want to go back to my place and play nurse?" he asked.

"They said you was just fine."

"I need you to rub some icy-hot on me after I soak. I'm gonna be sore."

She smiled up at him and brushed a lock of hair back from his forehead. "I suppose."

"And *now* she plays it cool folks. You got my head spinning Ms. Morgan."

She looked down. "I know. I can't help it. I have something to talk to you about anyway."

He flashed his sexy grin. "That's settled then, you're coming with me."

"I guess so." She didn't have any more excuses for putting off telling him, but she dreaded having this conversation. It made her feel like throwing up. *Oh well, we'll see where we are when the dust settles.*

21

"I'll draw your bath. Where do you keep the Epsom salt?" Cassie asked.

"Under the sink," he called from his bedroom.

She heard him groan. "You need my help?"

"I'm okay. I must have fucked up my shoulder. Had a little trouble taking off my shirt. You'll have to rub it for me later."

She knelt down beside the tub and tested the water temperature. *Just right.* She heard him and turned to look over her shoulder. He stood in the doorway without a stitch of clothing and she drew in a sharp breath. Perfection. He was so dark and beautiful. His partially erect penis, long and thick, nestled in the dark hair that trailed down from his navel. He was lean and cut, all taut and defined muscle.

Cassie swallowed hard. "Come here you," she said breathlessly.

She watched his gaze map her face as he walked to

her where she knelt by the tub. Palming his shaft, she stroked his length as he groaned. She buried her nose against his groin, nuzzling, inhaling the musky scent of him. She licked the underside of his cock, inching her way to the tip. She tongued the slit, tasting salt before sucking him inside her mouth. He cradled her head between his palms, fingers entwined in her hair. "Cassie," he groaned, thrusting inside

She sucked him hard while holding the base of him, cupping his sac with the other hand. His hands guided her as she took him in deeper, and smiled when his body shuddered. She moaned against him, savoring his taste and smell, loving that she pleased him. She withdrew then sucked him back in, as he gently thrust his hips. Tightening her mouth around him, her tongue swirled over his tip.

He trembled and cried out her name as he climaxed, reveling in the sense of power that gave her. *I love pleasing him. I did that to him.*

He pulled her up into his arms and held her, still breathing hard as he painted kisses at the hollow of her throat, behind her ear, her cheeks, finally settling on her lips.

"Thank you," he murmured into her mouth.

"Newsflash cowboy. You never *ever* need to thank me for pleasuring you. It's become my favorite thing to do. Now get in the tub and soak before the water gets cold."

He released her and stepped into the warm bath, bending his knees so he could submerge his upper body. Cassie laughed. "You make that tub look teeny."

"It kind of is."

"You want some music?"

"Naw. I kind of like the quiet."

"I'm going to go fix us a sandwich for when you get out. I'll see what else there is to scrounge up."

Eyes closed, he chuckled softly. "Good luck with that."

"I've been known to get pretty creative in the kitchen with very little. I'll check back in a while."

Cassie found some cold-cuts and cheese and a loaf of expired white bread, sans mold. She washed some lettuce, sliced a tomato real thin and set it aside. Opening a can of Campbells tomato soup, she emptied it into a saucepan to heat later, then opened a bag of chips. She went to check on her patient and found him toweling off in his bedroom. Grabbing the towel from him she said, "Turn around."

He turned his back to her and she rubbed the fluffy white towel over his skin, drying his shoulders and back then his delicious ass, teasing his crack before continuing down the backs of his thighs.

"Are you feeling guilty about something? You're being awfully sweet to me," he joked.

Her pulse, already racing from toweling him off, went into overdrive and heat rushed into her cheeks. "No. You're hurt, remember?"

"How could I forget. You do know that you're going to make me want to fall off more often, don't you? This could be setting a bad precedent."

"You go off again and I will strangle you."

He grinned. "That's my girl."

"Turn around and face me," she commanded.

"Bossy little thing aren't ya?"

She bit her lip to keep from smiling and, a little too roughly, rubbed his chest dry.

"Ow, you trying to take off a layer of skin?"

"Here." She thrust the towel at him. "You can get to the rest. Come on out when you're dressed. I'll throw the stale bread in the toaster and heat the soup du jour."

Cassie watched as Eli took a huge bite of his sandwich. A blob of mayo oozed onto his chin. She reached over and scooped it with her finger then stuck it between her lips.

"Are you trying to kill me?" he said.

She looked at him through her thick lashes. "Maybe." She was trying hard to distract herself from the conversation she was about to initiate as soon as they were done eating.

She grabbed a chip and nibbled on it. He, on the other hand, shoved several in at a time, the crunching sound making her lips curve up. *Such a guy.*

He raised his brows and said, "You said you had something you wanted to talk about?"

Cassie didn't meet his eyes. "Yeah, finish eating first. There's no hurry." She fidgeted with her watch band until she saw him looking at her.

"You seem nervous or something."

"Just eat already!"

His lips tightened, but he complied.

He finished his sandwich then wiped his mouth

with a napkin. "All done," he said. He leaned back and crossed his arms over his chest. "I'm ready. What's on your mind?"

Cassie chewed on her fingernail and tried to slow her breathing down. "I don't know how to even start," she confessed.

"I won't bite, I promise. Just say it."

"I...well...I'm...I'm pregnant," she blurted out.

His eyes widened in shock and she watched the surprise change to confusion then back to shock again. He sat back in his seat like he'd been body slammed. He stared into space looking stunned, and the silence stretched on for what felt like forever. Cassie waited... and waited. The longer the quiet dragged out the heavier her heart felt.

"Wait. What?" he finally managed to get out, his face drained of color, eyes glazed over.

She crossed her arms, hackles rising. "Is that the best you got? I think you heard me, I'm pregnant."

He ran his fingers through his hair and blew out a long breath. "Okay," he said, drawing that one word out. "Are you sure?"

She winced then glared. "I'm positive. Do you honestly think I would have come to you if I wasn't sure?"

He pinched the bridge of his nose. "No, but how?"

Through gritted teeth she said, "You know it happens sometimes when two people fuck and don't use protection. And FYI, I'm keeping it. You're under no obligation to help raise this baby. I just thought you should know."

He held up his hand. "Can you give me a minute

here. I um...this is the last thing I was expecting you to say."

Hiding her hurt behind a sarcastic and excessive Texan drawl, she said, "You poor dear. I'm sure it's come as such a shock to you. I must be nine kinds of selfish. What in the world was I thinking? Course, I wasn't the least bit surprised myself."

That seemed to sink through and he scrubbed his hands over his face then sat up and leaned forward. "I'm sure you were. I'm messing this all up. Listen Cass, I can tell you're hurt and I know I'm fucking this up, but I have a million questions and I'm not thinking straight right now. What, where, when, how long?" He paused as something seemed to dawn on him. "Wait. Is that why you were so mad at me after my ride, if you can call that a ride? And the other night, you were so off. Now it all makes sense."

She nodded her head, eyes still narrowed. "Yeah. I took the test right before you got there for supper the other night. I figured it was better to wait until after your ride to tell ya. I didn't want to send you into the competition with your head all screwed up. I was afraid something bad would happen...but it did anyway."

"I don't get it. We've been careful...except for that first night." His eyes widened. "That puts us at about six weeks if I'm not mistaken." She nodded her head again.

"You've decided to keep it. You sure about that?"

"I'm sure."

"I mean I'm only going by what you've said in the past...that you don't want kids," he trailed of when he saw her cheeks redden.

"Listen Cassie, I'm not trying to piss you off or to be insensitive."

"You may not be trying, but you're doing a hell of a good job of it."

"Look I'm sorry I'm saying everything all wrong. You've had a couple of days to digest this, I'm still in shock."

Cassie sighed and looked at the ceiling. "I know all that, which is why I haven't walked out that damn door already."

He suppressed a grin. "There's that smart mouth again."

"Listen, I know it's not what either of us had planned. We just barely got started ourselves. I'm planning on raising this baby all by myself. It's up to you whether or not you want to be in this child's life. If you don't, I understand. You didn't sign up for this and I know how much you like your freedom. If all you want is to be there for birthdays and holidays that's fine too."

"Oh no you don't. It's my baby, too. Am I surprised? Yes, but I got a thousand feelings competing for my attention and none of them are telling me to run."

"Is that a fact?" she drawled.

"I think you can tone down the sarcasm, Cass. I get it. You're pissed off at me. I'm sorry if I'm not having the reaction you'd hoped for."

She rolled her eyes. "Puleeze. I had no expectations."

"You're lying Cassie," he growled softly.

"Am I?"

"Yeah, you are. You wear your heart on your sleeve and I can see I hurt you. I'm sorry for that."

He stood and walked to her side of the table and getting down on one knee he reached for her hand. "You are not going to go through this alone. I'm in. One hundred percent."

Ignoring the fluttering in her chest, she said, "I won't be alone. I got Silas and Nash." Cassie's eyes stung with unshed tears, but they finally spilled over and down her cheeks. He reached up and brushed them away with his thumb.

Cassie's breath hitched. "Eli, the truth is I don't know what the hell I'm doing. I had no role-modeling for being a good mama. I'll probably screw the poor kid up but good. I'm scared out of my wits. But even so, I'm having this baby."

He gripped both her shoulders and gently shook her. "Babe, look at me. You mother everyone. Silas, Kiss, Dios, and as much as I hate it, Nash. Look how you were with Lily that night. Your instinct kicked in and you knew just what to do. You'll be an amazing mom."

She swiped the back of her hand across her cheeks. "Thank you for saying that."

He stood up and paced. "Have you told Silas yet?"

"No, just Nash."

He scowled. "Oh really? He was the first one you ran to?"

"Eli, he's my best friend. Course I told him. I was freakin' out."

"You should have come to me first," he said quietly. "Should we tell Silas together then?"

"No. I'll do it myself, but not till after the doctor appointment."

His jaw tightened. "Cassie, don't shut me out. I'm not letting you carry this alone and I'm not letting Nash take over my responsibilities. When it's time, we'll tell Silas together."

She stammered. "Eli…I'm…not sure…"

They locked gazes, his eyes glittering with frustration. "Well, I am."

She looked away. "But…"

He cut in. "When do you see the doctor?"

"I made an appointment for Tuesday coming up."

He stopped and turned back to face her. "I'm going."

"I don't know. Take some time to think this through. It's a lot to take in. I don't need you making promises you can't keep. I'd rather have no expectations than to be disappointed."

Hurt flashed across his face. "I understand, but I don't need to think about it. It's my baby too. I want to be there."

Her throat tightened. "Alright then. Appointments at nine in the morning."

He nodded. "Cassie we'll figure things out. But if you think you're going to cut me out of this, think again."

"I'll do my best. But Eli, I'm telling you, I don't want no flowery speeches or bullshit. I only want the truth. If you're scared or you want out, I need to know."

"That's not going to happen."

"If you say so."

"I do."

"Now take some ibuprofen and rest. You had a hard fall. If you need me, you know where to find me. I'm giving you some time to think things through. I'll see you Tuesday morning unless something comes up; if it does, I'll understand."

"What about your ride tomorrow?"

"I dropped out."

He rubbed his jaw, his brows drawing together. "Are you sure you don't want to stay here tonight and keep me company?"

"I'm sure."

Eli pulled Cassie in for a long hug. "I'm sorry if I hurt you Cass. That's the last thing I want to do. And I'm sorry that Nash pisses me off so bad. I know I can't compete with him; he's been there for you your whole life. But damn it, I want to be the first person you think to go to. I hope someday you will. But for now, we have more important things to focus on. Babe, it's going to be okay. *We're* going to be okay."

She nuzzled against his chest, memorizing his scent, the feel of his arms around her, his hard body. "We'll talk later." She pulled away and slipped out the door.

22

After Cassie left, Eli paced back and forth in his small living room. His thoughts churned. He wished she'd have stayed, but he also knew they both needed time to regroup. He'd certainly fucked that up royally. *And fuck Nash and the horse he rode in on.* It stuck in his craw that she'd told him first. Jealousy and hurt had ripped through his gut like a laser. But God, he hated that he'd been the one to cause that look of disappointment and hurt flash across her face. He shouldn't have made it about himself. To be fair, he was only human and he'd been shaken to his core. *I'm going to be a father and fuckin eh, talk about paradigm shift.*

His brow furrowed as he tried to make sense of his emotions. His chest tightened remembering Cassie's face when she'd shared the news. He'd caught that flicker of uncertainty before her defenses had kicked in. After that, she'd appeared unflappable and certain about keeping it, like she had it all figured out. Her composure, compared to how he felt, made him feel ashamed. He knew she'd have been every bit as shocked as he was when she'd taken the test. And she'd carried it alone, until now. *Yeah all except for Nash.* He wished she'd come to him right away...had leaned on him. It showed him she was still holding back...that she didn't completely trust him and that hurt.

He wished he could talk to someone about it, but that didn't feel right either. Too soon. He had no doubt his mom would be supportive, not to mention thrilled to have another grandchild, but he could already hear his father's disapproval. Elijah the ne'er-do-well son, fucks up again...literally. He scrubbed his hands over his face.

A kid. Definitely not a part of his master plan, as if he had one. Where did that leave him with his rodeo career? A muscle in his jaw twitched. He always thought he'd just keep going until his body made him quit. He'd always lived for that eight-second ride and it'd been good to him. Memories came flooding back. Seemed like yesterday he was leaving home with big dreams. Hard to believe he'd already been competing for over fifteen years.

He swallowed a lump in his throat. He was aware of a warm feeling centering somewhere in the chest area, replacing the confusion and previous apprehension. *Well, I'll be damned.* His mouth curved up in a smile. His pleasure at the thought of a baby growing...their baby growing inside of Cassie's belly was unexpected and welcome.

23

Tuesday morning Eli knocked on Cassie's door and shuffled his feet while waiting for her to answer. When she finally stepped out, he took one look at her and immediately forgot about his own nervousness. She was pale beneath her tan and her green eyes looked enormous. Her vulnerability tugged at his heart. Made him go all protector mode.

She'd kept her hair loose and it fell thick and wavy around her shoulders. The spaghetti straps of the sundress exposed her creamy skin and he fought the urge to put his lips there and trail kisses across her shoulders and neck. Maybe he could seduce those fears right out of her. He held out his hand and she took it, hers cool and clammy.

"How are you feeling? You look kind of pale."

"Morning sickness. I should have thought of that when I scheduled."

His palm settled at the small of her back as he

walked her to his truck. Opening the passenger door, he helped her in then shut it behind her. Climbing in behind the wheel, he turned to face Cassie before buckling himself in. Watching her closely, he reached over, resting his hand on her thigh, needing to touch her...to reassure her somehow...*or is it to reassure myself? Hell if I know*. "Nervous?" he asked.

"Very. I feel like jumping out of my skin between bouts of nausea."

Very softly he said, "Cassie, I want you to know that I'm glad you're keeping our baby. Once the shock wore off, I found myself getting excited."

Her eyes widened. "You did?"

"Yep. Not saying there isn't a little terror mixed in there as well, but hell Cassie, think about it. What are the chances? After one night? Can't help but wonder if maybe it was meant to be." His cheeks colored, slightly embarrassed by the admission.

Her eyes shone with tears as she studied his face. "What a sweet thing to say."

"What I really want to tell ya is that I've been thinking a lot about this whole thing. You, me, and the baby. I want you to come to Wyoming. Live at the Triple C, at least until the baby is born. I'll take care of you." He reached over and stroked her hair.

She nervously twisted her fingers, not meeting his gaze. "I can take care of myself. Plus, I'd never leave Silas. And Nash. It's enough to know that she'll have a daddy to love on her."

Forgetting his irritation at the mention of his nemesis, a grin split across his face, "A daddy. That's me. And did you say she?"

"Course I don't know, but it's a feeling I have." She rubbed her belly.

He couldn't describe his own feelings. It caught him off guard to hear her say *daddy* and *she*. Made it even more real somehow. He was aware of that warm throbbing in his chest again, like he was about to burst wide open.

He leaned across the console and touched her cheek with his lips. "We'll talk more about this later. Hell, Silas is more than welcome. He can park his RV on the ranch easy as anywhere else." He left Nash out of the offer. Latching his seat buckle, he started the truck and headed towards their appointment.

24

Elijah eyed the door leading to the examination rooms, anxious to get back to where Cassie was being prepped for a vaginal ultrasound. Doctor Thompson had decided to go ahead with the early test, since Cassie's job was high impact and demanding and it was her first pregnancy.

A nurse appeared and motioned Eli to follow her. They made small talk as they walked down the long fluorescent-lit hallway until she stopped and entered an examination room. The lights were low, which illuminated the computer screen. Cassie was in a paper gown, lying down on the exam table with her knees bent, feet in stirrups, and covered with a paper sheet. Dr. Thompson sat on a stool typing on a keyboard that was connected to the ultrasound screen, but glanced up long enough to smile at Eli.

"Go ahead and sit down beside Cassie," she said.

The nurse pointed to a chair by the head of the exam table.

He sat down and looked over at Cassie. She was chewing nervously on her bottom lip. "I guess they want to be on the safe side," she said.

"I think it's a good idea," Eli said. He slipped her hand in his and squeezed. "How ya holding up?"

"A little anxious, but excited too."

The doctor spoke in a calm reassuring tone, talking Cassie through the procedure step by step. Right before inserting the wand, she said, "This is going to feel a little cool and there will be some pressure. You tell me if anything feels uncomfortable, okay?" Cassie nodded, her eyes glued to the screen. Once in place, it began to transmit images directly onto the monitor.

Eli stared at the screen, trying to make sense out of what he was seeing. A grainy black and white image with a dark patch and a small white blob inside of that empty space, appeared like a bunch of nothing to him.

The doctor looked at him, smiled, then said, "Confused?"

"Yes ma'am. I don't have a clue what I'm looking at."

"See that fluttering there?" she asked. She turned up the volume of the machine and the swishing sound got louder.

He heard it first, then saw that the sound was in sync with the movement at the center of the tiny white bean and a grin split across his face. "That's the heartbeat?"

The doctor nodded, smiling at his excitement.

"No shit!" he said, his voice full of wonder. He glanced over at Cassie and saw that her eyes were brimming with tears. He stood and leaned over brushing her lips with his. "Cass that little bean right there is our baby."

She smiled up at him. "I read before it'd be the size of a sweet pea so I've been calling her that."

"That reminds me, doc, can you tell if it's a girl or a boy?" Eli asked.

"It's too soon, but by the next ultrasound we'll know. Everything appears to be fine. The position of the fetus is good, the heartbeat is good, the shape and size all normal," she said, withdrawing the wand. "I'll send you home with a picture. See you in twelve weeks. If you have any questions or concerns, please feel free to call the office."

She stepped out of the room and the nurse said, "I'll be right back. Go ahead and get dressed."

Eli couldn't wipe the smile from his face. "I'll see you out in the waiting room."

"I thought I was the one who was supposed to be glowing," Cassie teased.

On the drive home, Eli kept sensing Cassie's side-eyed looks. He was whistling, he couldn't help himself, while she seemed to be freaking out big time. They were about to spill it all to Silas.

"How can you be so calm? I'm as nervous as a long-tailed cat in a room full of rocking chairs and you're whistling, apparently without a care in the world."

"I can't help it," he grinned, totally disarming her. "I just saw my baby for the first time. What can I say? I'm happy. How do ya think ole Silas is going to take the news? This will make him a great-grandpa."

"I think he'll be worried first, then on cloud nine once he figures out that I'm okay."

"That's what I think, too. We're about to find out," he said, pulling up to the RV and killing the engine. He climbed out and went around to the passenger side and gave Cassie a hand down. "Just think, soon you'll be as big as a barn and I'll have to hoist ya out."

Cassie glared at him and put her hands on her hips. "I do declare, this cowboy has a death wish. Haven't you heard, Elijah Cane? You don't mess with Texas. My hissy fits aren't pretty."

With a broad smile he tilted his head so that they were standing nose to nose. "I don't care how big ya get, there'll be more of you to love on."

"Sweet talker."

"Let's get this over with," he said, weaving her fingers through his.

She took in a shaky breath and nodded. "I'm ready. You have the ultrasound picture?"

"Yep." He reached into his back pocket and pulled out the rolled-up piece of paper. "Our first picture of Sweet Pea."

"Look what the dern cat dragged in," he said, giving them both a once over as they sat down across from him.

"Hey grandpa," Cassie said.

The corner of his mouth quirked up. "You squirrels

look like you're 'bout to burst. Y'all fixin' to tell ole Silas something?"

Cassie sat wringing her hands in her lap and Eli covered them both with his large hand. She glanced up at him with a grateful smile and took in a deep shuddering breath and began. "Gramps, this may come as something of a surprise, I'm sorry there isn't a better way to tell ya. I...um...I...just please don't freak out on me."

Scowling, he drummed his fingers on the table. "Spit it out, Tater."

Cassie looked at Eli for support and he nodded his head encouragingly.

"The thing is...well...I want you to know that I'm okay, I'm actually happy...I..."

Silas glared at Elijah and said, "Dag gum it, can't ya help her git it out? I'm gonna die of old age by the time she's ready to declare. She normally talks the ears off a mule."

Eli grinned and pulled out the sonogram, handing it to Cassie. She unrolled it and handed it to Silas. "That little sweet pea there," she pointed, "That's your great grandchild."

He blinked. Then his eyes lit up as recognition dawned. "Well, I'll be. So you're sitting on the nest."

Eli barked out a laugh. "Leave it to you Silas. Yeah, you could say that."

Silas's eyes were suspiciously bright. His voice was gruff when he spoke again. "That's why yer not competing. Makes sense now." His faded silver blue eyes stared penetratingly at Cassie. "My baby girl is pregnant. How do ya feel about it?"

"I won't lie to ya, at first I was shocked and scared... you know my history. How am I gonna raise a baby, I never had a mama to show me how, you know the usual. I've never been around kids, I don't know the first thing about it, blah blah blah. But something happened when I saw that positive sign on the test wand. I felt an instant connection, you know, the minute I knew for sure. I already love this baby growing inside me. Then I thought of you and Reed; about how much love I had growing up. I reckon it doesn't really matter if it came from a woman or a man, you both nurtured me every bit as much as my mom would have."

Silas bowed his head, squeezing his eyes shut and pinching the inside corners with his large thumb and index fingers. When he looked up again, he directed his gaze at Eli. "What about you son?"

"Silas, you have my word, I will do everything in my power to take care of Cassie and this baby. I want her to move out to my ranch, at least until the baby is born. I got a big family that can watch over her when I'm on the road. But I plan to pull out of most of the remaining competitions this year, if I can convince her to move there. She flat out said no at first. I'm hoping you'll help me talk her into it. I truly believe it's for the best. She won't come without you, though. She can keep Kiss there, and more importantly Dios will love it. Our ranch can always use another hand. For pay, of course."

Silas's gray bushy brows furrowed as he huffed. "You don't need an old washed-up cowboy draggin' you youngins' down. Me and Dios will be just fine in Austin."

"Grandpa, that will be you, Dios and me then. My mind is made up."

Silas grimaced. "Cassie, I think Elijah is right. His ranch is the best place for you and the baby right now. You don't need to pay me no never-mind."

Cassie crossed her arms, lips tight, eyes narrowed, wearing a mutinous expression. "It's your decision gramps. If you think that's best for me, then I reckon you'll agree to come with me."

Eli suppressed a laugh, secretly placing his bet that Cassie was going to win this showdown. Best of all, that meant a win for himself.

25

Eli's heart was pounding as he punched in the ranch's home phone number. Three rings later his sister Becca answered.

"Hey sis."

"Elijah! What's the occasion?"

"Ha-ha. Is ma there?"

"Yeah, but you have to say more than six words to me before I go and get her."

Eli sighed loudly into the phone. "What do you want me to say?"

"You still seeing that barrel racer?"

"Yep."

"Seriously?"

Eli smirked at the shock in her voice. "Very seriously."

"Oh my God! I never thought I'd hear the day that my brother, the infamous Elijah Cane, would be tamed."

"Who said anything about being tamed? I have to keep my edge to be with this one. Cassie is as fiery as they come, can't have her getting bored with me."

She snorted. "Doubtful. Did you forget I've known you my entire life? You can't tame the wild out of you. But even wild horses can find their mate."

"Get Mom," he commanded.

"Hold on. Mom? Eli's on the phone."

Eli rubbed his ear from the sting of her piercing yell. Annoyed he said, "Thanks for puncturing my eardrum."

"Anytime. Here's Mom."

"Is anything wrong?" she asked immediately.

"Can't a guy call home without it being an emergency?"

"Some dutiful sons do, you know, to keep their poor mamas from worrying. But not you."

Eli massaged the back of his neck, guilt creeping in. "I'm sorry Ma. You know I've never been too good at that."

She chuckled. "I'm kidding. So, what's on your mind?"

"Are ya sitting down?"

"I can be." Eli heard rustling. "I'm sitting."

"Mom, our family is about to get a little bit bigger. My girl is pregnant."

Silence. "Ma? You alright?"

"Elijah Cane, I didn't think you were capable of shocking me anymore...but I stand corrected," she said.

"We just found out and I was waiting for the first doctor's appointment to tell y'all."

"I didn't even know you were in a serious relationship. We've never even met the girl. What's her name? Is it that Cassie girl I spoke with on the phone that time? How long have you known her?"

"We'll get to all that. Ma, I want her to come live at the ranch, along with her grandpa, at the very least until the baby is born but I'm hoping for something more permanent. She's amazing. I think you're going to love her."

"Do you? Love her?"

"I'm not sure I even know what love is, but I do know I want her in my life and I want to have this baby." He heard his mom sniffle. "Ma, are you crying?"

"Eli, I'm your mama, I only want what's best for you, you know that right? Who is this girl? Does she love you? Are her intentions good ones?"

"She's the best. She's smart and funny and independent as all git out. It took a hell of a lot of convincing to get her to consider moving to the Triple C. She wanted to do it all on her own, giving me visitation of course, but with no financial help from me or anyone else."

"How long have you been seeing each other?"

"Pretty much flirting around all summer, but it got more serious a couple of months ago. She's about seven weeks along now."

"I see." He heard her take in a deep breath.

"Mom, she's going to need you and Becca and even Sophia. She grew up without a mama; her mama died when she was only four. All she's had is Silas, who's like a grandpa, and his son Reed. They were family friends from her mama's past... Reed adopted her and raised her. Reed's gone now, so all she has is Silas. She hasn't had it easy not having a mom. She's scared she won't know how to raise this baby."

He heard her sigh and her voice was warm and soft when she responded. "Course we'll take care of her and her grandpa too. I'll get the spare room in the main house ready for you both. Is that what you're thinking?"

"That'd be great for now. Silas has an RV he can park there and live in. I told him we'd put him to work. He's a real character. Means a lot to me. Oh and his dog Dios...and Cassie's horse, Kiss. I told you, your family's getting bigger."

"I just have to ask, are you happy? About the baby? I never saw you settling down before you were in your sixties."

He laughed out loud. "You and the rest of the world, Ma. I guess I was ready and I didn't even know it. I knew I'd become bored with being a rodeo hotshot, the casual hook-ups, um...sorry mom... but Cassie's different. We're alike in some ways. Super independent. Stubborn, opinionated, but behind all that she's a sweetheart. I've never met anyone like her."

"And how do you feel about becoming a daddy?"

"I feel honored and humbled and determined to do this one thing right. Oh, did I mention scared to death?"

She sighed. "Elijah, you've done plenty right. And of course you're scared. It's only natural. That's why you'll be a good daddy. You don't need to worry about us accepting Cassie. I'll love anyone that is special enough to capture your heart. And, I'm going to have another baby to love on!"

Elijah smiled, his chest felt all warm and fuzzy and

weird. "Will you break it to the old man and the rest of the clan for me?"

"Yes, it's probably better that way. Don't you worry about a thing. When are you coming?"

"End of next week. Is that okay?"

"I'm chomping at the bit. As a matter of fact, I can't wait to set up the nursery. Your room will be big enough for a crib and playpen. Oh, and I'll have to get a changing table."

"Ma! Stop. Don't go overboard. You might want to wait on some of it and do it with Cassie."

"There'll be plenty to do. I'll tell the family tonight at supper. Gunner and Sophia are home, so the timing is perfect."

"When do they go on tour again?"

"First of next week. You'll probably miss each other, coming and going."

"Mom?"

"Yes?"

"Thanks. I don't know how I got so lucky, but you're the best."

Brushing off the compliment, she said, "I'll see y'all next week. Love you, son, and congratulations."

"Thanks. See ya."

Elijah put his hands behind his head and leaned back against the couch, planting his feet up on the coffee table. As he'd suspected, his mom had his back one hundred percent and he knew she'd pave the way with his dad. That didn't mean he'd be spared entirely, but at least it gave his father time to cool down before they arrived next week. He'd take it. Sometimes it's the small stuff.

26

Eli was dozing off on the couch when he heard a knock at the door. "Come on in."

The screen door opened and Silas stepped in, clutching a folder against his chest as he fidgeted in the doorway.

"Silas, come on in."

His shoulders slumped as he entered the living room and sat down on the club chair across from Eli.

"What's on your mind?"

Silas tugged at his shirt collar before answering. Blowing out a deep breath he muttered, "Eli, what I'm about to tell ya has to stay between the two of us, at least fer the time being."

"What's going on?"

"This goes way back...back to when Cassie was four. She don't know nothing 'bout what I'm going to say. Reed and me kept it to ourselves for Tater's peace of mind. I thought I'd tell her one day when she was older, but the timing never felt right and she never really asked us much about her past."

Eli sat up and held out a hand. "Stop right there. Silas, is this something that's gonna come between me and Cassie? If it is, I don't want to know. I'm a terrible liar."

"Boy, you're gonna have to trust me on this."

"Go on then."

Silas rustled around in the folder and pulled out an envelope. "See the thing is, Cassie don't know nothing 'bout her real pa, and how it is she ended up with the likes of me and my son."

"I thought her mom was raising her alone?"

"Partly true. She and Cass were in the witness protection program. The US Marshals. They found Cassie huddled in a motel hamper with a backpack and instructions. Her mom missing."

The hair on Eli's neck prickled and he knew he didn't really want to hear what came next. "So, how'd they find you guys?"

"Her mom left our contact information and named Reed as Cassie's father."

Eli prompted him to continue. "Start from the beginning, Silas."

"Cassie's mom and my son Reed was high school sweethearts. Had been inseparable since grade school. Head over heels in love, but they was young. Cassie's mom, Nicole Valentine was her name, had a voice like an angel. True God-given talent. Sang in the church choir." His eyes took on a far-away glaze. "She just so happened to have the looks to go with it. One of the most beautiful girls ya ever laid eyes on. Cassie looks just like her."

Silas continued. "Nicky had big dreams. So did my son. When they graduated from high school, they decided they was gonna go after their dreams before settling down together. He took off for the rodeo, following in my footsteps, and she left for Vegas. She worked singing private parties, weddings, networking, biding her time hoping to be discovered or some such thing. She auditioned for one of them fancy musicals and landed a lead role. Roxy Hart from that play *Chicaga*. You know the one I'm talkin' 'bout?"

Eli nodded and Silas continued. "Things were lookin' up fer her. Reed was doing good in the rodeo. Winnin' more than losin'. She and Reed kept in touch, by phone, letters, the whole bit. I reckon it was after she landed that part, things started to change. Reed thought it was because she was so busy, so when he hadn't heard hide nor hair from her, he went to see her show in Vegas. And he found out in short order why Nicky wasn't takin' his calls. That billionaire Casino owner had taken a fancy to her and swept her clean off her feet. She broke it off. It was like some dang spell had been cast on our Nicky. We always hoped she'd come back to her senses and back to Reed. Instead, she ended up marrying him, but from the sounds of her letter, she weren't over Reed neither." He pulled a folded piece of paper from the envelope and handed it to Eli.

"Where's her mom now?"

Silas's face clouded over. "God rest her soul, Nicky

is dead. Died in a car crash. Marshal service notified us she passed a year or so after she left Tater with us."

Eli shook his head. "Wow!"

"Here. It's probably best ya just read the dag burn thing."

My dearest Reed. If you are reading this, it's because he found me and we're in danger. I'm sure you can guess who 'he' is. My husband. I have been in the witness protection program, hiding with my daughter Cassie for the last three months. When I thought our cover was blown, I fled. You are the only person I can trust and the only place I know my daughter will be safe. I have identified you as her real father to my handler and left instructions for the Marshal Service to place her with you, and that you didn't even know she existed. I'm sorry that I had to lie about that, but I couldn't take any chances that you wouldn't be the one to raise her. Please forgive me. I know this will be a shock.

Reed, I have never stopped loving you. How I wish I could turn back time. I was a fool. Too young and dumb to know I was in over my head. I'm sorry for that. Maxim is an evil and dangerous man, unfortunately I found that out far too late. After my personal assistant tried to help me get away, then disappeared into thin air, I knew I had to leave. I had no choice. Maxim was determined to keep me at whatever cost. He owned me and I felt paralyzed with fear, because if my assistant could vanish, why not me? I had to think of Cassie. It's always been about his obsession with me. He will always be looking for me, hunting me down like his prey. If I'm lucky enough to escape again, I can no longer keep my daughter with me. To keep her safe, I have to let her go. I can never come back and don't try to find me. My wish is that you tell her that that I died and that I was raising her alone. That way she'll be safer from the truth and from danger. I'm hoping that this trauma will fade quickly and that she won't remember Maxim. She's only four. I know you'll raise her right. Please forgive me. All my love, always, Nicky.

Eli sat back, scrubbing his hands roughly over his face. "Why are you telling me this now?"

Silas rubbed his jaw, "Partly the nightmares and maybe I'm being skittish, but when we was in Austin on our break, Nash said some guy in an expensive car showed up sniffin' around askin' 'bout my son Reed and his next of kin. Nash was a tad suspicious, so he told 'em Reed was dead, the guy left and we didn't hear nothing more. Made me wonder...could someone be lookin' for Tater? And if so, why?"

"So, you're saying nobody has ever bothered to find Cassie before now?"

"Not so far as we know. No reason fer him to connect Cass with us. Reed adopted Cass and gave her his name. Early on, we got a note from Nicky telling us she was okay, so we knew she'd managed to get away from Petrov. Then nothing till the Marshals tole us she was gone," Silas said.

"So all Cassie knows is that her mama died and Reed adopted her. Wow, Silas. I have a lot of respect for y'all. That must have been tough, two single men, taking on a four-year-old, living on the road."

"Didn't make a lick of difference to him or me that she weren't our blood relation. She was Nicky's child and that was all that mattered." He paused and pinched the bridge of his nose. "Never seemed like the right time to tell Tater about her dad...or what we knew about their circumstances. We didn't see any good coming from her hearing the truth 'bout him. Far as we was concerned, better to let sleepin' dogs lie."

"I can understand your reasoning."

"Now, all this with that stranger in Austin might not amount to a hill of beans, but I felt like you should know about it. I'm figuring her bad dreams is probably old memories resurfacing, 'count a she's gonna be a mama herself."

"Makes sense. But is this the best time to tell her about all this, when she's pregnant? I'm not so sure," Eli said.

"Never a good time, see what I mean?" Silas shook his head. "I don't rightly know what the best thing is. I was hopin' you'd help me figure that out."

Eli felt a warm glow of affection for the old cowboy sitting across from him. "You're a good man Silas. I wish I could have known Reed as well. You're a perfect example that family has nothing to do with blood ties. Family is who ya love and the folks that will be there for ya no matter what. Cassie is lucky to have ya."

Silas's lips turned up at the corners. "We was the lucky ones." He nodded his head sadly. "Now ya know where she gets those singing pipes. Her mama had big dreams and look where it got her."

"One wrong turn can change everything. Listen Si, I

think Cassie could handle the truth, but maybe we should wait till after the baby is born."

"Let's sleep on it," Silas said. "I've waited this long."

"Yeah. Thanks for sharing with me, it helps me to understand her a little more." Eli cleared his throat, then continued. "For all intents and purposes, Reed was her father. Anyone can ejaculate—uh, sorry to be crude. Sperm doesn't make a father...love and nurturing does. You and Reed did right by Cassie."

Silas's eyes glistened and he rubbed the heels of his hands over them. His voice gruff, he said, "Eli, I'm glad she has ya, and I mean that boy."

"Highest compliment I could get. Thanks. I'll admit I've felt envious of her relationship with you a time or two. I never had someone like you in my life. Your approval means a lot."

"There ya go blowin' smoke up my arse. I'll take my leave."

"See ya round. Don't worry Si, I'll take good care of her and the baby."

27

Cassie brushed her fingertips across Elijah's naked chest, circling his nipples, tracing beneath his collar bones, marveling at how much she was into this man. The room smelled like sex, musky and raw, their scents blending together, pure sensual alchemy. He was stretched out on his back, eyes closed, with his arm wrapped around her shoulders, tucking her against him. She was sprawled out, her body languid, one leg slung over both of his, her cheek resting on his chest. She brushed across a small scar on his torso.

"How'd you get this?"

His voice sounded thick and relaxed. "I'd like to say it was something exciting like getting gored by a bull or parachuting from a plane, but the real story is that I fell out of a tree when I was a kid and impaled myself on a branch."

"Tough guy," she murmured.

His lips turned up. "I can't move."

She responded by snuggling closer and nuzzling his neck. "Do you think I'll fit in with your family?" She shivered as his fingers brushed up and down her arm, like feathers tickling over her overstimulated nerve endings.

Lazily he responded, "They're going to love you."

"Tell me what it's like there." Cassie craved reassurance, becoming increasingly nervous the closer it got to moving day.

"Well, let's see...Mom is the best. Gentle, but strong, kind, protective of everyone she loves, a great cook and the only one that can get through to my bull-headed father. Luke, the oldest, I've already told you that he lost his wife to cancer, and his son Clay is five and quite the charmer. We think he might be a child prodigy or something. He is already playing the piano and Gunner is working with him on guitar."

"Wow! That's amazing."

"You're no slouch yourself," he said. "You were all of what? Nine years old when you started to play?"

She bit his shoulder then prompted, "Go on."

"I'm probably closest to my sister Becca. She's the youngest, she's twenty-seven and sweet as the day's long but ornery too. She is the official concierge for the ranch along with a thousand other things she juggles every day, making it look easy. She fills in wherever she's needed. Bright, funny, easygoing. You'll get along just fine."

Cassie moved so that she was laying on top of him, stretched out full length across his body. Skin on skin. She craved closeness. She loved the feel of him beneath her. His cock twitched against her stomach and she lazily rubbed herself against him. Reveling in the sensations of his wiry hair surrounding his burgeoning erection, she licked and nibbled his neck. Her voice was smoky when she continued. "And Gunner? He's the country music singer and has a fiancée named Sophia, right?"

"Jesus, Cass," he said as she rocked harder against him. "Yes," he growled, flipping her onto her back so that he was on top, pressing her into the mattress. He gripped both her hands and held her arms over her head as he ground into her. She giggled when he peppered kisses along the delicate skin where her neck curved into her shoulder. "This interview is officially over," he said gruffly.

She squirmed beneath him, laughing now as he licked and nibbled his way down until he reached her ripe nipples. He released her arms so that he could massage her breasts as he suckled.

She reached between them to grip his shaft and ran her thumb over the crease at the tip of his cock, already leaking. She stroked him as he thrust into her hand. Returning to her lips, he slowly kissed her, licking inside her mouth, moaning into her as he explored the moist softness of her tongue and palate, sweeping across her teeth, sucking her lower lip between his lips. She was wet, tingling, aroused again. This man could bring her to the edge so easily. She was panting into his mouth.

"Elijah," she moaned. "Please."

Voice rough and deep he commanded, "Please what? Tell me."

"I want you."

"What do you want? Tell me."

"I want you to ride me like you're on a damn bronc," she hissed. "Your cock inside of me."

Chuckling, he spread her legs further apart and pushed deep, sinking his entire length inside her pulsating warmth. Cassie arched, raking her fingers down his back, gripping him with her vaginal muscles. He thrust slowly, rhythmically, and she rocked against him frenzied, encouraging him to go faster. He set the pace, not giving into her demands. She wrapped her thighs around him, urging him on.

He leisurely thrust his full length in again and again, his voice low and gravelly, "Baby, what's your hurry?"

Breathless, the heat slowly building, she surrendered, giving control to him, letting him have his way with her. When she let go, he slowly increased his tempo, driving into her, the bed banging against the wall with each thrust. He grunted and she squeezed her thighs tight, bringing them even closer together.

"God yes, Elijah!"

Then she was lost, suspended between this world an another, floating somewhere outside of reality. Her body spasmed and pulsated, sensation after sensation washing over her in waves. He grunted and with two more quick thrusts, she could feel him empty inside her, the warmth of his ejaculation filling her, then spilling out between her thighs.

He collapsed, his body melting into hers like warm putty. He licked and sucked at the juncture between her neck and shoulder, murmuring sexy dirty words that were almost unintelligible, but turned her body into molten lava. She couldn't move, didn't really want to move. This man was her kryptonite. And in the next few days things were about to get real. So, for now, she'd just relish being fucked into oblivion.

28

Cassie answered the soft knock at the door; Cissy and Lily stood on the stoop.

"Hey, Cissy!" Lily, whose arms were wrapped tightly around her mama's leg, peeked up shyly at Cassie. Opening the door wide, she motioned them inside, happy for the distraction.

Cassie crouched down to eye level with Lily. "Look at your pretty pink dress. And I love the cowgirl boots."

Lily smiled.

Cassie straightened. "I guess you heard the news... about the pregnancy and all. I'm done competing for the season. We head out to Wyoming tomorrow."

Cissy nodded, then looked down at her daughter. "We wanted to see you before you left. We have something for you. You want to give Cassie her gift?"

Lily lifted her hand and thrust a shiny blue gift bag towards Cassie.

"Aww, for me? Thank you. Should I open it now?"

Lily nodded. Cassie separated the white tissue paper and pulled out a framed picture. "Lily, did you draw this?"

"Yeth," she lisped.

"I love it." Tears stung Cassie's eyes as she studied the childish crayoned drawing of a happy family of three. The figures of a dad, mom and little girl, all huge egg-shaped heads with big U-shaped mouths, perched on top of sticks.

Cissy ruffled Lily's hair. "She could hardly wait to give it to you. I wanted to thank you for what you did for us. You, Nash and Eli. We're doing a lot better. Cody joined an AA meeting and has been sober since that night. You gave me courage Cassie. The courage to leave if I have to...to stand up to him. You'll never know how much your words meant to me."

Touched, Cassie felt an ache in her chest and hugged Cissy. "No need to thank me. We all help each other. And this isn't goodbye. I'll be around next season. I'm sure I won't be entering as many competitions but I'm not retiring yet." She looked down and rubbed her belly. "Who knows, I may be carrying the next Mary Walker or Trevor Brazile."

Cissy laughed. "If this baby takes after the parents, it'll be a shoe-in. And congratulations by the way... you'll be a great mom. Lily is excited that she might have a little baby to love on when you get back."

Cassie hugged herself. "It still doesn't feel real. Miss Lily, you're gonna have to learn your letters so you can read to the baby."

Her face lit up and she jumped on her tip toes. "I can weed a wittle."

Cissy imperceptibly shook her head, lips turning up. "We're working on it. She does know her alphabet."

Which prompted Lily to bellow out the ABC song as Cassie hid a smile behind her hand. "Wow. You're amazing."

"I hung onto some of Lily's baby clothes, if ya have a little girl I'll pass 'em on to ya," Cissy said.

"That'd be great. I have nothing."

Cissy gave her a lopsided grin. "We won't keep you. I know you must have a million things to do, but we'll see you next summer."

"Thanks for stopping by, and thank you, Lily. I will hang this picture in my new place, right over the baby's crib and I'll think of you every time I look at it."

Cassie closed the screen door behind them and sighed. She studied the picture Lily had given her, the innocence of the drawing, a belief in a happily ever after. She hoped that Cody could fight his demons and keep it together for his family, that Lily and Cissy would have a good life.

29

Cassie looked at Elijah's sleeping form slumped in the passenger seat and debated whether to wake him or not. Deciding to leave him undisturbed, she jumped out of the RV, yawning loudly as she stretched out her cramped body. The rest area was busy. There were a few semis parked with engines running and a number of vehicles in the lot. A sidewalk led to the buildings housing the bathrooms and visitor's welcoming area. A couple were walking their dog in the designated pet area and several groups of travelers were sitting at picnic tables catching a bite to eat and taking a break from the road.

It was their second day of travel and they had about six more hours to go before reaching the Triple C Ranch. Nash and Silas were alternating driving Elijah's truck, hauling the horse trailer with Kiss inside. She and Elijah followed behind in the RV. They'd parked in the designated truck area of a rest stop to take a break and use the restrooms.

"How ya holding up Tater?" Silas asked.

"Mm, okay, I guess. My hands may be permanently clenched from the death grip on the steering wheel, so this was perfect timing. I need to stretch out. The closer we get, the more nervous I am."

"Got nothin' to be scared about."

"Only that my entire life is changing and I'll be at the Cane family's mercy for the next seven months. What if they hate me?"

"They hain't gonna hate ya," Silas said, waving a hand dismissively.

"Whatever. How about you guys, staying awake?" she asked.

Nash grinned. "Silas's snoring is keeping me alert."

"I hain't sleepin' just restin' my eyes is all." He winked at Cassie.

Cassie suddenly felt a rush of emotion as she looked at her life-long friend. "Nash, thank you. I don't know where I'd be without you."

"Hey, you think I was gonna let you move, without me making sure the place was good enough for ya?"

"You know I'm not talking about today...I'm talking about my whole life. And this move...well...it's just temporary. Till the baby comes...then we'll see."

"See what?" Cassie startled and turned to see Eli standing there, rubbing his eyes and yawning sleepily. His shirt rode up as he stretched his arms overhead. She got an eye-full of ripped abs and the happy trail of dark hair disappearing into his low-slung jeans. It sent a wave of longing coursing through her.

Swallowing, she said, "See where we're going to wind up after this baby is born."

His expression darkened briefly, then cleared as his gaze roved over her. "Are you ready for me to take over driving?" he asked.

"Yes. I'm about to turn this into a Chevy Chase Vacation moment, you know the one, where he's driving asleep at the wheel," she said.

He chuckled warmly. "Can't have that."

Nash broke in. "Let's go Si, I need to take a leak. Cassie, will you hang with the trailer till we get back?"

"Sure. Go. I can wait. I'm not desperate." Nash and Silas took off for the bathrooms.

After they left Eli stepped closer and stroked her cheek with his thumb. "I'm going to grab a candy bar from the vending machine and hit the restroom, need anything?" he asked.

"I'll take a bag of peanut M&M's if they have it," Cassie said.

"What's your backup?" he asked.

"Snickers."

His face alight with amusement, he said, "Snickers, huh? I never would have taken you for a Snickers kind of girl...I'd have guessed Kit Kat."

"What about you...no let me guess...Reese's Peanut Butter Cups."

"Wrong! Almond Joy, and a bag of Twizzlers," he said.

"I forgot about Twizzlers! You have to share those with me. They're my favorite," she said.

In a low voice, he said, "Everything I've got is yours for the taking."

A current of electricity traveled down her spine and she unconsciously chewed on her bottom lip. "Chips?" she managed to squeak out.

He chuckled, low in his throat. "Uh huh. Anything else I can do for you?" He said waggling his eyebrows suggestively. Her stomach flip-flopped.

Finding her footing again, voice husky, she said, "Cowboy, you best back off or we might not make it to your ranch before nightfall."

"Can't have that now, can we? You know...my family is going to take one look at you and wonder how in the hell I even got close enough to have a chance. You're so damn beautiful, even with your hair all messed up and those raccoon eyes."

She pushed at his chest playfully. "Raccoon eyes? Who's got raccoon eyes?" She strode over to the pickup truck and glanced in the sideview mirror. "Oh, I guess I do look pretty rough."

He scooped her up from behind, holding her against his chest, burying his nose in her hair. "You smell so damn sexy..." He nuzzled her neck, sniffing again. "...all feminine...that hint of flowers, mm."

She squirmed against his strong hold as he restrained her. Giggling, she cried out, "That tickles!" He slowly released her and she felt a pang of loss without his arms around her. "I'm going to check on Kiss and give her another flake of hay and some water," Cass said.

"I'll be right back." He kissed the tip of her nose and walked away.

She watched him until he disappeared into the main building then tended to Kiss. She tried to imagine her life before Elijah had inserted himself into it, and could barely remember what it'd been like. She put trembling fingers to her lips and felt a vulnerability that shook her to her very core.

After taking in several deep breaths, she stepped into the horse trailer with Kiss. As she added a flake to the hay net, Kiss nickered and nudged Cassie with her nose. Wrapping her arms around Kiss, she nuzzled her neck. The smell of horse and hay soothed her, calming her anxious thoughts.

30

As they drove through the imposing pillars bracketing the wooden crossbeam with the Triple C logo burned into it, Elijah felt his chest tighten with pride. *Home.* "We're here," Elijah said, continuing down a long dusty lane running parallel to a wide creek bed. He checked his rearview mirror to make sure Silas and Nash were still behind them, then stuck his arm out the window, waving them forward.

He tried to imagine how it must look through Cassie's eyes, seeing it as if for the first time, too. As the lane curved, they passed the guest cottages nestled along the right, the tree-lined creek now hidden behind them. The main lodge was further ahead and the barns and riding arenas were coming into view to the left. By her wide-eyed expression and gaping mouth, he thought it must be as spellbinding to her as it was to him. Even though he'd been born and raised here, the land still gripped him every time—the majestic mountain backdrop, the spruce and pines, the old oak trees and fence-lined fields of grazing horses. It always drew him back home.

"Wow!" she said. "This is incredible. It might be the most beautiful place I've ever been."

He sighed, letting a deep low sound escape. "Yeah, pretty fucking amazing. Honestly, fall is my favorite time of year here. We've hit the sweet spot. September, October, this place erupts into flames. It's just starting to turn now. You just wait."

Before Eli had even cut the engine, a small boy was running towards them as fast as his little legs could carry him. "That would be my nephew, Clayton," Eli said, his gorgeous face split wide with a dazzling smile.

"Uncle Eli!" Clayton wrapped his arms around Eli's thigh as soon as he stepped out of the vehicle.

Close behind Clayton was a young twenty-something woman, slim with dark hair and sparkling hazel eyes and an older woman with graying hair, wearing an apron covered in flour and a warm smile.

"Mom, sis!" Eli said, slinging his arm across the older woman's shoulders and hugging her to him. He turned to look behind him and reached his free hand out to pull Cassie into the circle. "This is Cassie." Cassie stepped forward looking a little lost.

"Cass, this is this is my mom and my sister, and this little dervish is my nephew, Clayton. Mom, Becca, this is Cassie.

"Nice to finally meet y'all."

"I love that Texan accent," Becca said. Clayton snickered and imitated Cassie's drawn out 'y'all' and everyone laughed.

"Don't be rude, dude," Eli said.

Puzzled, his face a study in innocence, Clayton said, "But that's how she sounds."

One of their ranch hands appeared and was talking with Silas and Nash. Eli inclined his head and said, "That's Beau. Our number one ranch hand and my best friend. He'll get Kiss settled in. He's a horse whisperer, no lie."

Elijah waved his arm and called out. "Silas, Nash, Beau, come on over here."

Beau led them over and introductions were made. Silas pulled off his cowboy hat, revealing his mussed and thinning tufts of snow-white hair. Bowing, he said, "Pleased ta meet ya, ma'am. You too," Silas said, as he nodded at Becca.

His mom smiled warmly. "The pleasure is all mine. Please call me Abby. That goes for all of you."

"Nice to meet you, Silas," Becca held out her hand and they shook.

"Nash, this is my mom Abby and my sister Becca, this is Nash. He and Cass have been joined at the hip since they were Clay's age," Eli said.

A slight flush washed across Nash's tanned cheeks as he shook Becca's hand. "Um, pleased to meet you, miss, um Becca." Nash said. He nervously rolled the rim of his cowboy hat, his deep denim-blue eyes downcast. His blond curls hung over one eye, and he brushed them back before plunking his hat back onto his head. Eli suppressed a grin. He often forgot that his sister was a knockout. Poor Nash didn't know what had hit him.

Becca sized Nash up, but good. Her gaze boldly

swept from his face down to his dusty cowboy boots then back up again. Eli met Cassie's gaze and smirked. She bit her bottom lip to keep from giggling.

Beau thrust his hand toward Cassie. "I'm Beau."

"Hi. Eli tells me you'll be getting Kiss settled in?"

"Sure nuff," he said.

"Are you sure you don't mind? Want me to help?"

"No way. I've been looking forward to meeting the star filly of the rodeo. Eli tells me she's a real competitor."

"Yes, she is. Her heart's all in. Thanks for taking care of her, Beau. Will she be turned out or stalled today?"

"I thought I'd turn her out to pasture with Gunner's mare, Amitola, for company. Tonight, they can sleep in stalls right next to each other. Amitola is kind and she gets along with most everybody in the herd. That'll give your girl an edge when we turn her out with the rest of 'em."

"That sounds great. I'll find you later then?" Cassie asked.

"I'll be somewhere around the barn. I'd best get her out of that trailer. She's been cooped up long enough."

Cassie rolled her eyes. "You can say that again."

Eli noticed how tired Cassie looked; the dark smudges beneath her eyes seemed darker than before, almost appearing bruised. *But damn she was still beautiful.* He studied her, the thick dark brows emphasizing her emerald green eyes, rich brown hair cascading around her shoulders, the dusting of freckles across her dainty nose, then finally coming to rest on her luscious, kissable mouth.

She arched a brow at him. "Something you got to say, cowboy?"

Embarrassed at being caught, he cleared his throat. "I'll give you guys the grand tour later but," he swept his arm towards the log cabins nestled in the trees, "those are the guest quarters, and that large chalet over there is the lodge slash dining hall, replete with a bar of course. There's a pool thataway," he gestured behind the lodge. "Our homestead is the white house further up the lane."

Cassie inhale deeply. "Smells so clean and fresh here, like pine trees and sage."

"Don't forget the horse poop," Clayton piped in.

Cassie laughed. "I guess I automatically tune that out since it's the soundtrack of my life."

Clayton's brows knitted. "Don't you mean smell-track?"

"What? Oh!" Laughing, she nodded. "Yes the smell-track of my life." He flashed her an impish grin.

Becca motioned for everyone to follow her. "Come along to the lodge. We'll feed you then get ya settled in." She looked over at Nash. "Eli said your flight is day after tomorrow?"

"Yes ma'am."

"Dear Lord, puleeze don't call me ma'am. I'm only twenty-seven."

Nash smiled. "Okay Becca. Yeah, now I'm kinda wishing I'd have made a vacation out if it and stayed on for another week."

Cassie grabbed his arm. "It's not too late. Change your flight. Please."

"I can't, but I'll be back. I promise."

They all fell in step, Eli wedging himself between his mom and Cassie, arm slung across both of their shoulders. Silas and Nash walked along side Becca as she prattled on about the history of the ranch, and Clayton ran ahead then stopped to wait impatiently for them to catch up before running ahead again.

"Hey Bec, Gunner and Soph left on tour?" Eli asked.

"Yep. And Dad and Luke couldn't be here to greet you either. They're meeting with an advertising group to work on marketing strategies all day. They should be back by supper. Guests arrive tomorrow."

"Business as usual," he said.

"Pretty much."

"Good to be home."

31

Cassie sat on the edge of the king-sized bed, willing her stomach to settle. She rubbed at the tightness in her chest.

The room was lux, with a private en-suite, fireplace, and four-poster king-sized bed. Beautiful western artwork added color against the buttery cream walls. Soft rugs were scattered over cherry hardwood floors and the smell of fresh linen permeated the air. In the far west corner of the room sat a crib, playpen, and changing table. A colorful mobile dangled over the crib, and stuffed animals were piled high. On top of the dresser was a blown glass vase with fresh flowers and above that, a white poster board with colorful lettering saying, **Welcome Home Cassie!**

Silas would live in his RV for now. *Lucky man*! That could change later, Abby had explained. When the ranch closed down during off-season, he could move into a guest cabin.

Her nerves jangled and she felt like a virgin bride as she waited for Eli to finish showering and join her in bed. She'd deliberately kept it as unsexy as she could get, long baggy boyfriend tee over old ratty boxer shorts, white cotton briefs, hair pulled up in a tight bun and her face scrubbed bare. She heard the shower stop and tensed.

A few minutes later he entered the room, naked except for a white bath towel wrapped around his waist. He held another towel against his head, his arm muscles flexing as he rubbed his black hair dry. She swallowed; her mouth watered and her body heated. She couldn't tear her eyes away from his muscular chest, strong and cut, wanting to kiss her way down the light dusting of dark hair that trailed to the towel slung low on his hips.

His gaze met hers. "Hey," he said.

"Hey."

"You alright?"

She plucked at the quilt. Gathering up her courage, she took a deep bolstering breath. "Um...not really. This is all too weird. Why did your mom put us in the same room?"

"Don't know. I guess she did mention it to me and I didn't think anything of it. She assumed by the way I talk about you that we're...um...a couple?"

"Big assumption. Besides, being a couple and living together are like separate universes. And the crib?"

"Yeah, what about it."

"Isn't that a little freaky?"

"How so? Last I knew, we *were* having a baby. They do sleep in cribs, don't they?"

She squirmed uncomfortably. "It seems a little presumptuous to just take it upon themselves to make those decisions without us."

"Look, Cass, I come from a large family. Everyone is up in everyone else's bizz. I know you're not used to that, but they mean no harm. They're trying to help."

"I'm not comfortable with it. What if I wanted to pick out my own stuff?"

Eli hung the towel around his shoulders and sat down on the edge of the bed next to her. "It's a crib and a changing table! Is that really a big deal? Look, it's going to take time to acclimate, Cass. You're not used to all that mothering."

Her jaw set. "I don't need mothering."

He slapped the side of his head. "What a moron, I forgot. The badass Cassie Morgan doesn't need anybody."

"And did it ever occur to you to ask me about our living arrangements and what not?"

"I'm sorry, but no, it didn't. Maybe setting up that baby stuff was their way of trying to make you feel welcome and maybe, just maybe, they're excited too."

"Well, y'all should've discussed it with me. That's all I'm saying." She sniffed. "It would have been nice to have been asked is all. When you heard she was putting us in the same bedroom, why didn't you explain the situation?"

"Did I miss something? What exactly *is* the situation? We've been spending a hell of a lot of nights together...sleeping in the same bed as well as other extracurriculars. We're having a baby together. To me it makes sense that we'd share a room and try this cohabitation thing. I've told you before, I miss you when I wake up all alone," he said softly, reaching up to brush her cheek with his knuckles.

"I don't like feeling cornered, like I don't have choices in the matter," she said, her jaw tight. "Eli, all this," she spread her arms wide, "I come from a trailer park, now I'm like the princess sitting on the damn pea. Maybe I should settle in with Silas."

The muscles in his jaw twitched. "You just got here. Can't ya give it a damn minute? Christ Cass, you're tired, I get it, but your being over-dramatic. Just chill."

Cassie stiffened and when she replied she could hear the ice-cold anger in her voice. "Chill? You returned to your multi-million-dollar ranch, your *home*, everything is familiar, your cozy, *perfect* all-American family, *your family*. Not mine. They're all a bunch of strangers, far as I'm concerned. Everything is upside down and I'm freakin' the hell out. I'm pregnant, I haven't a clue about having a baby, I'm shacked up with a guy I've only been seeing for a couple of months, whose mother and sister are already decorating and planning my life out."

He looked stunned as he sat there staring at her. He took a long time before answering, then he said, "Wow Cass, way to kick me in the balls."

"Just forget it. Why did I think you'd ever understand? I'm ready for bed. I'm tired and I need sleep. Make sure you stay on your side of the bed, ya hear?"

"That will *not* be a sacrifice, trust me on that."

She snorted. "For me either."

Eli stood and removed his towel from around his waist, shaking his head as he strode to the bathroom.

She willed herself not to look at his ass. She huffed out a breath then reached to switch off the bedside lamp. Curling up onto her side, Cassie buried herself underneath the covers and squeezed her eyes tightly shut. She suddenly felt so alone, her eyes stinging with unshed tears.

Eli returned and crawled under the sheet, with what felt like an ocean between them on the king-sized bed. She felt him turn away, rolling onto his side with his back to her. *Well, it is what I asked for, right?*

He switched off his lamp and said, "Night Cass. See ya in the morning." She didn't respond, she was too afraid she'd give herself away, so she smothered her sniffles and buried her emotions in her pillow.

32

"How'd you sleep dear?" Abby said warmly, as Cassie came down the massive curved staircase.

"Fine. Thank you."

Abby was still in a bathrobe, reading glasses perched on top of her salt and pepper hair, looking like the quintessential perfect mom. "Guests come in later this afternoon, so there'll be no sleeping in for me after today, or for the next several weeks."

"I remember Becca mentioning that yesterday," she said quietly. "Have you seen Eli? He was already gone when I woke up."

Abby frowned. "No, I haven't dear." She eyed Cassie thoughtfully. "Everything alright? Your room comfortable?"

"Yes. More than comfortable. Thank you."

"You need anything, you let me know. Maybe we can go out shopping soon and buy some baby things.

You're going to need some maternity clothes before long, too."

Cassie lowered her eyes, not responding.

Abby walked over to Cassie, gently placing a hand on her shoulder. "You look tired. Honey, I know it's a lot. Being pregnant, moving to a brand-new place with all new people to get used to."

"I'll be fine," Cassie said, quickly.

"You sure you're feeling okay? You look a little pale. You're bringing out my mother hen."

Cassie stuck her hands in her front jean pockets to keep from fidgeting. Her mouth tightened and her eyes narrowed. "No need for that. I think I'm used to not having a mother by now, since I haven't had one since I was four." She dared another glance at Abby and was pierced by the compassion she saw in her warm brown eyes. *Or was it pity?* "Well, I reckon I'll go find Silas and Nash and tend to Kiss."

"You have to have some breakfast first," Abby said, firmly.

"I'm fine. Silas has some cereal in the RV. Don't worry about me none."

"Of course I'm going to worry about you. You're family now."

Cassie sputtered, gulping for air. "Family?"

"What did you think of the crib?" Abby asked.

Cassie bit down on her tongue. "Nice."

"Becca and I couldn't resist that darlin' mobile. It plays music, too. 'Somewhere Over the Rainbow.'"

"I've got to go," Cassie croaked, and practically ran out of the room.

. . .

Sitting across from Silas in his kitchen, munching on a bowl of cheerios, made her feel somewhat normal. Her shoulders began to lower away from her ears and the knot in her stomach was lessening. Mouth full, she said, "I can't take someone looking over my shoulder and hovering. I'm not some helpless kid."

"Don't mistake kindness for pity or nibnosin'. I'm sorry I couldn't prepare ya more for the outside world. We was just the two of us for so long after Reed died. Nash of course. But ya didn't have no women in yer life to mother ya."

Cassie rolled her eyes. "Thank God. I don't like it."

"Too soon to tell. How do ya know if ya don't give it some time."

"I already know. Makes my gut clench. Do you know they already bought a crib and toys and a musical mobile? She wants to take me shoppin' already! For baby things and maternity clothes."

Silas chuckled. "She's trying to make you feel welcome, I spect. Show that she cares."

"Not about me. Just the baby. Like Eli. He's doing all this for the baby, not me."

Silas glared. "Cassie Morgan! Ya sound like an ungrateful brat. You got a nerve ta say that. He's been nothing but supportive fer as I can tell. Were ya hoping he'd run away so you could blame him and continue on with yer life, seeing fit to do whatever you like?"

Cassie gaped. Silas rarely snapped at her like that. "I don't know what I was hoping for. Certainly not motherhood."

Concern etched Silas's face as he studied her. "Listen Tater, life takes us places we never would've gone ourselves. So many gal darn twists and turns we never see coming. If ya stay open, ya might find out that you kin fall in love with something ya never even dreamed of wanting."

She fought back tears. "I'm scared, Grandpa. It feels like too much. It's not even the baby, it's Eli, his family, moving, giving up the rodeo for now. I was worried his family wouldn't like me and now I just wish I could be swallowed up and ignored. I hate that my first reaction is to distrust and put walls up, but that's who I am I guess."

Silas patted her hand. "That's fear talking. That's not who you are. You're gonna have to draw deep Tater. Find yourself some faith. Trust a little. Let your guard down. These are good people. I like 'em."

"I don't know how."

"Remember, we get the lessons we're ready for. You'll learn. Let Elijah help ya."

"He hates me now."

"I doubt that."

She sniffled. "No, he does. I picked a fight last night and had the audacity to criticize his family. I'm sure he thinks I'm a terrible person. Hells bells, I think I'm a terrible person. I'm afraid I'm more set in my ways than I thought. He was gone before I woke up."

"He'll come round."

She shrugged. "I guess we'll meet Luke and Mr. Cane tonight since they missed supper last night. I'm nervous as all git out about that too."

"You know your way around cowboys, you've been

around 'em since you was knee high to a grasshopper."

"I hope you're right. I've sure stuck my foot in it so far. His mama probably thinks I'm nuttier than a fruitcake after running away from her like she was the devil incarnate. She probably hates me now, too."

He chuckled. "I spect she's willing to give ya more than a few chances."

Cassie finally let her lips turn up. "You think so?"

"Yes. And Cass, think about it. Who're you drawn to? The people who have fallen and got back up or the ones sittin' in their ivory towers? I reckon them scars make us better people. Nobody's perfect. It's the folks that have been hurt, maybe even broken, that come through it, that are the bravest. You're strong and resilient. Yer not broken anymore, kid. You fought fer years to overcome your losses, you're loyal, you love deeply, you got a good heart. Let people see the Tater I know and love."

She threw her arms around Silas's neck and hugged him tight. "Don't you ever even think about leaving me. Ever. I love you so much."

"I tole ya before, I hain't going anywhere anytime soon. Now go find yer cowboy and talk it out."

"I'm going already!"

He swatted her bottom as she walked out the door. "Love ya, Tater."

"Love you more."

"And Tater?"

She turned. "Hm?"

"Let go of that pride for a minute. It gets ya in trouble."

Cassie rolled her eyes. "Yes, Grandpa."

33

Cassie tipped her head back, letting the sun warm her face as she made her way to the barn. The mid-seventies temperatures were perfect riding weather and as expected, she spied Elijah galloping in the outdoor ring on his mustang, Freak. Shirtless, his bronzed skin, black hair and black jeans contrasted dramatically against the white coat of his horse. He looked dangerous, his brows furrowed, lips compressed into a tight line.

She stepped up on the rail and watched him. He hadn't noticed her yet. Her heart was in her throat as they took a three-foot jump like it was nothing and approached the next jump, sailing over it like Freak had wings.

She knew the second Eli noticed her, because his body stiffened. He transitioned to a trot and circled the ring several times before riding over to where she perched.

His face was inscrutable and set in stone as he greeted her. "Morning."

"Morning. How'd you sleep?"

"Took a while to get there, but I managed to grab a couple of hours anyway."

Cassie fidgeted with the hem of her shirt. Head bowed, she ventured, "Do you hate me?"

His warm voice stroked her, deep and husky. "I could never hate you, Cassie."

Her eyes darted up to meet his gaze. "You couldn't?"

He shook his head. "No, but I'm frustrated as hell. I don't like the feeling that I have to walk on eggshells around you."

Cassie hiked one shoulder, her lips tilting up. "I've never professed to being an easy keeper."

He snorted. "No one will ever accuse you of that."

Cassie sighed, relieved that he appeared to be softening. "I'm sorry about last night. Your mom probably thought she was making concessions to bunk us together and I took it all wrong. I'm all muddled." She shook her head like a dog shaking off water.

"It's no wonder you have whiplash, Cass. Don't be too hard on yourself. I thought a lot about it last night. Your whole world has turned upside down."

"So has yours," she said. "And you're not acting crazy as a loon."

He grinned. "I've got a great poker face. Besides, as you so eloquently pointed out, this is my home, everything is familiar. My family, my home. You were right."

Cassie felt her cheeks heat. "I may have been right, but I sounded like a spoiled child. I'm embarrassed."

"Don't be. It stays between me and you. Mom will

never know that you questioned the Cane family's hospitality."

Cheeks flaming, she said, "Well...about that. I kinda acted like an ass to your ma this morning."

His eyebrows rose. "How bad?"

"Pretty bad, but I meant what I said...it's just that I could have said it a whole lot better."

"Cass, where'd ya ever get that idea that someone being kind to ya had strings attached or some ulterior motive? Can't ya lighten up a little? You know how good it feels to do something nice for someone? Maybe it's time to return the favor, let someone do something nice for you."

"I'm not used to being under a microscope."

He laughed at her. "You're like a spitting kitten, Cass. But don't worry about my mom, she's got pretty thick skin. I'm sure it'll be fine between ya."

"But Eli, I'm really not ready, you know, for all that fussing. I hope you can be patient with me. It's a lot."

"It is, but remember, that patience goes both ways." He jumped off Freak and opened the gate to walk through. Cassie closed and latched it behind them and fell in step beside Eli, as he headed towards the barn.

"I'd like to help out around here. I'll go stir crazy if y'all don't give me something to do," Cassie said.

Eli nodded, biting the inside of his cheek. "Beau could always use help around the barn. There's plenty of work to be done around this place."

"Good. That suits me just fine."

. . .

That evening, they all gathered at the table for supper. The entire Cane tribe, except for Gunner and Sophia, were there. The lodge served dinner family style, long picnic tables and benches seating up to twelve guests each were arranged comfortably, for maximum mixing and mingling. Full capacity meant only twenty-five guests in order to fulfill the promise of a personalized vacation. At present, the room was full of excited chatter from the new arrivals.

The dining hall was one large open room with huge exposed log beams, polished hardwood floors, large windows letting in natural light and incredible views of the mountains and trees. Western art and woven Native American tapestries adorned the walls.

"Them's the best collards I've ever eaten," Silas said as he polished off his second helping. He patted his belly and chuckled. "I think I outdid myself."

Abby smiled. "Chef James is fantastic. We lucked out when we found him. He's been a life saver. I still manage breakfast and lunch, with a lot of help of course, but he covers supper five days a week."

"I reckon you'll pass on my appreciation?" Silas said.

Nash swallowed a mouthful of food and agreed. "Mm, real good Mrs. Cane."

Becca's eyes seemed to permanently sparkle, and now that gleam was focused on Nash. Her disposition was always positive, cheerful and slightly mischievous. In comparison, Cassie felt like the Winnie-the-Pooh character Eeyore to Becca's Tigger. It was intimidating. *Funny, here I was worried about the infamous Bill Cane and he's being a total cupcake. It's Abby and Becca that put me on edge.*

Bill Cane's booming deep voice broke through her thoughts, "So Cassie, are you getting settled in?"

"Yes sir. It's so beautiful here. From what I've seen, this place runs as smoothly as a thoroughbred on the racetrack. You must be so proud."

He chuckled. "It's a family affair," he said, darting a pointed look at Eli. "For the most part." Eli glared and folded his arms across his chest.

"Well as far as I'm concerned, this is the perfect vacation destination. I'm so thankful to y'all for making me feel so welcome." She happened to catch an eyeroll from Eli and kicked him under the table.

Clayton said, "Grandpa said maybe Uncle Eli will come to his senses now."

Luke looked at his son sternly. "Clayton."

Wide-eyed Clayton replied, "What? That's what he said."

"You don't have to repeat everything you overhear," Luke warned.

"But..."

"Clayton, I said enough," Luke's dark brows were drawn together, brooking no argument.

Clayton's bottom lip jutted out and he crossed his arms mimicking Eli. It was all Cassie could do to not break down laughing. Between their identical postures and the slip from Clayton, it was like the laughter in church syndrome. She glanced around the table, biting her lip to keep silent. Bill appeared unconcerned that he'd been caught talking behind Eli's back and Luke still wore the stern parental mask.

Abby reached out to stroke Clay's cheek and murmured, "You know what your daddy is trying to say?"

Clayton shook his head, expression mutinous, arms still folded across his chest. "I wasn't telling no lie."

"Yes, but you were repeating something someone said to someone else, that you overheard. It wasn't for you to tell."

"But what 'bout when you told Aunt Becca what you heard Nash say 'bout her?" A snort of laughter shot out of Cassie, and she quickly covered it with a cough. She glanced first at Becca then Nash and they both looked like they'd rather be anywhere but sitting at this dinner table.

"Yes...well...that was different." You could see Abby was struggling to come up with a response.

Forehead puckered, Clayton said, "But why is it different?"

Luke cleared his throat. "We'll discuss this later Clay. Finish your supper."

"No fair," he whined.

"Clayton."

Sulkily, he muttered, "Okay."

There was a prolonged silence, then everyone seemed to start talking at once.

"Cassie?" Silas nudged her. "Bill was asking you somethin'."

"Oh, I'm sorry."

Bill Cane repeated himself. "Becca was telling me that you're quite the accomplished barrel racer. Beauty and talent. I'm impressed. How did you end up with the likes of my son?"

Cassie felt her cheeks heat and she stole a glance at Eli, whose lips were drawn in a tight line. "Lucky, I guess. We were kind of thrown together this summer; we entered most of the same rodeos this year. It just kind of happened."

"I think Eli's a little old to be bronc riding, don't you? Got to grow up sometime." He shook his head. "I gave up on talking sense into him long time ago."

"You know Dad, I *am* sitting right here listening to this," Eli said, scowling.

As if he didn't hear him, Bill Cane continued. "You seem like a smart and sensible girl. Maybe you'll be able to convince him to grow up. Now with a baby on the way, I'm hoping a little old fashioned common sense will kick in."

Cassie squirmed in her seat, not sure how to redirect the conversation away from Eli, but she had to try. "Mr. Cane, was the Triple C always a dude ranch or was that something you thought up?"

"Well, it used to be a family ranch, raised cattle. We had three log cabins we rented out to hunters. After college, I visited a dude ranch in Montana and the idea took ahold of me. I was inspired. I researched it and with my parents blessing, I took the bull by the horns and moved forward with the idea. We started out small and went from there. Little by little." His eyes sparkled warmly at her.

"Wow! Now it's big as Dallas!" Cassie said, smiling. She couldn't help herself, she liked Bill. She wouldn't want to be his child, but she knew his type. Highly competent. Hard as nails. Expects everyone to be as capable as he is. Asks too much of his kids, but nothing more than he's willing to do himself. Outspoken, impatient, but if one happens to win his approval, it'd be like a long soak in a warm tub.

"Would you like to take a ride after supper? I'll take you out on the four-wheeler and show you the lay of the land. Give you the grand tour. I'm sure my son hasn't taken the time yet."

The Canes all looked surprised by the invitation, especially Eli. She swallowed. "Um, that would be lovely." She looked to Eli for approval, but his eyes were narrowed at his father.

"We just got here. I had plans to show her around after her company left," he ground out, nodding at Nash.

"No need to get defensive boy, it wasn't an admonishment. I'm happy to show this beautiful young lady around." This earned a wide-eyed, open-mouth stare from Eli. Cassie blushed.

Becca said, "Not to change the subject, but do you really have to leave tomorrow Nash?"

"Yeah unfortunately. I hate to leave. This is a little bit of heaven ya got here."

"You'll have to come back when you can stay a spell."

"I'll do that. Thanks."

"Cassie, Mom says you want to go shopping. Let's make a plan for after Nash leaves." Becca said. "We can work around the guests.

Cassie shot a dirty look at Eli, then waved her hand dismissively. "I don't want to be any trouble. Eli and I can do it."

"Pshaw. What does Eli know about shopping? Let us women take care of you."

She pleaded with her eyes for Eli to save her and wanted to strangle him when he nodded his head and agreed. "Yeah, Mom and Bec are much better at shopping than me and I'm pretty sure you'll need all the help you can get." He grinned at her. *Don't smile at me Mr. Innocent.*

"But we don't want to add to their already busy schedule," she said, making one last attempt to extricate herself, smiling with her lips while simultaneously spearing him with her eyes.

Becca cheerfully shot her down. "We love to shop! That's like dessert for us. It gets us away from all the chores staring us in the face."

"Well, um, if you're sure it's not too much trouble," she trailed off.

Silas grinned at her. "They'll make a girl outta ya yet."

"Don't count on it," she replied. Under her breath, she whispered, "Who's side are you on?"

Cassie felt like she was suffocating. Too damn many Canes. First Bill Cane taking her off on some joy ride after supper, then locked down for that shopping spree with Abby and Becca, next thing she knew she'd be forced into joining some damn quilting bee. *Breathe.*

Bill Cane stood up, towering over the table, all six foot four-plus inches of him, and said, "Well Cassie, are you ready?"

She plastered a smile on her face and stood. "Yes. All I have to do is change my shoes. Where shall I meet you?"

"I'll pick you up in front of the house."

She cocked an eyebrow at Eli. "Walk with me?"

He stood. "Let's go." He reached for her hand, but she pulled hers away, purposefully striding ahead of him into the lobby and out the front door. He caught up to her as she stepped off the front porch. "Hey, didn't you invite me to walk with you?"

"Yes, so I can give you an earful," she hissed, looking over her shoulder to make sure no one else could hear her.

"What'd I do now?" He did his best to look innocent, but the smirk he bit back gave him away.

She huffed, "As if."

"What was I supposed to do? You've got to jump in with both feet. My family already loves you. They're trying to make you feel at home."

"I hate to break it to ya, but it's having the opposite effect. I feel fenced in."

"Fenced is in your own mind, Cass. Quit making everything so damn complicated. I really don't know shit from Shinola about shopping for a baby, and you've got to admit, we do need to start buying stuff."

"Here's the kicker, your dad as my tour guide? My nerves are shore nuff shot right about now."

Elijah held up his hands, "Wait, I had nothing to do with that. My dad seems to have taken a shining towards ya which, by the way, is a miracle in itself. That never happens. He usually takes forever to warm up, warm being relative mind you. I was as surprised as you were. By their expressions, so were Ma and Bec."

She raised a skeptical eyebrow. "Is that the truth?"

He flashed her his sexy grin, slipping an arm across

her shoulders. "Yeah. God's honest truth. Maybe I've finally done something right by my old man. Found a good woman that can kick my ass." He chuckled.

She shook her head, but couldn't help smiling up at him. "I'll make sure to put in a good word for you."

"I never doubted it."

They reached the house and he placed both hands on her shoulders, turning her to face him. His expression serious, he said, "All you ever have to do is to be yourself, Cass. No one can possibly resist that." He touched her face and her pulse skittered.

"You make me crazy, you know that? One minute I'm ready to strangle ya, and in the next, I want you to kiss me senseless," Cass said.

He chuckled warmly as he brought his mouth down to hers. Planting a soft kiss against her lips, her body responded immediately and she slid her palms up his chest, wrapping them around his neck. His warm breath against her cheek, the masculine scent of him, all had her breathless, then his lips found a sensitive spot at the curve of her neck and she shuddered.

"I'd better go get ready; I'd hate to lose favor with your dad so soon."

"We'll continue this tonight. That's a promise."

Still breathless, she said, "You've got yourself a deal. Wish me luck."

He winked. "You may be *my* key to the old man's heart."

She smiled. "More pressure. But I can take it I suppose. See you later." She left him gazing after her, the hunger still burning in his eyes. *Good. Least I'm not the only one.*

34

Cassie had settled into a routine in the month since she'd arrived, her mornings taken up with helping Beau and the other ranch hands muck stalls and tend to the animals. She picked up the wheelbarrow and went to empty it into the manure spreader at the back of the barn. Lenny and Clifford happily followed her, tails wagging. She was often joined by Silas and Dios, but today he was busy helping Clayton put together a model airplane.

She was slowly getting used to being around a large family. Unlike her, Silas had needed no adjustment period. He loved every second of it and Clayton clung to him like he was a superhero.

To her surprise and delight, she'd been asked to lead a group of guests out on a couple of trail rides. Elijah had taken her out riding plenty of times, so she was comfortable with the terrain and knew the best spots to show the guests. It made her happy and she could easily see herself doing it until she got too far along and her baby belly got in the way.

She rested her palm against her abdomen, although not noticeable to anyone else yet, she and Eli could certainly see a baby bump. Some nights when she and Eli got in bed, he'd place his mouth close to her belly and talk to their baby. He'd tell stories, or talk about the day, sometimes he'd read a children's book from a shelf already full...thank you very much Abby and Becca. But for some strange reason, she minded their involvement less and less.

Abby's gentle touch and soothing presence had slowly worked its magic, putting Cassie at ease. So much so that Cassie had invited her to go with them to meet their new pediatrician, scheduled for the following week.

Cassie sighed. She'd felt lonely since Eli had left for a competition in Texas. He'd only been gone three days but still...she really missed him. He'd be home tomorrow and that couldn't get here fast enough. She frowned. *Gawd! When did I become so needy?*

"Here let me empty that for ya," Beau said.

"I got it, but thanks Beau." She smiled warmly at him. He was a real sweetheart and he'd been one of the main reasons she felt less overwhelmed. He was her people. A cowboy through and through. He reminded Cassie a little of Nash, and not just the blond hair and all-American good looks, but his warm, kind eyes and the way he was with animals. He put them and her at ease without even trying.

"Aw, come on. I feel guilty. That wheelbarrow is heavy," he said.

"I'm used to it and the experts agree it's better for the baby and me to stay active and in shape. If it's activities my body is used to, there isn't a risk."

Beau's green eyes squinted as he sized Cassie up. "You sure about that? Eli will have my ass if he thinks I'm working ya too hard."

"Don't you worry about Eli, I can handle him."

Beau chuckled. "I never thought I'd see the day someone would domesticate that wild stallion, but I have to hand it to ya, Cass. He's definitely whipped."

Cassie held in a smile. "You really think so, huh?"

Beau winked. "I know so." Cassie didn't want to admit to herself how much that pleased her. Her body felt all warm and tingly thinking about it.

"Becca said you're taking another group out this afternoon. I'll stick around and help them tack up."

"I'd be grateful for your help, Beau. It's a green group of riders. Two of them don't have a lick of experience. One is a city slicker who'll probably wear his Gucci loafers to the barn. Raised on concrete. I'm terrible. I shouldn't make fun of the guests."

Beau grinned. "Don't bother me none. I do it all the time. Don't mean no harm."

"Exactly." A huge smile split her face. "Glad we're on the same page. I'm going to finish the last stall then grab me some lunch before I take the group out."

"What time should I meet ya back here?"

"One o'clock work for you?"

"Yep. I'll be here."

"Thanks. See ya in a bit," she said. She finished mucking the last stall then headed for the dining hall.

. . .

Cassie had to fight the temptation to roll her eyes at Beau when the city slicker strode up and introduced himself. He had on an expensive pair of black Lucchese alligator cowboy boots.

First chance she got, she whispered to Beau, "Look at them fancy-ass boots. Brand spankin' new, too."

He bit back a smile and nodded. "Yeah, they set him back at least five grand, I'm guessing."

She grinned, then turned her attention back to the rest of the guests. It was a small group of seven.

One guest raised her hand, "Hey Cassie, how long have you been riding?"

"Since I was about five," she said. "Don't let that intimidate you none. It's never too late to learn. We put you all on real good beginner horses."

One of the women said, "Thank God! I'm so nervous."

"Don't be. I swear we wouldn't put you on a horse we didn't trust. These are all veterans. Doesn't mean they won't test you, but not in a mean way." Cassie smiled.

Clarissa, a guest from Ohio, asked, "Where you from Cassie?"

"Texas," she replied. "Can't y'all tell?" she teased. "Grew up there. Okay everybody," she said, "Beau will check to make sure your cinches are tight, then please head over to the mounting block and I'll help ya hop on."

Beau checked them one by one, then Cassie helped them mount. Holding Pirate's reins, she steadied him while the guest climbed on. When everyone else was settled, Cassie mounted Kiss and trotted to the front of the group.

"Y'all line up behind me single file. Andrew and Clarissa, I want you right behind me since you don't have any experience. Alright? Y'all ready?" They all nodded, their bright eyes and smiling faces expectant, which made Cassie want to make sure their ride was special.

"We'll start out at a walk and after everyone feels comfortable, we can pick up a trot," she called over her shoulder. "If I stop and hold up my hand, stay quiet and look around. Lots of wildlife round here we don't want to scare any off till ya get a good look."

Cassie nudged Kiss into a faster walk and let herself relax with the sway of her horse's barrel. Kiss blew out a noisy sigh and Cassie smiled. Kiss had adjusted well to her new home. Like Beau had predicted, she and Amitola had formed a bond and were inseparable when turned out with the herd. The sun was bright in the cloudless azure sky and a warm breeze blew in from the west. She brushed back a stray lock of hair that tickled her cheek, tucking it behind one ear. She twisted around to make sure everyone was keeping up, then faced forward again.

Pitching her voice loud enough to reach the last in line, she said, "It's not hard to imagine this land centuries ago. It seems unchanged somehow. Only two of the original eleven Native American tribes that lived in Wyoming are left, the Shoshone and Arapaho. They live on the Wind River Reservation."

"Are there any wild buffalo around here?" Clarissa asked.

"Best place to spot them is Yellowstone. They've made somewhat of a comeback from a couple dozen to five thousand free-range. They were practically hunted to extinction, not by the natives mind ya, but by European settlers. They're definitely a symbol of the wild west. The Native tribes depended on them for survival. Not just food, mind you, but for food, clothing, shelter, and even tools. It's sad that they almost got wiped out. Chances are we won't see any, but we may spot some elk or antelope."

"That'd be cool," A voice responded from the back.

"So, Cassie, how did you end up here in Wyoming?"

"Lucky I guess," she answered, sticking with the simplest answer. "Everyone ready to pick up a trot?"

A chorus of yeses answered her question. "Tap them with your heel, click your tongue and squeeze your legs a bit, then say trot. They'll follow my lead though." Cassie couldn't help grinning as she listened to the group clicking tongues, giggling, groaning and complaining when the horses continued to walk. She clicked her own tongue and Kiss transitioned to a trot. She looked back, satisfied to see that their horses were finally complying. Horses were geniuses at sizing up their riders and acting accordingly. She imagined them all secretly grinning with pleasure at their successful power play. With everyone trotting comfortably, Cassie concentrated on what lay ahead.

They rode at the faster pace until Cassie held up her hand and called out, "Whoa." She brought Kiss to a standstill and pointed ahead and off to the right. "See the moose over there? Unusual to see them this time a day. They're usually snoozing." The small herd had their heads lowered at the stream's edge, grazing.

"Wow, look at the size of those antlers. They must span at least four feet!"

"Oh my God! They're huge!"

"Believe it or not they're smaller than the Canadian Moose," Cassie said. This was her first-time seeing Wyoming moose. She couldn't wait to tell Eli. She'd been reading up on the wildlife and history of Wyoming, so she could keep the rides she led more interesting. But a little talkin' went a long way so she kept it light. The beauty of the land spoke for itself. It seeped into your soul and changed a person. Nobody ever came away disappointed.

There was a sense of being tucked away somewhere between the peaks and meadows, the grasslands, trees and meandering trout-filled streams, all under the endless big sky. It made Cassie feel small and, strangely enough, that was comforting. She could feel the whispers of ancient cultures, like ghosts still roaming the vast land. Her heart felt full, and a peaceful calm washed over her every time she and Kiss explored this sacred ground. Like the Kacey Musgraves tune, "Oh What a World," there's all kinds of magic!

35

Elijah pulled his carry-on from the overhead compartment and waited for the passengers to clear the aisle before exiting the plane. He had a weird sensation in the pit of his stomach, kind of the same feeling he'd experienced when riding the downhill side of a rollercoaster. In fact, every time he thought about Cassie at the ranch, sleeping in his bed, living with him, carrying their baby, he was impatient as hell to get home to her. He spotted Beau waiting for him and after exchanging a warm greeting, they fell in step together.

"How'd ya do?" Beau asked.

"First place."

"Yee haw. You're on fire."

"How'd it go here while I was gone?"

"Good. Cassie took the guests out on a couple of trail rides. She seemed pleased as all git out."

Eli smiled. "Good. How about Silas?"

"He acts like he's lived here his whole life. Clayton still won't give him a moment's peace. I swear, that kid could talk the legs off a chair."

"That just about describes our Clay." They reached the truck and they both climbed in. "Damn, feels like I've been gone for weeks," Eli said as Beau pulled out.

"That's what love will do to ya, tames even the wildest beast," Beau said, biting back a smile.

Eli narrowed his eyes. "Watch it there, don't dig up more snakes than you can kill."

Beau laughed. "Wash off your war paint. I'm just yanking your chain. No need to get all het up about it."

"I've still got my old man's comments running around loose in my brain." Eli's lips twisted. "My loving father...telling Cassie that maybe she can make me grow up and shit like that. As always, he couldn't wait to jump on me with all four feet. He's relentless. And he wonders why I stay away. Christ."

"I'm not gonna sugarcoat it, he's always been harder on you for some reason. He's old school that's for sure."

"Old school my ass. Kind way of saying pig-headed. But hey, thanks for the reality check."

"I'll bet if ya quit the rodeo he'd come around purdy quick."

"Maybe. That's what he's always wanted. Me and Gunner here to help run the ranch. Now that a baby is on the way, he may just get his wish."

"I can't say I'd mind having my best friend around all the time," Beau said.

"Aww, getting all sappy on me?"

"Maybe. Got a problem with it?"

Eli put his fist over his chest, drumming it like a beating heart. "Naw, I feel ya dude."

Beau looked over at him and snorted, taking his hand off the wheel long enough to flip him off. "Fuck you."

All wide-eyed innocence, Elijah said, "What? You know I love ya, big guy."

Beau chuckled. "You never change, bro."

Suddenly serious, Eli said, "I hope that's not true. I've pretty much been a selfish prick most of my life. Now I want to be more than that."

"Aww, going all sappy on me?" Beau grinned, pleased to be throwing Eli's words back in his face. Beau suddenly grew serious. "For the record, you've never been a selfish prick. Wild yes, aggressively going for what you want, fer sure, but you've always been honest to a fault. I ain't ever heard ya pretending to be anything you're not or making promises you have no intentions of keepin'."

Eli felt a tightness in his chest. "Thanks B. That means a lot."

"You're a lot more than your hype," he said grinning.

Eli guffawed. "My hype? That's priceless."

"It's true though. Your dad has it all wrong. A wild heart ain't nothin' like a mean one. Nothing wrong with sowing some wild oats before ya settle down. Know what I mean?"

"No, maybe you could explain it to me," Eli teased.

"Some other time, champ. Here we are," Beau said. "Home sweet home." He parked the truck and Elijah grabbed his bag and jumped out.

"Thanks for the lift."

"Anytime."

Eli strode briskly toward the lodge, making a beeline for the kitchen where Abby was stirring a large vat of stew. "Hey Ma, where's Cass?" The savory smell of herbs pricked Eli's nostrils, reminding him that he hadn't eaten since seven that morning. He grabbed a leftover muffin off the counter and ate half of it in one bite.

"Hello, dear. I think she was taking a group out on a trail ride."

He polished off the muffin. "Thanks. I'm going to park my bag; I'll pick it up later."

"No hug for your mom?"

He grinned and grabbed her from behind in a big bear hug, kissing the top of her head. "Love ya, Ma."

"Go find her," she said smiling.

"That's the plan."

Swallowing hard, he watched Cassie crest the hill, perched on Kiss's back, leading a small group of guests in from their trail ride. His gaze roved over her body, so comfortable and relaxed on horseback, and sexy as hell. Her head tilted back as she laughed with the group. *God, I've missed her*. He wanted to haul her off to his bedroom and have her all to himself. Heat and desire coursed through him.

He knew the moment she saw him as he watched surprise then longing flit across her face. He could have imagined it, because it was quickly shuttered behind a neutral mask.

He walked up to Kiss and grabbed the reins, holding them while Cassie dismounted. "Hi," he said in a soft growl. "Did you miss me?" The top of her head just reached his broad shoulders so she had to look up to meet his gaze.

Her eyes challenged him. "Who wants to know?" She led her horse away from the guests and he followed.

"I missed you," he said.

She narrowed her eyes. "Sure about that? Hard to tell since you didn't bother to call."

His eyes widened. "That's not true. I called you practically the minute my plane landed."

"Then didn't hear hide nor hair from you."

"It honestly never occurred to me. I haven't had a steady girl since high school. Doesn't mean I wasn't thinking about ya though, fantasizing about you all night long...that you were in bed next to me...doing things."

Her penetrating stare bore into him, weighing whether or not she should believe him.

Teasing, he kept his voice low and intimate. "You know...talking dirty to me...touching me."

She put a hand on her hip. "Amazing. You had all that time to think and yet you didn't call me."

"You know, you could have called me if you missed me that much. I didn't know you'd be here moping around without me. We could have had phone sex or something." Her eyes hardened to green shards of irritation. He immediately realized his mistake in teasing her. *Damn but she was good at giving the stink eye.*

She turned her back to him and addressed the

group who were already untacking their horses. "Don't forget to pick their hooves. There are carrots and apple slices in the tack room."

Eli leaned down and whispered close to her ear. "What's with the fancy dude over there?"

She curbed a smile. "He's actually very sweet. A complete greenie."

"Sweet huh? I don't like the sound of that." He wrapped his arms possessively around her waist, staking claim and making sure there was no room for doubt. Leaning down he kissed the corner of her mouth. "You could hug me back, even if it's just for show."

He smiled as she slipped her arms around him.

"I'm sorry I didn't call you," he said softly. "Forgive me?"

She nodded her head, her face still buried in his chest. He heard her take in a deep breath, then she said, "You smell pretty good cowboy."

He smiled into her hair. "Miss Morgan, are you talkin' dirty to me?"

"You're insufferable," she said, laughing as she pushed him away.

36

"You rang?" Eli asked, leaning against the doorframe of the office.

His father was bent over the computer and barely glanced up. Pushing his cowboy hat back from his brow, he barked, "Finishing up. Sit."

Eli glared at his father but obeyed, plopping down and crossing his arms over his chest, waiting. He let his gaze wander around the office. He never really took the time to appreciate how far the ranch had come. When he was a kid, this office hadn't even been built. His dad had done the bookkeeping at their kitchen table. The old lodge had slowly been replaced with the current deluxe chalet and five more guest cabins had been added in the last ten years.

Bill Cane switched off the computer and leaned back in his chair, eyeing Eli speculatively. "Since Gunner's making a name for himself and spending more time in Nashville, I was wondering what your plans are now, with a baby on the way."

"No solid plans yet. I pulled out of the rodeo for the rest of this year. I need to be here for Cass. Not sure about next season. I'm available to work the ranch for now." Eli resisted the urge to squirm as his father stared at him in disapproval.

"That's it then?" Bill Cane said, steepling his fingers.

"What did you have in mind?" Eli said, not even attempting to curb his sarcasm.

"You've got to grow up sometime, son. A baby's on the way. Seems like the time to call it a day on your rodeo *career*," he said, his fingers making air quotations around the word career.

Eli bristled. Through gritted teeth he said, "Dad, why have you always had it in for me? What did I ever do that was so terrible?"

"Every father wants his son to succeed."

"Succeed? And how do you measure that? Huh? Being the best bronc rider and repeated champion obviously doesn't qualify. Making big money either. What does my success look like to you, old man?"

"Being a responsible adult with purpose, for starters."

"Give me a break. I've been on my own and paying my way since I left home. You always picked on me. Why?"

His father's brows shot up in surprise. "I don't know what you're talking about. I treated you same as the rest."

"No, you didn't, Dad. You were always on me about something. My grades weren't good enough, when I played quarterback in high school, I didn't throw the ball hard enough, at home I didn't do the chores the way you wanted me to."

Bill scoffed. "You and Beau were always getting into trouble at school, caught drinking beer too many times, coming in way after curfew. Could have killed yourself riding the horses like ya did. Nothing too wild, nothing too high to jump, nothing too fast. It was almost like you had a death wish."

Eli shook his head in disgust. "I was a kid."

"Maybe you reminded me a little too much of myself. My dad had to come down hard on me too. Kept me in line. I'd never have amounted to anything otherwise." The emotion behind his softly spoken words sounded uncharacteristically unsure.

Eli leaned back in his chair studying his father's face. "I'm sure you raised us the way you thought best."

Bill cleared his throat. "Your mom and I aren't getting any younger. You never know from one day to the next. I was hoping you'd sowed your wild oats and were ready to settle down here. Managing the ranch with your brother Luke. He the financials, you the operations manager. We'd like to travel a little. Not full on retire, but step back some."

Eli frowned. *Is my father showing a glimpse of vulnerability? Good Lord the skies are going to open up and swallow us all!*

"Dad, I've never heard you talk like this. You and ma okay? You feeling good?"

"Yes, nothing like that, except I get tired at the end of the day. So does your ma. I'd like to show her something besides the ranch, see a little of the world before we die."

Eli felt his chest tighten. "I didn't know you and Mom were thinking that way, you know, about slowing down."

"We only recently started talking about it." He waved his hand dismissively. "As for the way I raised you kids, I did what I thought was right, can't take it back now."

"You know Dad, maybe for you, the old-school child rearing worked out, glad it worked out for you, but for me...well...let's just say it was something for me to overcome."

"I'm sorry you feel that way. Just so you know, I always thought you were special...you had a wild streak yes, but that meant you had courage and daring, you were smart. I wanted to train you to use it to your advantage."

"And all I ever wanted to do was get the hell out of here."

"I see that now. I'm sorry if you think that was my fault." He cleared his throat. "I hope you'll take a little time and think over my offer. If you say no, I'll try to respect that. We'll have to hire someone from outside the family in that case. Something I'm hoping we won't have to do."

"I'm not saying one way or another until I've had time to think about it and talk to Cassie. She only committed to living here until the baby comes."

"If you decide to take the job, we'll build you and Cassie a home of your own. It's no good you having to live here with your parents. And son?" Eli's brow rose.

"I really like her. You did good. You seem all in and I'm glad. I hope it works out for you."

"You're not the only one." Eli stood. "Listen Dad, I'd already been thinking about my future, fatherhood and the likes, so your timing is good. I'll get back to you."

"That's all I can ask. Try to look at the whole picture. You have a baby to think about now and the mother of your child. Rodeo is too risky. Anything can happen. Look at last year."

"Nothing I haven't already thought of. If I would accept the position, I won't have you micromanaging me and breathing down my neck twenty-four seven. We'd have to have some strict boundaries in place. Like who is in charge of what. Do ya think you can handle that?"

His lips turned up at the corners. "Your mom and I have discussed that already. I suspect y'all will keep me on the straight and narrow."

Eli softened, feeling a slight thaw towards his father. "I reckon if Ma has my back on this, it'll happen. Your hard head at least has sense enough to listen to her."

"Watch your smart mouth boy. I'm still your father."

"As if you'd let me forget. I'll get back with you soon. And Dad, thanks for the vote of confidence."

"Nobody knows this ranch better than family and no one loves this land more than us. It's the Cane legacy."

"Is that it then?" Eli asked. At his father's nod, he saluted and said, "Catch ya later, Dad."

37

After Eli left his father, he decided to take a detour and check in with Silas.

"Silas," Eli called out, through the screen door.

"Come on in."

Silas was standing in front of the sink washing dishes. He grabbed a kitchen towel and dried his hands before turning to greet Eli. "Don't just stand there, take a load off." Eli sat at the kitchen table and Silas grabbed a couple of bottled waters, passing one to Eli before taking the seat across from him.

"To what do I owe the pleasure?"

"I wanted to ask ya about something."

"Spit it out son."

"Cassie has had a few of those nightmares lately. In her sleep she keeps repeating something about a tree or Dee. When she wakes up its always the same, a young man hiding with her in a closet. Just wondering if you have any advice. I have an idea about it and I wanted to get your opinion." Eli cleared his throat. "Also, my dad wants me to quit the rodeo and become a respectable family man. Wondering what you think my odds are of convincing Cassie to join me here?"

Silas's bushy brows drew together. "Well now. Let's start with the dreams. I know it can be startlin' getting woke up like that in the middle of the night. Best thing I know is to hold her till she comes out of it." He held up a finger. "Wait here." Standing, he disappeared down the hall. When he returned, he had a large stuffed animal tucked under his arm. He set it on the table. "Now don't laugh. I'd like ya to meet Benny." Eli's white teeth flashed against his tan skin. "Cassie had this with her when she first showed up and has always kept it on her bed. Might seem silly, but why don't ya take it home with ya."

"How can I resist? He seems a bit bedraggled, tells me he's seen a lot of action."

Silas chuckled. "You could say that. I've been thinking a lot about this dream business. Maybe it's past time lettin' her read the letter from Nicky. Telling her 'bout her real dad, what her mama went through, could help her to heal from her past. Least it would fill in some of the missin' pieces, best case she'll get over havin' them bad dreams."

Eli scratched his head, nodding thoughtfully. "You could be right. After all, she's 'bout to be a mom herself."

"Hold on, if we're gonna go there, let me show ya something." Silas ambled back down the hallway, returning with a wooden box about the size of a briefcase. He set it on the table between them and unlatched a brass hook, opening the lid. Inside looked to be full of photographs, letters and documents which pricked Eli's curiosity. Silas rooted through the box.

"What ya looking for?" Eli asked. Silas pulled out an envelope and Eli recognized it to be the one from Cassie's mother he'd read. Silas set it aside, then lifted a photograph of a young couple in formal attire and held it out to Eli.

Eli whistled. "Holy hell! You weren't kidding when you said Cassie looks just like her ma."

Silas smiled. "Nicky's hair was a little lighter, but other'n that, spittin' image."

"Your son was certainly handsome. They both look so happy here."

"They was. That was their senior prom picture."

Eli grabbed a stack of photographs from the box and looked at the one on top of a young child of about four. It was Cassie. "Damn she was cute." He leafed through them. Cassie on a horse, Cassie with Reed, Cassie missing her front teeth, Cassie playing guitar, a collage of her life after the age of four. At the bottom of the pile, he noticed a picture of Cassie with her mom and a tall man with olive skin and a menacing appearance and a handsome young boy who couldn't have been more than ten or eleven. The boy looked like a young version of the man he stood next to. Eli studied it. Cassie in her mom's lap crying, Nicky looking unhappily into the camera. "I take it this is her father?" Silas nodded.

"Who's the boy?"

"Don't know."

"Has Cass seen this one?"

Silas looked at Eli, wearing regret like a blanket. "No. Nicole had put that and two other photographs in Cassie's back-pack. That one there...with him and the boy, and a picture of Nicole by herself and another one of her and Cassie together. I'm sure she wanted Tater to have something to remember her by. Not sure why she put that one with him in there. Maybe so we'd be able to identify him if we needed to. Don't know and don't care. He's not her daddy now. We was going to tell her more when she got old enough, but when Cassie started havin' them nightmares, we decided it might be best to keep the past in the past, best we could anyhow." He reached back into the box and pulled out several pages ripped from a magazine and several newspaper articles. Handing them to Eli, he said, "This is the other reason we've kept it on the down low."

Eli whistled softly as his eyes skimmed over the articles with pleas from the wealthy casino owner Maxim Petrov, offering a million-dollar reward for any information leading to his missing wife Nicole Petrov, alongside her photograph. "That's after we already had Cassie."

"Wow."

"Don't s'pose he cared that much 'bout finding Cassie in the first place; Nicole was the prize. But there was no trail leading him to us anyhow, Marshals made sure of that. Far as I know anyway, he didn't know about Reed. When Reed adopted her, he gave her his name."

"This kind of puts a whole new light on things. Maybe we should let sleeping dogs lie after all, because I sure as hell don't know what's best."

Silas smiled sadly. "She keeps a picture of her ma in her jewel box, least she used to."

Eli was mesmerized by the picture he held of Cassie and her mom. He could see that Nicole had that special something...she was beautiful yes, but she also possessed that intangible that separated her from the ordinary, a star quality that some people were just born with. Like his brother, Gunner. The photo captured such a look of love shared between mother and daughter, Nicole laughing down at her while Cassie gazed up at her mom adoringly. Eli felt his heart squeeze for their loss. He drummed his fingers on the table.

"By the way, Cassie's appointment's at eleven tomorrow, then we're grabbing some lunch. We'll stop by after and tell you all about it."

"Sounds good."

"How about this, after the ultrasound, we talk about it some more before we decide what to do."

Silas huffed out a breath. "I s'pose."

"Si, don't worry, we both want what's best for Cassie. I still have to wonder if she'd be better off knowing the truth. At least she'd know those boogey men fears aren't made up in her head."

"I wish I knew. It's just...I still see her as that traumatized little thing that showed up on our doorstep. What if the nightmares get worse?" Silas bowed his head. "I reckon I can't protect her forever."

"The question is, should we keep her from the truth? Her mom loved her enough to risk her life to keep her safe. That is the truth. She'll have a better understanding of why she has the nightmares and they might make more sense to her. That can't be a bad thing, can it?"

"Let's think on it fer a bit. As fer you taking the job here and moving back home, only you kin answer that, but I'll tell ya, this place is special and Cassie seems to be bloomin' here. She's thriving bein' round yer family. She's belongin'. Only family she had was me and Reed. Nash a course, but here...she's got all ya."

"You really think so?" Eli cringed at the hope and eagerness he heard in his voice.

"Son, I promise ya. Even if she's still havin' them damn nightmares, she's calmer and less prickly."

Eli felt like a weight had been lifted. He jumped up and paced the floor of Silas's kitchen. "That's music to my ears Si and makes me give more weight to my father's proposition."

"I can't speak fer Cass, she may not even know it herself. But I kin see it."

"There's hope at least. See ya at dinner?"

"I spect."

"Later. Thanks, Si."

38

Cassie crawled into the back of Eli's Silverado, leaving the front passenger seat free for Abby. Once they were buckled in, Eli pulled out of the physician's parking lot heading to town for lunch. He was practically bouncing off the cab with excitement.

"I liked the doctor a lot." Eli said.

"She was very nice and seemed to genuinely care," Abby said. "And, I'm going to finally have another grandchild. Just think, next visit you'll find out if it's a girl or a boy!"

She turned in her seat to look back at Cassie, her eyes shiny with tears. "Thank you for asking me to go with you. It somehow made it feel real."

Cassie felt overcome and utterly unworthy of the love and admiration she saw pouring out of Abby's soft eyes. Love directed straight at her. It pierced her, and she needed to push it away, put some distance between them. Suddenly she couldn't breathe. "No need to thank me, you're Eli's mom after all. It was only right that you be there."

Abby's face momentarily clouded, but she recovered quickly. Clapping her hands together she said, "I know! Let's go shopping! This week. Just us girls. You, Becca and me."

Cassie suddenly felt panicked. It was all so much. Too much. The doctor's visit...hearing the heartbeat through the stethoscope, birthing classes, all of it had made it real for her as well. "It's too soon," Cassie blurted out, sounding panicked and much harsher than she'd intended. There was dead silence and Cassie wanted to be swallowed up and spit out to sea. Eli looked at her from the rearview mirror, his brow furrowed with concern.

"Babe, you alright?"

"Actually no. I can't breathe right now." It was true, she was hyperventilating, gasping for air, having a full-blown anxiety attack.

Abby unlatched her seat belt and gracelessly climbed over the console and into the back seat with Cassie. She wrapped her arms around Cassie, holding her close. Cassie stiffened and tried to pull away, but Abby held on tight.

"Shh, I felt the very same way," Abby murmured comfortingly. She rocked Cassie in her arms like she was a child. "When I found out I was pregnant with Luke, I was only twenty-one and scared to death. My mama was already gone. I hadn't a clue how I was going to raise a child when I was still a child myself."

Cassie tried to hold on to the last ounce of control she had because if she let go, she feared she'd never be right again. Her teeth began to chatter. Abby continued, keeping her voice calm and steady. "I doubt that you and I have the corner on that market. It is the scariest thing I can think of. Suddenly you're on a rollercoaster ride and have no control over anything. Add to that, zero experience." Miraculously, Cassie felt her anxiety lessening, only to be replaced with grief and tears that silently ran down her cheeks.

Abby continued to rock Cassie while stroking her hair. "There, there. You're not alone my dear." It was almost as if she'd read Cassie's mind. "We're all in this together, that's what family does. We stick together. You're family." Eli pulled out a hanky from his pocket and tossed it to his mom. She gently wiped Cassie's tears.

"I...I'm...so...sor...sorry. I don't deserve this. I...I... I've been terrible to you."

"Nonsense!" Abby said sharply. "You've been overwhelmed and who could blame you. We're an intimidating bunch. Cassie, we love you already."

"But how can you? I'm not loveable. I feel like such a mess and you're all so together."

She snorted. "Oh really? We must be putting on a good show then. Hang around the Canes long enough and you'll change your tune."

Cassie found herself smiling through her tears. She slipped her arms around Abby's waist and hugged her tight. She smelled of baking bread and flowers and if comfort had a smell, it would be Abby.

They rode in silence for a while; the only sound was the truck tires on pavement. Cassie lifted her gaze and met Eli's in the rearview mirror, his eyes burning with a fierceness she didn't quite understand. His body appeared tense, alert, almost protective, as if ready to jump to action if necessary. His voice was thick when he said, "You okay?" When she smiled at him, she saw his shoulders relax and then she knew, this alpha cowboy had been worried about her, was right there in the frying pan alongside her and had been from the git go.

39

After Eli dropped his mom and Cassie off at the house and parked, he jogged over to Silas's place. Silas raised his brows looking behind him for Cassie.

"Today was a big day, a little too big. Cass had a meltdown on the way home from the doctor's. She's fine now. But I came by myself to fill ya in. It was so awesome...hearing the heartbeat, talking about scheduling classes, pre-natal stuff—it scared her."

"Why? Is the baby all right?"

"Yes, it was nothing like that! It brought up all her fears about mothering and not being good enough. Thank God Mom was there. She worked her magic and brought Cass down. It's all good. No need to worry. But definitely not the time to hit her up with something else. Let's postpone it for now."

"A course. I trust you know what's best." Silas said. Eli swallowed a smile, pleased by the compliment.

"I'm going to take Cass out for a trail ride later, pack a picnic and eat our supper by the stream. Full moon tonight. See if I can cheer her up. Get out and let nature take its course and have its way with us." He grinned.

Si nodded his approval. "Best way I know of."

"See ya around then."

"Thanks for looking out for Tater."

He winked. "Takes a village."

Several hours later, Cassie and Eli were sprawled on their backs on top of a blanket, Eli's arm curled behind Cassie's neck, her head nestled in the crook of his arm. They'd finished the picnic he'd packed and were now enjoying the peaceful beauty surrounding them. The gurgle of the stream over the rocks, the breeze stirring the trees and the horses' occasional snorts of contentment were all that broke the quiet of the vast landscape.

"I think Kiss has a crush on Freak," Cassie said. Eli chuckled, his husky tone kicking her craving for him into overdrive.

"I'm pretty sure it goes both ways," he replied.

They watched nature's colorful show as the sun set. The sky was awash with a spectacular display of vivid oranges, yellows and purples, streaked across as if they'd been painted by an artist's brushstrokes. "Best show in town," Eli said.

She turned to study his handsome face, the warm breeze ruffling his dark hair. "You can say that again." Tracing her fingertip along his thick dark brows, she feathered down his nose before outlining his lips.

Nuzzling into the crook of his arm, she said, "I love the way you smell, all sexy...and spicy."

Cassie rolled onto her side and snuck her hand under his tee-shirt, palming his lower abdomen. Her fingers roamed over his happy trail of hair, her insides quivering in response to touching him. His erection was immediate and she resisted the urge to unzip his jeans and pleasure him right then and there. Instead, she skimmed her palm up his chest and teased his nipples with featherlight strokes of her fingertips.

He groaned. "Yes, do that."

She crawled on top of him and rubbed herself against his bulge. Leaning down, she touched his lips with hers, her tongue darting out and licking his bottom lip before biting him. Then she soothed the mistreated lip by drawing it into her mouth and suckling gently. He cupped her buttocks roughly with his large palms and pressed her snugly against him. She rocked her hips with more urgency.

"Cassie, what are you doing to me?" Eli roughly pulled her tee-shirt from her jeans and slid his hands up to cup her breasts, kneading them as his thumbs rolled over the silk-clad nipples.

She threw her head back and arched. "Yes," she panted.

He reached behind her and unclasped her bra, freeing her breasts and allowing him better access. She gasped as he pulled her down and settled his open mouth on her nub and sucked her in. She moaned as his tongue licked and swirled around her areola. Cassie felt like there was an electric channel that ran directly from her breast to her center of desire. Each tug made her throb with need. He switched his attention to her other breast, giving it the same erotic treatment until, without warning, he flipped her onto her back.

Trailing his mouth down her chest, he nuzzled her belly before unbuttoning and unzipping her jeans. Dragging them down her legs, she moaned as he licked his way up and buried his nose in the crease of her thigh. "You like that?" he said.

"Mm."

"Tell me Cass," he commanded gruffly.

"Yes. I...ahh..." She jerked as his hot mouth tongued her through her panties. "Yes, I like your mouth on me."

Slipping his finger under the elastic leg band, he slid a finger against her wet opening and plunged inside. She thrust against him, needing to feel him. "More," she whispered.

He slipped a second digit in and began pleasuring her with his fingers, burying them up to his knuckles, which pressed against her sweet spot with each thrust. Eli's breath was quick and shallow as he pressed in and out, again and again, until she was writhing with abandon. Her fingers were buried in his hair as she panted. "Eli, I can't...hold on...I..." She cried out and bucked as sensations swallowed her up. He continued his assault on her senses, nuzzling between her thighs as she rubbed herself against his hot mouth. When her trembling subsided, Eli crawled up and pulled Cassie into his arms and cradled her against his chest, murmuring unintelligible pillow talk into her hair.

As Cassie's breathing returned to normal, she felt Eli's stiff cock pressing against her thigh. She slid one hand into the waistband of his low rider jeans and cupped his erection, pressing hard against him. He undulated in her hand and she fisted him through his underwear. His breath was hot against her neck as he buried his face into the curve of her shoulder and ground into her hand.

"Cass," he groaned.

She continued to stroke him, gripping his chin to bring his lips to hers. They kissed, hot wet kisses, their tongues exploring, licking, sucking...Eli panted into her mouth as his arousal took over. Cassie unbuttoned his jeans and pulled out his hard cock, sliding from the base to the tip of his head and back down again, milking him as he groaned. Still fisting him, she let her hair tickle his chest and abs as she slid down to kiss the tip of his straining erection. He tasted salty and his musky scent made her want to bury her nose. He hissed and jerked as she slipped the head of his cock between her lips.

"God, Cassie!" he growled.

She suckled and stroked until he reached down and gently cupped her face in his hands, lifting her mouth from him. "I'm about to come," he gasped. She continued to stroke as his climax ripped through him.

The full moon illuminated them, casting light and shadow across the land. When Cassie tried to sit up, Eli held her against him. "Not yet," he said.

"Okay." They continued to relax on the blanket, both reluctant to break the spell.

"I can't believe how bright the moon is." Her hushed voice revealed the awe she felt at the haunting stillness of the night sky. The cricket and insect sounds were magnified, a cadence resonating like a symphony, all perfectly synchronized. Just then, the sound of an owl pierced the night, followed by another.

"You're hearing a duet," Eli said. "There's two of them. Great Horned Owls."

"Oh my God! We're being serenaded!" The soft low hoots soothed her further.

"Yeah, but don't be surprised if they let out a screech."

As if on cue, a loud screech pierced the air and Cassie laughed. "That sure enough could make your hair stand up on end."

He pulled her in, kissing the tip of her nose. "Cass, I have something to run by you, but I don't want you freakin' out."

"Didn't ya ever learn not to start out leadin' a conversation like that? You just set my teeth on edge, now I'm spectin' the worst."

Eli sat up, propped up on his elbows. Uncharacteristically fidgety, he said, "Cass, my dad offered me a position as ranch manager, and said he'd build us a house if we were to stay on here. I told him I'd have to talk with you about your plans before I could give him an answer. My parents want to free up more time to travel. Not retire exactly, but semi-retire."

As the air grew thick between them, Eli's gut clenched. His anxiety turned to frustration when Cassie remained silent. "When did you want to have this conversation? As the back door hit you in the ass when you're waltzing out with our child?"

"Hold on a hot minute. Hell if I know what I'm doing besides getting through each day!"

"You like it here, right?"

"Yes. You know I do."

"You like my family? Seems like you're growing close to everyone."

She nodded.

"I like to think that includes yours truly."

She sighed. "You know it does. Elijah, next to Silas and Reed, you're the best thing that's ever happened to me."

"Well then?"

"Are you asking me to give up the rodeo? Are you ready to do that? Does having a baby mean we can't do what we love anymore? It's a lot to think about. Give it some time to digest. We'll talk more later. Right now, we're both tired and it is getting late."

"Ready to head back?"

"I guess."

"I can't keep my father hanging forever. He's talking about hiring someone if I don't want the position."

Standing, he pulled Cassie to her feet, then rolled up the blanket and stuffed it in his duffel bag.

"Eli, you know you're the only one that can decide about the job. I know you need to know where I stand, but about working here, for your family, that's something you have to feel right with."

"You're a part of my life Cassie. We're in this together, so no, it's something we both decide."

"You're the father and my lover and...oh it's so damn complicated."

"You're right. Let's let this simmer and talk about it when we're fresh. I think we got everything. Let me give you a leg up." Kiss waited patiently as Eli grasped his hands on either side of her hips and lifted her easily into the saddle. She swung her leg up over Kiss and settled her feet into the stirrups. Eli attached his duffle to the back of the saddle and mounted Freak. With a click of his tongue, they headed towards home.

Cassie sighed, staring up at the huge golden globe of the full moon, its glow washing over them and lighting their path. "Eli, a year ago I never could have imagined that this would be my life. For the first time in as long as I can remember, I feel full...I don't feel like I'm missing anything, you know? It's like that emptiness I'd felt from my childhood isn't there right now...like it's quiet. In answer to our future, I can't visualize leaving all this behind." She laughed, suddenly feeling embarrassed by her admission. Eli was quiet and she bit her lip to keep from filling the silence.

When he finally responded, his voice sounded thick. "Cassie, if I could give you that moon right up there, I would. I am glad you're finding your way here. I hope I'm a part of that peace you're feeling right now."

She laughed. "You big lug-head. You're the romantic male lead of this story."

"That's good then."

They arrived home and untacked their horses, putting them into their stalls for the night. They walked hand in hand back home and let themselves in quietly, careful not to disturb the sleeping household. They brushed their teeth together, Cassie smiling at him through the white foam, loving the intimacy of this simple ritual. Then they fell in bed together wrapped in each other's arms and were asleep as soon as their heads hit the pillow.

40

Cassie and Eli had volunteered to pick Sophia and Gunner up from the airport and now waited for them to disembark from the plane. No longer a Gunner Cane virgin, she knew all of his recorded songs by heart and could even play a few of them. It was official. She considered herself a closeted Gunner Cane fangirl.

"Gunner!" Eli yelled, waving to his brother.

Cassie caught sight of a super gorgeous redhead walking beside a drop-dead sexy guy oozing charisma from every pore of his perfect body. Sophia and Gunner.

Gunner smiled at Sophia then loped over and grabbed Eli in a big bear hug. "It's been a minute bro," he said.

"Too long. Congratulations on topping the country chart." They fist bumped then Eli grabbed Soph in for a hug. "Hey Soph. My brother treating you right?"

"He has no choice," she said, flashing him a dazzling smile.

Cassie felt about as exciting as a sack of potatoes standing next to these three.

Eli turned at that moment and grabbed Cassie's hand, pulling her forward. "Hey this is my girl, Cassie. Cass this is Gunner and Sophia."

Sophia stepped up to her and pulled her in for a hug. "Look at you, you're every bit as beautiful as everyone said!" Her smile was warm and contagious, her dark brown eyes sparkled with devilry, and Cassie found herself relaxing. Sophia linked her arm through Cassie's like they'd been besties their entire lives.

Gunner caught Cassie's eye and winked. "I finally get to meet the girl my brother's so sweet on. He tells me you're no slouch in the talent department. He's been talking you up. I quote, 'Cassie can sing and play guitar like an angel.'"

Cassie felt her cheeks heat. "Now that's embarrassing, seeing who it is he served that up to." Gunner laughed, a warm hearty sound that made him seem approachable and down to earth, not at all who she'd conjured up in her imagination.

Eli stuck his face next to Gunner's and said, "Now tell the truth girls, who's prettier?"

They all laughed and Gunner shoved him away.

"Better question, who's the biggest bullshitter?" Gunner said.

Cassie liked seeing the interaction between the brothers. It tickled something in the back of her brain. A flash of memory swept through her of a tall handsome teenager, playing with her and reading to her. Then it was gone.

"Let's get out of here," Eli said. He grabbed their suitcase, rolling it behind him to the exit.

"How are my hounds?" Gunner asked.

"Don't you mean my hounds?" Eli replied.

Sophia held up her hand. "Actually, they seem to prefer me."

Cassie cleared her throat. "Um, they've been sticking pretty close to me lately."

"Well, I reckon if I plied them with treats at every turn, I could bribe them to 'prefer' me," Eli teased.

Sophia rolled her eyes. "Uh-huh. I've caught you slipping them treats a time or two."

"I see you fancy yourself a version of super-sleuth Amelia. How is she, by the way?" he asked, referring to Sophia's childhood friend. They'd come together for a vacation at the Triple C last year and Sophia wound up working as their pastry chef and falling for Eli's brother.

"She is living the dream," Sophia said, chuckling. "Footloose and fancy free, always broke, but happy." She shrugged.

"Get her out here for another visit. Hank is lonely."

"I'll tell her you said that, but I think Hank has plenty of pretty girls hankering after him. Bartenders are like rock stars to women."

"Plus, he's got me now," Gunner said.

"Bro, not the same," Elijah said, shaking his head.

. . .

The following day, since they were guest-free until Friday, Becca pitched the idea of a softball game. The old-fashioned, friendly, throwdown variety. The suggestion was met with enthusiasm, so now here they were, gathered and preparing the field, waiting to figure out teams. Eli had invited Beau and Hank to join them, which brought the participants to an even twelve.

Cassie had to laugh at Sophia, who was jumping up and down, punching the air like she was preparing for a boxing match, rather than a softball game. Her Cub's ballcap was pulled low on her brow, her long red ponytail snaked through the back, bouncing with each jab. Gunner could barely keep his eyes or hands off of Sophia, and their exchanged glances were so full of desire that Cassie thought she might need a cold shower after the game...or a moment alone with her man. Those two were as solid as a couple could get.

Her eyes wandered to Elijah as he used spray paint to mark the bases, and she felt a tingle run down her spine. His laughter pealed at something Clay had said, then he suddenly looked up and caught her staring. Their eyes locked and her breath hitched. He made a fist and tapped his chest, sending her pulse racing. *Gawd, I'm practically swooning.* But she smiled and blew him a kiss.

Clayton came barreling over at full speed, grinning from ear to ear, almost knocking her down as he threw himself at her and wrapped his arms around her waist. Her heart ached and she cupped her belly, rubbing the soft swell of her baby bump.

"Cassie, Eli says I can be on your team."

"You'd better be, cause we're going to serve them up some humble pie."

Gunner chimed in, "Pull in your horns Cassie. This is a friendly game."

"Ah-huh. Sure, it is," she responded. "I heard ya earlier. Already scheming."

"Busted," he said, grinning.

Abby approached and linked her arm with Cassie's. "We'd better parcel out us old fogies evenly."

"Are you kidding me? I want you on my team Abby. You're as tough as nails."

Abby chuckled. "Maybe in the kitchen."

"Or with her knitting needle," Clay chimed in. "Huh Gramps?"

Bill Cane looked as relaxed as Cassie had ever seen him. A John Deer ball cap perched on top of his head, with his steely gray hair just brushing the nape of his neck. His normally stern expression softened as he smiled at his grandson. "Your grandma may surprise you. She played softball in high school. Was pretty good swinging that bat."

Clay's eyes sparkled with glee. "Really?"

"Yep. It's been a couple of years since we've had a family game, but last game we played, your grandma hit the ball that brought our runner in. Sewed it up but good."

Clay looked at Abby with amazement. "Will you be on me and Cassie's team?"

Abby's warm brown eyes could melt the frozen alps as far as Cassie was concerned, and she found herself craving the loving look that was shining on Clayton right now. "I wouldn't have it any other way, my dear. We're going to show 'em what's for." He pumped his little fist and let out a whoop.

Sophia approached, pouting. "What am I, yesterday's leftover chopped liver?"

Clayton scrunched up his face. "I knew you'd want to be on Uncle Gunner's team and Cassie don't have no family 'cept Silas, so she needs me."

Cassie took in a sharp breath and her heart melted. She crouched down and pulled Clayton against her, tears stinging her eyes. Whispering into his ear, she said, "You're sweeter than honey. Do you know that? Thank you for looking out for me."

He shrugged one bony shoulder. "I don't have a mom either."

Cassie swallowed around the lump in her throat. "That means we have to stick together, right? You know what else?" He shook his head. "Your mama would be so proud of you!"

"Daddy says she's in heaven and is watching over me. He says that I can talk to her whenever I want and that she'll hear me. I'll bet your mom is up there watching over you too."

"You're probably right. And look how lucky you are to have four women right here lovin' all over you."

He grinned impishly. "And sneaking me candy and stuff."

Cassie ruffled his hair. "Exactly my point. You catch on quick."

"Okay, friends and foes gather round," Becca announced. "Cassie, Mom, and Clay have already teamed up. I'm assuming, since Eli can't be apart from his girl, he's tagged for team one. Six per team. Beau and Luke, you can join them on team one. That leaves the rest of y'all on team two...the winning team." Becca pumped both fists in the air then gave Sophia a high five.

"We'll flip a coin to see who goes first. Who has a coin?"

Silas pulled a quarter from his pocket. "Here ya go."

"Go ahead Si, you do the honors," Becca said. "Team two calls heads."

Silas threw the coin in the air then slapped it onto the back of his hand. "Tails." Team one cheered. Then the teams huddled together to make decisions about batting order and pitching.

They had set up enough camp chairs for everyone to use while benched. It was sunny but cool, with temperatures hovering around sixty-eight degrees. Hank was pitching for team two, and he winked at Clay, first up, tossing the ball gently, aiming right at Clay's bat. Swing and a miss.

"You can do it, Clay," Abby called. Everyone held their breath as Clayton stood at the mound, bat gripped tightly, tongue out and brow furrowed in concentration. On the second pitch, the ball made contact and Clay threw down his bat, and took off towards first base with everyone from both teams screaming, "run Clay."

He made it to first base and Grandpa Bill clapped him on his shoulder, smiling proudly. "Atta boy, Clayton," he said.

Next up, Eli. He looked sexy as hell in his black jeans and hoodie. He turned to smile back at the peanut gallery, stepped up to home base, and took a batter's stance. Hank chewed his gum, blowing a bubble cockily before throwing his pitch. Gunner and Becca heckled him from the outfield, as Eli swung and missed.

"Strike one," Becca hollered gleefully.

The next swing sent the ball far into the outfield and Clayton made it to home base, scoring their first run. Eli was now on third base and Abby was up to bat.

Hank gestured with his index and middle fingers pointing in a V at his own eyes then at Abby's. She grinned wickedly, and said, "Give it your best shot, Hank."

Hank wound up and Abby walloped it hard. It sailed into right field, but unfortunately landed right in Gunner's glove. He waved his mitt in the air, calling out, "Sorry, Ma." Abby grumbled, but her lips were curved up in a smile.

"Out!" Becca the town crier added, for effect.

Luke was able to bat Eli in, then got tagged at second leaving one out to go. Cassie stepped up to the plate, biting her lip in concentration, her face scrunched. Wiggling her hips, she held the bat in a death grip and proceeded to strike out. "Sorry guys. Did I fail to mention that I suck at baseball?"

Clayton patted her arm, "That's okay, Cassie."

Eli bent down and brushed the corner of her lips with his, "You could have given me a heads up." She smacked his butt as he headed for the outfield.

In the first inning, Silas scored for his team, surprising everyone including himself, when he hit a home run first time up at bat. Clay was so excited, that he left his position by Eli in outfield to run the bases with Si. In the end, it wasn't enough. The final score was six-four in team one's favor.

"We won!" Clayton said. His cheeks flushed with excitement as he high-fived the entire team. Eli slung his arm across Cassie's shoulders and she was so content in that moment that she thought her heart might burst. Eli's warm body nestled next to hers, took away some of the autumn chill she felt now that they weren't moving.

Abby had already prepared potato salad and green beans with ham hocks to go along with the hot dogs and hamburgers. All they had to do was fire up the grill. For Cassie it was almost like a fairy tale.

"What're you thinking about?" Eli asked.

Cassie met his bright hazel eyes, so vibrant and full of life. "About how surreal this all seems at times. You know? It's as if I rubbed some genie's lamp or some damn thing. I went from me and Silas to a baseball team for God's sake." She laughed. "It's a lot to take in sometimes."

Eli frowned. "It's not too much is it?"

"Gawd no! I like it so much it scares the bejesus out of me."

Eli's face relaxed into a lazy grin. "Why don't we head to the bedroom and discuss this a little further before supper."

"Um, that would be a hell no. I'm not about to get on Bill and Abby's bad side by getting out of chores. We've got mouths to feed." Eli kissed the tip of her cold nose and escorted her to the lodge.

41

When Eli entered the house and saw Cassie and his mom sitting in front of the fire knitting together, it did something to him. His mom had been teaching Cassie how to knit for the last month and she had a pretty large swatch of pink blanket laid out on her lap. He stood there for a minute watching them before making himself known. The house was decorated for Halloween, large paper spiders crawling up door frames, ceramic jack-o-lanterns and black cats adorning the fireplace mantel.

"Well now, aren't you two a sight for sore eyes."

Cassie looked up at him, her big green eyes sparkling. She held up her pink project for his approval. He grinned and nodded. "Nice. Peanut is going to love it."

"Come over here cowboy," she said patting the cushion beside her. He shrugged off his jacket and hung it up on the coat rack, toed off his boots and joined them in front of the blazing fire.

"Close your eyes and give me your hand." He complied and she placed his palm against her belly. Cassie leaned back against the couch and watched him.

It wasn't too long before he felt it. His eyes popped open wide, his gaze darting to Cassie's face. "Is that what I think it is?" She nodded, her eyes dancing with excitement. "Well, I'll be."

"I know. I'm beside myself. I've been feeling little twinges for the last week, but this here is something."

"Just shy of four months already," Eli said. He put his mouth next to her belly and said, "I feel you, baby girl. You gonna be a soccer player or what?"

Abby laughed. "You two are adorable." She stood up and groaned, massaging her neck. "I sat too long. I'm going to go throw in a load of laundry. Here Eli, you take over my sweater for me." He reached for her yarn and needles and studied the piece to see what stitch she was on, then he began to knit.

"You snake in the grass. You've been holding out on me!" Cassie said, surprised to see him holding his knitting needles like a pro. He smiled without looking up. When a thick lock of hair fell across his brow, he felt her fingers gently brush it aside. "Your nose is still pink. Must be cold out there."

Without his concentration, he replied, "A little brisk, one could say."

Cassie snuggled against him, nuzzling his ear. "Did ya miss me?"

"Hm mm," he murmured, biting back a grin as he

continued to knit, curious to see how far Cass would go to distract him. He liked it.

He detected a pout in her voice when she said, "How's Kiss? I haven't stepped foot in the barn for three days. I'm getting lazy."

"She's happily in love, bunked in the stall next to Freak."

"At least *she's* getting some attention," Cassie mumbled under her breath, but loud enough for him to hear.

Eli set the knitting aside and swiveled to face her. He tilted her chin up with his knuckles. "Is my baby getting bored?" She shook her head and narrowed her eyes, lower lip jutting out. He leaned in and sucked her plump bottom lip into his mouth. She resisted for about a millisecond, then opened to receive him.

When he lifted his head, she said, "It's about damn time. I'm starting to feel like a piece of furniture round here."

He guffawed. "You're kidding, right? I treat you like a princess. I do have to pull my weight around here. As tempting as it is, I can't sit around feeding you bon bons and pork rinds all day." He pushed her down and lay down next to her, pinning her with his thigh. Peppering her face with tiny kisses, she squirmed and giggled.

"Why not?" she said, gasping for breath.

They broke apart as someone cleared his voice. "Sorry to interrupt," Gunner said, smirking. "Dad wants you to work the combine today."

Eli sat up, pulling Cassie with him. "Your turn, bro."

"Dad's call," he said, suppressing a grin. "Guess he likes me better."

"As if that's news," Eli grumbled as he stood up.

"Oh, I don't know. He seems to have softened since you brought Cassie home."

Cassie batted her eyes up at Eli. "See, you'd better treat me right. I'm your lucky charm."

Eli rolled his eyes in response. "Thanks, Gunner. I can always count on you."

Abby entered the room and smiled proudly. "Aren't my boys the most handsome things you ever saw?" They both preened comically, puffing out their chests and grinning wickedly.

Cassie tried not to laugh, but couldn't help herself. "I do think y'all have a screw loose."

"Babe, why don't you sit with me in the combine and keep me company?"

Cassie's eyes widened. "Seriously?"

"Yeah. I'll bring snacks."

"Sold!" she said, jumping up from the couch.

Gunner whistled. "You know you're in love when riding in a combine excites ya."

Sophia walked in and overheard her man teasing Eli and Cassie. She put a hand on her hip and said, "Look who's talking. Gunner's favorite date is taking a nap together."

"I'll go fix you up a snack pack," Abby said.

"I'll go change," Cassie said. She smiled at Eli. "Wait for me."

His eyes burned as they roved over her tight leggings and wooly cropped sweater. Her loose dark hair fell in thick waves around her shoulders. Cassie's breasts were fuller with the pregnancy and her baby bump was the sexiest thing he'd ever seen. "I'm not going anywhere."

42

Eli glanced over at Cassie who was bebopping to whatever tune she was listening to through her earbuds, eyes closed, a smile playing on her lips. *Damn she was beautiful.* Their John Deere combine was a nineteen eighties model, antiquated by today's standards, but plenty good enough for their needs. They only grew enough corn, oats and hay to feed their cattle and horses. The oats and hay had already been harvested, so the corn was the last yield of the year.

Harvesting could be monotonous, but for Eli it was an opportunity to get quiet and think. Currently, he had a whole lot of thinking to do. He always knew his father's master plan was to have him come home. But would his dad really let go of the reins? Could Cassie be happy here? Could *he* be happy, giving up bronc riding?

Honestly there was never a dull moment, from early spring, all through tourist season and right up until late fall and the bitter cold months of winter. There was always something to do. Planting, harvesting, branding, guests, it was a small operation with huge responsibility. His family's legacy, born from a dream, hard work and a bit of luck.

He sighed heavily. Really, as much as he needed to get away when he was younger, out from under his dad's thumb, he loved this land, the ranch, his family. His dad appeared to be softening and their conversation was still fresh in his mind. No doubt they'd always butt heads to some extent, but he was beginning to appreciate all his father had accomplished to provide for his family. Especially since he was about to have a child of his own. And knowing how his father had been raised gave him some insight into his heavy-handed strategy at parenting.

Like she often did, Cassie sensed something was churning inside of him and she pulled out her earbuds, smiling over at him. And that's all it took for him to feel all kinds of hope about their future together. Eli got the feeling sometimes that Cassie was psychic, or connected by some invisible thread, as she reached over and touched his arm.

"You okay cowboy?" she said, talking loud over the noise of the combine.

"Yeah. Just thinking."

She arched a brow. "About?"

"You and me, the baby."

"Hmm. Likewise. Especially after our conversation the other night. Until that night, I'd intentionally been avoiding thinking too far ahead. You know me with my propensity for freakin' the hell out."

"I'm familiar with that aspect, yes."

"So let's just say, theoretical mind you, that you was to take on managing the ranch...I hate to break it to ya like this," she grinned wickedly, "but, you are quite a bit older than me."

He shot her a dirty look. "Your point?"

"Well, what if I was to continue with barrel racing, you know, picking and choosing my favorite venues, for a couple more years," she held up her palm as he was about to protest, "No, it's a lot safer than bronc riding and you know it. No reason we both have to quit."

"Hm. Okay, I'm hearing ya. So we'd live here together and you'd enter some races, and then come right back home to me? Make this your permanent address?"

"That's what I'm proposing as one alternative. Now mind you, I still can't speak for you, pertaining to what's best for you."

He bit the inside of his cheek. "After that spill I took last year, I'm not gonna lie, it's been on my mind that I might not be so lucky next time. Then when we wound up pregnant, changed everything."

She nodded. "Well, my other thought is, now that I'm all grown up and having a baby, what's right for everybody, you know? It's no longer just me...or you and me...we have someone that will be depending on us for everything. Kind of ties up the next eighteen years or so. But I'm also a firm believer that parents get to have a life too. If we're fulfilled, we'll teach our baby how to have a happy life by example."

Eli laughed. "I like the way you think."

"How do you see it?" she asked.

"It must be contagious, because I agree."

"Blame me, I can take it," she said. "Problem is, what do I want? What do you want? You know? I like it here. I think maybe I could phase out racing over the next couple of years, especially if I have something to look forward to here. I really enjoy leading the guests out on the trails. I could help gentle new horses, tend to the herd...stuff like that."

Eli clasped her hand. "Can you really see staying on here at the ranch? Making a life here," he swallowed, "with me?"

Cassie brought their hands to her lips and kissed his. "Elijah Cane, you never cease to amaze me, you know that?"

"Why's that?"

"Well, I don't know...a million reasons...mostly because you just do."

"That clears up everything," he said, chuckling.

"Every time I turn around, you're surprisin' me. Before, I thought you was some hotshot rodeo cowboy with an ego the size of Texas, not a care in the world; turns out, you're a big ole softie. But back to your question, I'm happy here, and if it scares me a little to be so damn content, I'll admit it. I'm trying on different scenarios, to see what makes me feel a green light inside. None of what we're talking about makes me feel dread or heavy. This ranch is a perfect place to raise a child."

She continued, "I still have baggage, stuff I haven't worked out from my past. I don't need to tell you that though, you've had to hold me through enough of my bad dreams. Makes me feel weak. Like I'm not equipped somehow. I can be skipping along, thinking

I'm doing fine and the anxiety takes hold and suddenly I feel like I'll never be right."

"Cass, you're already right. Everybody feels overwhelmed and anxious sometimes. You're one of the strongest people I know. You're not broken, I promise you."

Her green eyes were pools of uncertainty. "You really believe that?"

"I do."

She took a deep breath and exhaled slowly. "Thank you for that. You want to know what I do know? Here's what I know...right this minute...I'm not ready to go anywhere, maybe never will be. I like it here, with you, with your family, Si's in heaven. It feels right. I feel safe and taken care of. The rest will sort itself out. I know you need to work out your part with your father, but no matter what, I'll support you. What's best for you is best for us. Right Clara Bell?" she said patting her belly, then snorted with laughter at his shocked expression.

"Um that would be a no," he said.

"Well Elijah Cane, I reckon Clara Bell is a fine old-fashioned name that's stood the test of time."

"No."

"We'll see about that," she smirked.

He rolled his eyes and mumbled, "Whatever."

Her eyes sparkled with mischief. "I love a smart cowboy."

He shook his head and huffed, "Clara Bell."

He turned his face towards her, keeping his eyes on the endless rows of corn and pursed his lips. "Give me some sugar."

And she did.

43

Cassie smiled to herself. She and Eli along with Becca, Luke, Bill, Abby and Silas sat around the dining room table, playing poker. Clayton sat on Silas's lap helping him. Thanksgiving was tomorrow so there was a festive air to the gathering.

Sighing dramatically, Clayton said, "Silas, when can we play sumthin' else? Puleese! This is boring."

"We're almost done bubby. Why don't cha hop on down and get your Legos? You kin git started and when I finish kickin' the stuffings outta these bumpkins, I'll join ya."

"Deal." He jumped down and ran to his toy box, and pulled out his bag of Legos.

Cassie pressed her thigh against Eli's, her feet wrapped around the legs of her chair. She tried to keep a poker face, which was torture for her. She watched as Eli arranged the cards in his hands, dying to sift through his thick hair, worn longer these days, long enough that it brushed his shirt collar. She liked it that way. He hadn't shaved yet today and his jaw had that designer stubble she found sexy as hell.

Gunner and Sophia were out on a trail ride, opting out of poker night. She happened to catch Abby looking at her with such a maternal expression that Cassie thought she'd melt like a stick of butter from the warmth of it. Abby wore her reading glasses... making her look even more huggable as she smiled at Cassie. There was a time that would have had Cassie running for cover. *My my, what a difference a little time can make.*

She smothered a laugh when Abby's maternal look suddenly morphed into daggers, as she stared directly at her husband. He quickly snatched his hand back from the bowl of chips he'd been reaching for.

"And tomorrow, no gravy or turkey skin. I'll be keeping my eye on you. The doctor said you have to lose weight," she said.

"Yeah, Gramps. The doctor said you have to be good," Clayton added his two cents from the floor as he sorted his tiles by color.

"I know, I know already. How many of you are going to tell me the same thing over and over? In my opinion the holidays should be exempt," Bill grumbled.

Clayton squealed when the hounds began nosing through his neat piles, scattering his Legos, ruining all his efforts at organization. "Lenny, Clifford, no!" Their tails wagged synchronistically, looking very pleased with themselves. Dios pushed his way into the circle, yapping at the two large dogs as if scolding them. "Dios, you're my buddy aren't ya?" Dios climbed onto Clayton's lap and he buried his nose in the dog's soft fur. "Good boy."

Becca shuffled the deck of cards. "I think we should cut Dad some slack. It's not like he has that much to lose and besides that, the doctor gave him a clean bill of health."

"He also said prevention is worth a pound of cure," Abby said.

"After the holidays," Becca insisted.

"Alright, but after tomorrow, we'll work on it."

The crackling fire roared in the fireplace and the house smelled of wood and bread baking. Laughter along with Clayton's constant chatter, filled the air and Cassie wondered how this had happened to her. The baby kicked as if to say, *yo, you're welcome.* She giggled.

"What's funny?" Eli asked.

"The baby just kicked me right when I was wondering how I ended up here in this fairy tale life."

"Taking the credit?"

"Exactly." He chuckled and squeezed her thigh.

The following day, Cassie and Sophia set the large dining room table after adding two leaf extensions. Abby had thrown on a tablecloth with big fat turkeys which color coordinated with the centerpiece the children had bought for their mom. It had five tapered candles, which Sophia now lit, that were nestled in an arrangement with a variety of chrysanthemums in fall colors of orange, rust, burgundy and gold. Indian corn and dried wild grasses added flare to the centerpiece.

"Turkey's coming out," Bill called, carrying a huge platter with the golden-brown bird, partially carved, and setting it by the head of the table. It smelled divine, of rosemary, sage and poultry seasonings. Becca brought several casseroles out from the kitchen, setting them down and returning for more.

"What can I do to help?" Cassie asked.

"Go ahead and have a seat. You can help with clean-up," Abby said. "You too, Eli."

"I get to sit between Cassie and Silas!" Clayton said, grabbing the seat next to her as soon as she sat down. Silas chuckled and took the seat on his other side.

"My lands, is that a green bean casserole?" Silas asked.

"Yep. Mom makes the best," Eli said.

Becca had returned with more food and huffed, "I made that casserole, thank you very much!"

Eli widened his eyes comically and covered his mouth. "Oh no! Mom's taken to poisoning us."

"Hardy har har. Don't eat it then. Next year you can cook the entire meal yourself. About time Mom and I get a break, you ungrateful brat." She put a hand on her hip. "Come to think of it, Sophia baked the bread and the pies for dessert, Dad stuffed the turkey, Gunner mashed the potatoes, and Luke made the cranberry salad. Silas brought in the wood for the fire, Cassie stirred the gravy and Mom did everything else. And you did what, exactly?"

Cassie bit back a smile. She loved the sibling banter, envied it a bit, really. She'd often pined for a brother or sister, which was why her bond with Nash meant so much. He was the next best thing. It brought up the loneliness she experienced growing up, despite how awesome Silas and Reed had been. That ache for something intangible. Shaking off those thoughts, she eyed the huge bowl of mashed potatoes and gravy carafe greedily.

"I opened the wine bottles," Eli retorted.

"Some things never change," Becca said, shaking her head in disgust, but the look she shot her brother was full of adoration.

Clayton cupped his hand over his mouth and pulled Cassie down so he could whisper in her ear, loud enough for everyone to hear. "Cassie, did your mom cook thanksgiving supper for you before, you know, before she went to heaven?"

Cassie swallowed. "Um, I don't rightly I know. I don't remember. I was real young, like you were." Luke, who was sitting directly across from them, narrowed his eyes as if about to intervene, but Cassie shook her head and he stayed silent.

The lump in her throat grew to epic proportions when Clay reached for her hand and grasped it with his small slender fingers. They felt as fragile as a tiny bird in her palm. He looked up at her with his huge brown eyes full of empathy, well beyond his years. She bent down and gently kissed the top of his head. "You're really something special, Clayton Cane." Suddenly shy, he buried his face against her arm. Cassie met Silas's gaze over Clay's head and the corner of his lips crooked up.

"Am I the only one that's starving?" Gunner complained.

"Bring it on," Eli agreed.

Bill took his seat at the head of the table and Abby sat down to his right. Everyone started passing food around the table, and the feast was officially on. Chatter, pleases and thank yous, cutlery clinking against serving bowls, the fireplace crackling, plates passed to the head of the table to be loaded down with turkey, and sent back like a well-honed assembly line. The smells from the roasted turkey, baked pies, and steaming side dishes sent Cassie into an olfactory high.

"So Cassie," Gunner said, swallowing a mouthful of food, "what do you say that we have us a little jam session tonight? Never know when I might need a backup singer. Keep it in the family...know what I mean?"

Cassie felt her cheeks flush. "I was hoping to avoid that topic. Seeing as you've opened for my idol Miranda, the answer is no."

He chuckled. "Come on! Don't be shy now. I'm looking forward to some amazing harmonies."

"Oh yeah, trust me, she's that good bro," Eli said. Cassie shot him a dirty look.

"So I've heard. Si, what do you say? You on banjo, Cass on guitar, you in?"

Silas grinned. "Yep. I think we kin twist someone's arm a little."

Clay reached over and tried tickling Sophia, "Please, Cassie, please."

She held up her hands in surrender. "I give. Okay, I'm in but don't be comparing me. I'm strictly amateur."

Gunner winked. "She's pretty easy Eli, I don't know why you keep saying she's difficult."

Sophia elbowed Gunner in the side. "Trouble-maker. Behave."

"Yes dear."

Thanksgiving cleanup was a piece of cake, even with their overfull bellies. Eli washed and Cassie and Sophia dried, while Gunner had the fun job of putting the dishes away. As usual Luke had disappeared immediately after supper, like a thief in the night. He rarely laughed or even smiled for that matter. Cassie knew his grief ran deep, but she worried for Clay. It was obvious that he adored his father, but was always trying to make him smile or win Luke's approval.

"I'm almost too full to move," Sophia complained.

"Me too," Cassie said.

As Gunner reached over his head to shove a frying pan in the overcrowded pantry, he said, "Cassie, you do know that you're the only girl to ever get my brother to stay put in one place long enough to grow roots? He's like a damn oak tree...roots for miles now. You've gone and done it. Elijah Cane is officially grounded."

"Is that so? If my memory serves me, I had the misfortune to observe him in action the last couple of years. He is legendary, so I wouldn't be too sure 'bout those roots if I was you," Cassie fired back.

Eli raised his brows. "Really Cassie? What's it gonna take to prove my love, huh?" He grabbed her from behind with wet dishwater hands and blew raspberries against the delicate skin of her neck.

She shrieked. “Stop! That tickles.” He lifted her from the ground and she wiggled to free herself.

“Take it back,” Eli commanded.

“Okay. I give...you’re a changed man. Now let me go.” Her pulse skittered. *Don’t read too much into that.*

Lenny and Clifford suddenly deciding it was too much excitement to resist, circled them, barking joyfully. Dios stayed on the sidelines observing.

Breathless from laughing, Cassie panted out, “See, even the dogs are on my side.”

With one last nibble on her neck, he looked at the hounds and set Cassie back on her feet grumbling, “Traitors.”

44

Cassie could see her own breath in the frigid December air as she mucked the last stall of the evening. Bundled up in her Carhartt overalls, jacket, and knit hat, she was toasty warm everywhere except for her cheeks and nose. She took off her gloves and palmed her face, trying to warm them up.

"Buddy, have some hot chocolate," she said, as Clayton reappeared. She twisted off a lid, then handed Clayton a thermos filled with hot cocoa.

He tilted his head back and drank, then smiled at her with chocolate milk rimming his upper lip. "Yummy. Thanks Cass."

"Gotta keep our strength up," she said, then took a large swallow.

Clayton's eyes widened as he locked onto something behind her. Cassie turned to see the tall dark silhouette of a man standing at the barn aisle entrance.

"Hi, can I help you?" she asked.

With the sun going down, she couldn't make out his features in the dimly lit barn. He walked towards her, stopping when he was several feet away.

"Cassie?" he said.

Her heart lurched in her chest as he got close enough for her to make out his features. Cassie racked her brain to place this handsome man, who she was sure she would never forget meeting. He reeked of power, money and confidence. His black hair, vivid blue eyes and gorgeous olive complexion wouldn't easily be forgotten. Yet Cassie couldn't place him. Somehow, she knew him, but she didn't.

She set her rake down and grabbed the stall door for support. All sorts of memories and sensations suddenly flooding her senses. "Do I know you?" she asked, her voice sounding small and tentative.

"I'll go get Uncle Eli," Clayton said, and took off running towards the office.

"Cassie, you probably don't remember me...it was so long ago..."

"Dee," she whispered.

His smile was warm as he nodded. "Yes, that's right. I'm Dimitri. It's been so long. My God. You look exactly like your mom."

"You knew my mom?"

"Yes, I've been trying to find you. Is there a place we can go and talk?"

She stared at him, taking in every last detail, as a warmth spread through her entire being. Her hands were shaking as she tentatively reached towards his face, as if to touch it. "My brother." The words came out of nowhere, surprising her.

He jolted, looking surprised. "Yes. It's been a very long time. I wasn't sure if you'd have any memories of me."

She blinked back tears, as she nodded. "I, um, I, keep having these dreams...and you're in them, except it's not you, I mean, you're young, a teenager, and we're hiding together or sometimes we're playing with my stuffed dog Benny, but in the bad dreams we're hiding and people are fighting and yelling and I'm crying and you're holding me...and I..." she buried her face in her palms. Cassie felt a firm hand press against her back.

"I'm Elijah Cane, what can I do for you?" He protectively stepped in front of Cassie, placing himself between them.

Dimitri stuck out his hand and said, "Hello, I'm Dimitri Petrov. I'm sorry to show up unexpectedly, but I've been trying to find Cassie for the last ten months. When my PI finally located her, I was so excited I didn't take the time to think things through, I just hopped in my plane and flew here."

Eli frowned, concern etching his face. "What business do you have with Cassie?"

Cassie touched his arm and said, "It's okay Eli. He means no harm. He's my...my, um, my brother."

Eli's mouth gaped open, eyes widening, suddenly putting it together. "Petrov."

"Yes. Is there somewhere we can go to talk? Preferably someplace a little warmer?" He smiled, his eyes keen with intelligence, yet kind.

"Of course." Elijah looked at Cassie and said, "Let's see if Silas is home. I think he'd like to be in on this conversation." Cassie nodded her agreement.

"I sent Clayton home to warm up and get ready for bed," Eli said. "Follow me," he took Cassie's gloved hand in his. They left the barn in silence.

A flood of emotions warred for her attention as they trudged through the snow to Silas's cabin. He'd reluctantly moved out of his RV and into a cabin for the winter, at everyone's insistence.

Eli stepped onto the front porch and knocked before trying the knob. It was unlocked so he stepped inside, calling out, "Hey, Si, are ya home?"

A gruff voice called out from the back of the house. "Comin'. Don't git yer panties in a twist." Dimitri smiled at Silas's comments as Eli turned to let them in.

45

Dimitri followed Cassie and stood just inside the door, his lithe body a few inches taller than Elijah's six-foot frame. Cassie's eyes were glued to his face as she studied him, remembering his deep blue eyes and dark hair. She recalled the sense of warmth and safety he'd provided for her all those years ago. It all came floating through her consciousness like a mist, a sensation, then an image, then a childish impression of hero worship. That she had loved this boy/man, there was no doubt. Once upon a time, he'd been everything to her.

Silas stiffened and stood stock still, his eyes flickering with recognition, when he saw the tall man standing in his entry. "I s'pose you should come on inside and take a seat," he said. "I'll put on a pot a coffee. Hang yer coats up on those pegs by the door."

Eli helped Cassie take her coat off and Dimitri's eyes widened when he saw Cassie's pregnant belly.

"You're having a baby?" He asked.

"Yes."

"Wow! Congratulations."

"You have any kids?" she asked.

"No."

There was an awkward silence, then Silas said, "What cha waitin' fer, come on in and have a seat fer cryin' out loud." Dimitri bit back another smile.

"Where you from?" Cassie asked, as they sat down at the small kitchen table.

"Vegas. I own several hotels and casinos on the strip. Well, they were my father's, now I'm running them."

"Oh, sounds exciting," Cassie said, even as something niggled the back of her brain. She'd never been to Vegas, least she didn't think she had, but an image of gilded banisters and marble floors flitted through her memory.

Silas pulled out the half and half from the fridge and grabbed a sugar bowl, setting them both on the table. Eli sat with his arms crossed, distrust hovering over his dark expression. His knitted brows and clenched jaw were a deviation from his normally open and friendly countenance.

"How did you find us? You mentioned a PI?" Eli asked.

"Yes. Our father," he paused, seeing Cassie's face blanch, "passed away in February. That's when I started looking for Cassie."

Cassie looked puzzled. *Our father?*

Silas held up his hand. "Wait a minute, son. Reckon we should slow down. Hain't no hurry now, is there?"

"No sir."

"Eli would ya do the honors and pour the coffee? I'm gonna go get something from the back."

"Sure thing, Si. Careful now," Eli said, filling Dimitri's mug. "Silas's coffee is known to put hair on your chest."

Dimitri chuckled. "Got enough of that."

Cassie couldn't take her eyes off of Dimitri. Not only was he handsome, but she was amazed at how self-possessed he was. If he was uncomfortable, he certainly didn't show it. She on the other hand, had to clasp her hands to keep from fidgeting. Eli handed her a mug of steaming hot coffee and she was grateful for something to do. She poured a heap of creamer in and stirred before taking a sip.

Dimitri stirred creamer into his coffee. A gold Rolex watch gleamed against his tanned wrist, which was covered with a light dusting of dark hair. Even the way he stirred his coffee was elegant and poised. It was slightly intimidating. He was kind of the antithesis of the cowboys Cassie'd grown up around.

Silas returned with a couple of photographs, which he handed to Cassie and Dimitri, before sitting down. Shards of memories pierced through as she studied the photograph of herself sitting on her mom's lap with a young Dimitri and presumably the father he'd referred to. She *had* known him. Had surely loved him. *But he wasn't a man back then. He'd been a boy, barely a teenager.*

"It's you," Cassie said, voice hushed. Her eyes met Dimitri's. "I do remember you. Your eyes. How nice you were to me."

"Our father was Maxim Petrov. We had different mothers."

Cassie looked at Silas. "But...I...I thought we didn't know who my daddy was?"

"Reed and me always meant to tell ya when ya got bigger, but never seemed like the right time. You never acted curious 'bout it, so we avoided the subject. When ya started with them nightmares, we decided it best to let the past go." Eli slipped his arm around her waist, resting his palm on her hip.

Dimitri's voice was low and urgent. "I was devastated when you and your mom left. But I was a kid and powerless to do anything about it. And I understood why she had to leave. Our father was a son-of-a-bitch. You and Nicky were the only bright spots in my life when I had to be at my father's. Before your mom came along, I hated it there with every fiber of my being. She made it tolerable."

Dimitri grimaced, and for the first time Cassie saw a crack in his polished persona. "It wasn't always horrible for your mom. They seemed happy when they first got together. I was six. My parents were already divorced. Dad worshipped your mom. At some point something changed and things got dark. I loved her, Cassie. She was so special. I loved you, too. I was a lonely rich kid, sequestered from the world, and then you came along. You were the only sibling I had. You adored me...and that meant everything. And your mom, well, she was like a beautiful angel. I was beginning to doubt that I'd ever find you." His voice was gruff as he said, "I'm astounded by how much you resemble her. You really look exactly like her."

Silas interrupted. "I don't mean to offend, mind ya, but how do we know that your old man hain't behind this and didn't put ya up to it," Silas said.

Dimitri held up a satchel he'd been carrying and tilted his head towards it. "It's all here. I've got the death certificate, the obituary."

Cassie's brow furrowed. "I can't wrap my mind around everything." Feeling panicked, she glanced at Eli, seeking comfort. His warm gaze made her throat tighten. She pleaded with her eyes.

Eli immediately took charge. "Listen Dimitri, Silas, as much as I know there are things that need to get sorted, how about we shelve the revelations for tonight and visit. I think we've gone far enough down memory lane for one night. Let's let Cass and her brother get reacquainted for a bit, then call it a day. We can pick up where we left off tomorrow." Cassie's body sagged with relief.

Silas took inventory of the situation and agreed. "I agree. Too wet to plow anyhow. Break will do us some good."

Dimitri said, "Good coffee. Warming me up from the inside out. It's colder than hell out there."

"Where ya staying boy?" Silas asked.

"Didn't make arrangements yet. Figured this time of year, it wouldn't be too difficult to find a place."

"How 'bout you stay right here with me. I got me an extry bedroom."

"I appreciate the offer, Silas."

"We kin have us a nice big breakfast in the mornin', then compare notes."

Dimitri put his hand on Cassie's shoulder. "You look like you could curl up and fall asleep right now."

Cassie wrinkled her nose. "I'm not gonna lie, it's a pretty big shock, you showing up out of nowhere. I don't know up from down."

"I'm sorry. I don't think there is such a thing as perfect timing. I was so happy to finally know where you were that I came immediately. Honestly, when I decided to find you, I didn't know if you were dead or alive. I only knew I needed to find out one way or another. But you're here and safe and, I...I'm so very very glad about that."

Cassie tilted her head. "Why were you looking for me? After all this time, why now?"

"I think Eli is right." Dimitri said. "Let's save that conversation for tomorrow. I wouldn't mind having a friendly game of cards though. Anyone else?"

Cassie smiled. "Perfect."

Silas stood and stiffly walked to a kitchen drawer, pulling out a deck of cards. "Poker?"

"Of course, what else is there?" Eli said. "I'll light a fire." Eli threw a couple logs in the fireplace and before long, a toasty warmth emanated from the fireplace. They sat around a small four-chair kitchen table and Cassie dealt the first hand. Happy for the social ice-breaker, relief coursed through her and she began to relax.

"Anyone want a snort of whiskey?" Silas asked.

"Sounds good to me," Dimitri said.

"Me too," Eli agreed.

They settled in for a night of cards and getting acquainted. Before long, Cassie spotted glimpses of the boy she had known with his ready smile and warm eyes. He was also loads of fun and had an easy-going countenance that put everyone at ease.

"I swear Cassie, you still have that same determined look you wore when you were four," Dimitri said, chuckling. He imitated her, the tip of his tongue out, scowling at his cards as if willing them into submission.

"I don't look like that, and anyhow, look who's talking," she chided. "For a guy who grew up in a casino, you sure give lots of tells. I can see whether your cards are good or not, like the second you fan them out."

He winked. "Don't be talking trash, sore loser isn't a good look on you."

She sputtered. "I don't see a pile of coins sitting in front of you!"

"Hey, at least I have a bigger pile than you do." She glanced down at her winnings and grinned up at him.

By evening's end, her walls had crumbled and her heart was full and open, inviting him in. She almost couldn't believe it was true. *I have a brother! He had loved my mama and me.*

46

The next day, after breakfast, they were congregated right back where they'd been sitting till one am the night before. In Silas's kitchen.

"Feels like déjà vu all over again," Eli joked.

"I s'pose, even I know that's a tired-ass joke," Silas said, lips twitching, his right cheek rounded with chewing tobacco.

"I can't be hilarious one hundred percent of the time; even I have my limitations," Eli said, and Silas snorted.

Dimitri sipped his coffee, expression suddenly serious. "I have some things to say, but when I was trying to get to sleep last night, I realized that this is just the beginning. I found my sister and we're going to have a relationship that spans our lives. It all won't all get said in one visit."

He ran his hands through his dark hair. "Cassie, I

don't know how much you've been told about why your mama left. Suffice to say, I couldn't risk trying to find you or your mom while my father was still alive. Even after I'd turned eighteen, I knew he would never forget or forgive. I couldn't risk leading him to you. I figured if he'd given up, you were probably impossible to find anyway. It killed me not to know what had happened to you both. All my father would ever say is that Nicole left, abandoned him without a reason or as much as a goodbye note."

Cassie shook her head sadly. "That must have been so hard for you Dee."

"It really was. I missed you guys and I worried that something bad had happened to you." Cassie looked down at her clasped hands and nodded.

Silas cleared his throat and said, "Now's good a time as any I spect. I have a little information to share with y'all." He opened the wooden box; the one Cassie had been curious about since he'd sat down with it. Cassie noticed Silas exchange a look with Eli before nodding his head slightly. Silas pulled out some old photographs, shuffling through them before passing them to Cassie. He reached back into the box, pulling out an envelope. He studied it, his weathered face suddenly looking every bit his age, his expression sad.

Handing the letter to Cassie he said, "This here letter was from your ma to Reed. It's gonna be hard to read. Just know that she loved ya that much. Okay, Tater?"

Cassie slid the letter out slowly, holding her breath. *I am holding a letter my own mama wrote.* The enormity of that hit her and she squeezed her eyes shut. "I don't know if I can read it right now."

"It's up to you Tater, but ya know we're all her fer ya."

Eli stepped behind her and clasped both her shoulders firmly. "Whatever you want to do."

She tentatively unfolded the letter, her chest tightening at seeing her mother's beautiful cursive writing. The slanted letters and flourished loops gave her a glimpse into her mom's personality, soft, feminine, creative...*my mama wrote this.* Eli leaned down and wrapped his arms around her waist.

My Dearest Reed, If you are reading this it's because...

Cassie's hands trembled as the words poured out onto the page. Her eyes filled with tears and she didn't even notice that they spilled over and down her cheeks. When she finished, it was like she'd found the missing jigsaw piece. The moment her past and present came together. Now she knew who the boogey men were. They'd been real and they'd taken her mama away... Her mother who'd done everything in her power to protect her baby. *To protect me.*

Staring blankly into space, she handed the letter to Dimitri and he began to read. Like Cassie, his blue eyes shimmered with emotion as he read. Dimitri slowly folded the letter and wedged it back inside the envelope. He stood and walked to Cassie's side. Pulling her to her feet, he wrapped her up in a big brotherly bear hug. "You had the best mama, Cassie. She loved you so much. I have so many photographs to show you. Of you and me and Nicky. The way she looks at you in those pictures tells the story." He kissed the top of her head and with one last hug, released her. "We have a whole lot of catching up to do. I have to fly out today, but we've got time."

Her eyes were burning and surely red-rimmed. She sniffled and smiled up at him, then over at Eli. "Our baby is going to have another uncle to love all over her. She's gonna be spoiled rotten."

"You have no idea!" Dimitri said, his eyes sparkling.

"I would like to finish up with a little business... leave it here on the table, if you don't mind? Let's have a seat," Dimitri said. "So, Cassie, I need you to hear me out until the end. Okay?"

"Depends. What's this about?" She took her seat, crossing her arms over her chest.

"The root of all evil, of course. So, I'm sure by now you've figured out that our father was a very rich man, we're talking billions, okay? Not only did he have the hotels and casinos, he'd invested heavily in stocks and did well. Also invested well in the entertainment industry. Some of his dealings were shady; I knew nothing about them until now. I'm still working with lawyers to sort it all out and stay out of trouble myself."

"Surely you can't be responsible for his choices, can you?" She heard the panic in her voice, and Dimitri reached across the table and covered her clasped hands with his.

"I'm not going anywhere, Cass. I won't disappear from your life. Okay? I promise."

She sighed. "Knee jerk reaction."

"I understand."

"Once the estate is settled, you'll take your place as

an equal heir." Cassie sputtered and he held up his hand. "Rightfully so," he said firmly.

"No. I don't want a dime from that monster."

"You may not, but what about your baby?"

Eli interjected, "I can provide for my family. We don't need dirty money."

"Thanks a lot!" Dimitri pinched the bridge of his nose. "Listen, I am bringing everything out in the open, anything that's not legit is gone. I plan on making our legacy something to be proud of. Using our fortune for good. You can't fault me or yourself, Cassie, we didn't do anything wrong, but we can leave the world a better place. Money can do that."

"Dimitri. Thank you from the bottom of my heart. You were as much a victim as Mom and me. And no, we didn't do nothing wrong, but I trust you to do something amazing, truly, I know you will and I'll be cheering you on! But...and I mean it...leave me out of it. End of story."

"Cass..."

She interrupted him, "I can't talk about it anymore. My head is spinning."

"I'll give for now. Things are tied up pretty tight for the moment anyway. I hear what you're saying, but I want you to think about it. Give it a little time. For now, we'll shelve it for another day."

"Dang, I sure kin tell y'all are related," Silas grumbled. "Stubborn as mules."

Dimitri stood. "Get some rest Cass, you look like you've been run over, then they backed up and ran over you again."

She laughed. "I thank you for the compliment."

They went up to the house so Dimitri could say his goodbyes, then he left for the private airport, to return to his glamorous but complicated life.

47

Cassie smiled, listening to Eli singing off key in the shower. A Christmas song no less. "Deck the Halls." *He sure as hell didn't get blessed with the singing gene*. It did something to her...*he* did something to her. His joy was contagious. He was just plain ole fun. Rarely moody, what she used to mistake for shallowness and an 'I don't give a shit' attitude she now knew was his even-tempered disposition. He did care. A whole lot.

She heard the shower stop and soon he was walking towards her wearing only a towel wrapped around his hips. He gave a low wolf whistle as he caught sight of her sprawled out atop their king-sized bed in just a pair of lacy white panties and bra, now two sizes too small. The soft swell of her baby belly was unmistakable.

"I think I've died and gone to heaven." His heated gaze raked over every inch of her naked skin. He threw off his towel, exposing a massive erection. Diving onto the bed, he tugged the cup of her bra aside and nuzzled her engorged breasts. His tongue lapped at her nipple before he sucked it into his wet mouth. She groaned as he suckled and gently bit down on her pink nub. Her fingers slid through his hair and she grasped and pulled hard when he bit down again.

"Mm," he said. "I like that." He slung his thigh across hers and rubbed his stiff cock against her. It was long and thick and she could feel his moist arousal against her hip. She groaned when he slipped his hand beneath the lace and dipped his finger inside her.

"You're so wet for me," he growled.

She spread her legs wide, inviting his touch.

"Roll onto your side."

She complied, rolling away from him and pressing her buttocks against his hard shaft. He bit her shoulder and she shuddered.

"Please," she moaned.

"What baby?"

"Eli...please."

He unclasped her bra and slid the straps down her arms then tossed it aside. Kissing her shoulder, licking and nibbling his way up her neck, he pulled her heavy curtain of hair aside and sucked her skin at the sensitive spot below her ear as his hands returned to her full breasts. When he pinched her nipples she bucked against him, grinding into his groin.

"You like that?" He asked.

"Yes." A hand slid down her waist and he tugged her panties over her ass and thighs, then toed them the rest of the way off.

The head of his cock pressed against the cleft of her buttocks. She arched her back and he slid between her legs. Gripping his shaft, he positioned it at Cassie's wet entry, hovering there, teasing her, while she moaned for him. Reaching back, she spread herself, giving him better access as she ground against him. With one hard thrust, he was fully seated. He stilled for a long moment until Cassie squirmed against him, half-crazy with want. Then he began to pump, slowly at first, sliding in and out languidly. Her receptive vagina gripped him hard and he grunted, then began to thrust in earnest, picking up speed, pounding as she let out a soft cry.

Holding her hips, his fingers dug into her soft flesh as he rocked with more force, riding her, murmuring in her ear, "Cassie, you feel so damn good. I'm not going to last long." Panting, his open mouth sucked on her neck and reached around rubbing his fingers against her sweet spot. She could tell when he was about to come, because his rhythm became unsteady and his body jerked, then stiffened.

Suddenly he climaxed at the same time she exploded into orgasm. She called out as they rode wave after wave together. Her body shuddered, racked with sensation, she reached behind to grab his hair and weave her fingers through the black strands, tightening her grip as he hissed in her ear.

His voice was low and gravelly. "Cassie, I've never desired anyone as much as I do you. You're like a drug. I'll never get enough."

She sighed, her tremors subsiding, now more like aftershocks. Her body felt lazy and relaxed, and utterly satiated. She reveled in the feeling that she'd been consumed by Elijah. A satisfied smile played around her lips, as she snuggled her back against the soft fur of his hard chest. Yawning she said, "Tell me more, cowboy."

She felt like liquid fire was licking her skin as he began to kiss his way down her spine, all the way to her crease, then back up again. "Mm," he growled low, into her ear. "I love your body, Cass. I love you."

She froze. "Um, what?"

"I said, I love you."

She turned over to face him, running her fingertips across his chest as she looked up at him through her thick lashes. "You do?"

"Cassie, I've only said that to one other girl in my life and compared to what I feel for you, it was a complete overstatement of epic proportions."

Cass slid her palms up his chest, then wrapped them around his neck. Pulling his head down to hers, she let her tongue sweep across his bottom lip before sucking it in. She continued kissing him, letting her tongue dart in and out of his mouth with small kitten-like licks, until she felt his cock kick against her swollen belly. She reached down between them to stroke him, then whispered, "My my, quite the recovery. Could be a record."

He chuckled then grabbed her wrist and pulled her hand away. "Cassie, let's be serious for a minute. Now that Gunner and Soph are planning on moving to Nashville full time, their house will be available for us. That means we wouldn't have to build...that is, if you're still planning to stay on here. With me. We could move in the first of January."

Cassie smoothed his full bottom lip with her thumb and squinted up at him. "I reckon."

Rolling his eyes, he said, "You reckon?"

She thoroughly enjoying teasing him, but the doubt in his eyes made her cave. "You know that old song, about not letting your babies grow up to be cowboys? Thank God Abby ignored that little piece of advice. I'd have missed out on the best thing that ever happened to me. I love you, Elijah Cane. Every single inch of you. And yes, I want to stay and raise our babies here."

"Babies?"

"You heard right. I didn't grow up with siblings, I'm not about to let that happen to Clara Bell."

"We've got to come up with a name, before this one sticks," he grumbled.

"How about Piper?" she said.

"Hm. Piper, it's alright, better than Clara Bell."

"Let's try it on for size," she said.

"I'm all on that." He pressed his lips to her belly and said, "What do you think, Piper?"

48

Elijah held his camera, scanning the scene in his parent's living room, waiting to capture just the right moments. He felt a lump in his throat, catching Cassie and his father in the lens. Their heads were bent over together helping Clayton assemble his transformer, left by Santa in the wee hours of the night. He clicked, then studied the image. *Keeper.*

The massive tree was full of twinkling, multi-colored lights which reflected off the tinsel and ornaments. Gunner strummed his guitar, singing "Silent Night" while Silas picked his banjo. Sophia sat on the floor next to Gunner, leaning against his chair, her hand cupping his calf. *Click.*

Eli smirked when Cassie began to harmonize, he knew she couldn't help herself, any more than she could forget to breathe. Music was inside of her. He glanced at his mom, who was watching him, and nodded. She nodded back and he quietly slipped unnoticed out of the room.

He reached into the back of his drawer and pulled out the jewelers' ring box, and lifted the lid...just to be sure it was still there. The vivid green square-cut emerald was surrounded on two sides by sparkling diamonds. The emerald reminded him of Cassie's eyes. It was perfect.

When he entered the living room, Cassie's brows rose in question and he casually shrugged. *So much for unnoticed.* Eli waited until Becca and Luke returned from the kitchen because he wanted everyone there. Behind Cassie's back he stuck his thumb up at Gunner, who winked.

Gunner began picking out notes on his guitar, a beautiful prelude that captured everyone's attention. Everyone that is, but Cassie, who was the only one unaware of what was coming. Gunner began to sing, and the beautiful words and melody of Train's "Marry Me" filled the air like an achy caress. It was perfect.

*Forever can never be long enough for me...Forget the world...*When Gunner got to the line *Marry me,* Eli watched Cassie's head lift, her eyes urgently seeking out his. He could barely breathe around the tightness in his chest. As he approached and sank down on one knee, her eyes shimmered with tears.

Elijah's voice broke, "Cassie, just like the song says, love surely has shifted my way. I never knew it could be like this. I need you by my side, I want to wake up every single morning and see you first thing, the second my eyes pop open. I want to grow old with you, raise a family. You and me, babe. Will you marry me?"

The tears spilled out and ran down her cheeks.

Eli leaned in a kissed them away. "I love you, Cassie."

There was a long pause.

"Why is she crying? Is she gonna say yes?" Clayton said, unable to contain himself another moment. The room erupted in laughter.

Cassie smiled through her tears and threw her arms around Eli's neck, burying her face. Her voice muffled, she said, "Yes, yes, yes."

Silas's eyes were unusually bright. "I'm 'bout as happy as a hog in mud."

Much later as they prepared for bed, Cassie met Eli's gaze in the bathroom mirror and grinned. "Pinch me right now. If I told anyone that country star Gunner Cane would serenade me during my weddin' proposal, they'd think I was a few pickles short of a barrel. That was the most romantic thing ever. Topped every romantic movie, even *Sleepless in Seattle.*"

"Wow. I think I've gone and shot myself in the foot. How will I ever impress you again?"

She turned him to face her and stood on her tiptoes to reach his lips. Pulling his head down, she pressed them softly against his. "You impress me every damn day. I am so happy right now I could burst."

"Me too. Let's go to bed." Eli scooped her up into his arms and carried her to their bed. He crawled in beside her and tenderly kissed her lips.

"You taste like toothpaste," she said.

"You smell like summer," he replied. Yawning he said, "Turn around." She turned her back to him and he spooned against her, legs entangled, her soft bottom tucked close against his groin, their bodies a perfect fit. He reached behind him to turn off the bedside lamp and then buried his face in her neck, holding her close. They were both asleep within minutes.

EPILOGUE

EIGHTEEN MONTHS LATER

Cassie and Eli were on the road, Vegas bound, heading for a meeting with Dimitri. "He was so mysterious on the phone. What do you think he's up to?" Cassie asked.

"Hard telling."

"I'm sure it has something to do with that damn inheritance he's trying to shove on me. He was so insistent we meet."

Eli chuckled. "We're so close it was kind of a no brainer. You act like he's trying to poison you or something."

"Feels like the same thing. Poison my soul."

"Aren't you being a little dramatic?"

"Far as I'm concerned, the man who will remain unnamed ruined my mom's life."

They pulled up to the entrance as instructed and the valet parked their Silverado. Trying not to be nervous, Cassie clung to Eli's arm for support. *I suppose*

Dimitri is Vegas royalty. Certainly, his father had been, and now he'd assumed his position and was worth billions, a very rich man indeed.

When they entered the opulent Golden Gate Casino, they'd been met by several beefy security guards who then escorted them through the grand lobby to the elevators leading up to Dimitri's private office suites. Cassie tried not to gape at the extravagances as they fell in line behind the guards. She held Eli's hand in a death grip and he smiled down at her encouragingly.

Leaning down, he whispered against her ear. "It's going to be fine. It's Dimitri after all, but I won't leave your side."

Cassie gazed up at him, chewing on her bottom lip. "This place is intimidating as hell."

One could practically smell money as the elevator doors swished open, directly into the swanky waiting area. The entire outer wall were windows, providing a breathtaking view of the Vegas strip. No expense had been spared.

The furnishings were luxurious with plush leather couches and chairs, a wet bar, and a large screen TV running a silent, continuous loop of dazzling photographs of the Petrovs' Vegas real estate. Soft jazz played in the background. The thick plush carpeting buffered any other sounds, lending to the sense that they'd been swallowed into the lap of luxury, an invitation to partake of the riches being offered.

Sacha, who'd introduced himself as Dimitri's assistant, had taken over the minute they exited the elevator and the beefcake goons had vanished. After motioning them to sit, he disappeared, leaving Cassie and Eli alone.

"What if he won't take no for an answer?"

"He's not some monster, Cass. He wants what's best for you."

"I know."

"We don't even know what he wants yet. It could have nothing to do with an inheritance. Let's not borrow trouble."

A gorgeous statuesque blonde appeared from the back offices, wearing a tight navy skirt with a matching blazer, the neckline of her white silk blouse plunged daringly low, revealing ample breasts. "Can I offer either of you something to drink or to snack on? A cocktail perhaps?"

"No thank you," Cassie said.

"We also have coffee or water, even soft drinks. We have a killer shrimp or scallop appetizer. I can order anything you like. Just say the word. Mr. Petrov will be with you shortly. His conference call is running over. He asked that I apologize for the delay."

"No problem," Eli said. "I'll take you up on that offer of a bottled water though."

"Certainly." She strode confidently in her stiletto heels; reaching the wet bar, she pulled out a bottled water from the fridge.

Cassie leaned in close and whispered, "Professionalism, Vegas style I'm supposin'." Eli suppressed a grin.

"Here ya go. I'll check back in a few minutes. Hopefully you won't have to wait too long."

"Thanks," Eli said, unscrewing the cap and slugging down half the bottle.

"Okay, we're here, and I'm still as nervous as a cat on a hot tin roof," Cassie said. "You're so damn calm it's irritating," she hissed.

"You want me to be freakin' out too?"

"No, guess not." Eli tilted her chin up with his knuckles and planted a soft kiss at the corner of her parted lips, just as Petrov's assistant re-emerged.

Sacha bowed his head slightly and said, "Follow me. Mr. Petrov will see you now."

Their footfalls were swallowed up as they made their way silently along the long wide corridor. When they reached the very end, they were ushered inside another office with an even more breathtaking view of the city that never sleeps. Cassie's heart squeezed when she looked into Dimitri's warm eyes. That surreal feeling she'd had before pierced through her again. Flashes from her childhood that left as quickly as they appeared, leaving her unsettled.

"Cassie, Elijah, welcome. Have a seat." He waved to the comfortable club chairs and loveseat.

He walked around his massive desk and sat down on a chair across from them. His deep blue eyes roved over Cassie's face, taking in every detail. "Thanks for coming."

"Of course."

"How's my goddaughter?"

"The best. Waiting for us back at the rodeo. When are you coming for a visit?"

"Soon, Cassie, I know I've been saying that but I promise, soon. I'm sorry I've been so secretive about this visit."

"Ya think?"

He shrugged. "I think you'll understand why very soon."

He nodded to his assistant who pointed a remote at the huge screen mounted on the wall and the screen lit up.

"Watch this," Dimitri said, his eyes sparkling with barely contained excitement.

The short feature film was done documentary style. The opening title said **The Nicole Valentine Foundation** above a stunning photograph of her mother taking up the full screen. Next was a video clip of a beautiful life-sized bronze sculpture of a woman, her long hair and dress windblown, a hand cupped above her brows, appearing to be looking off at the distant horizon. Cassie swallowed hard. Next to the woman, a small child in a dress and cowboy boots, clung to her mother's leg, staring up adoringly. The statue sat in the middle of a fountain, the water cascading around the feet of the woman and child.

Cassie whispered, "It's beautiful."

Dimitri said, "You like it?"

Cassie nodded, afraid to try and talk around the lump in her throat. The film continued, and Cassie tuned into the words. It was about a non-profit center being built in Las Vegas for abused and battered women and their children, or any women who found themselves homeless for whatever reason. A temporary safe haven that would retrain and help women find jobs, provide food, clothing and shelter until they could get back on their feet again. It was on a grand scale with plans to expand to other states.

The film ended with a portion of the letter Nicole

had written to Reed. And there it was, for the whole world to see. Her last unselfish act, one of desperation and love. *He will always be looking for me, hunting me down like his prey. If I'm lucky enough to escape again, I can no longer keep my daughter with me. To keep her safe, I have to let her go. I can never come back and don't try to find me. My wish is that you tell her that her that I died and that I was raising her alone. That way she'll be safer from the truth and from danger. I'm hoping that this trauma will fade quickly and that she won't remember. She's only four. I know you'll raise her right. Please forgive me. All my love, always, Nicky.*

The credits rolled then at the very end a dedication filled the screen.

Dedicated to an angel that walked among us, whose short life exemplified a mother's love and sacrifice. Nicole Valentine, may your spirit soar forever and may no woman ever be faced with the impossible choices you made.

Eli stood and pulled Cassie into his arms, settling back on his chair with her in his lap. She sobbed like her heart was breaking. She cried for her mom, she cried for herself, she cried for Reed and Silas and Dimitri. But somehow when her tears subsided and became hiccups, she felt at peace. This center honoring her mother's memory, her courage, meant everything. Somehow, she felt like Reed and Nicole were together, and that this one thing gave purpose to the unthinkable.

"Thank you, Dimitri," she said from Eli's lap.

"I love you, sis."

"I love you too, Dee."

. . .

An hour later Eli and Cassie were back on the road returning to the rodeo camp grounds where Silas, Clay and baby Piper were waiting. Cassie had a big competition the following morning.

"Can you believe he did that for Mama?"

Eli took his hand off the wheel, long enough to stroke her cheek.

"He really loved her. And you. Yeah, it is something pretty special. It's way cool too, Dee asking if you wanted to help with the center."

She wrinkled her nose. "I'll have to think on it." She patted her belly. "With Junior on the way, I doubt I'll be doing much barrel racing the next couple of years, so it could work."

"Up to you, but worth considering. I think it'll be rewarding. Most of it would be online. Some back and forth to Vegas, he said."

The hum of the highway soon lulled Cassie to sleep and she didn't wake up until they were parked with Eli kissing her awake.

"We're here."

"Um...give me five minutes."

"No, wake up. You can go straight to bed and I'll take care of Piper, but you have to get in your own bed. You've got a big competition in the morning."

"Oh, alright bossy." She crawled out of the truck and practically sleep-walked to their trailer. Silas greeted them, told them Piper and Clay were already asleep, then went to bed himself. Cassie washed her face and brushed her teeth then collapsed onto the bed. By the time Eli had finished in the bathroom, Cassie was fast asleep.

Elijah held his fourteen-month-old daughter on his hip, pointing to the barrel racing entrance. "Piper, there's your mama. See? She's getting ready to start."

"Mama ma ma," her tiny face split in a wide grin, her chubby fingers pointing in the direction of Kiss and her mom. Eli couldn't look at his daughter without wanting to squeeze her tight. He rubbed his chin against her soft downlike hair. She smelled of baby lotion and shampoo.

"That's right."

"Da, da, da, da."

"Yes, pumpkin, I'm your daddy."

She grinned, then buried her face in his neck and his heart ached with a love so fierce, he couldn't have described it if his life depended on it. Primal. Abiding. Unconditional.

Clayton climbed onto the rail so he could have a better view of his latest obsession, his little cousin Piper. He grabbed her tiny cowboy boots and snickered. "Those are the smallest boots I ever saw. Okay, Piper, see those big barrels? Red, white and blue, you know those colors?" He grabbed his shirt and pulled it away from his chest and looked down. "See, my shirt is red. Do you get it? Now look over there." He pointed to the barrel, then his shirt. "Red and red. See my blue jeans? Blue, and blue. Your daddy's shirt is white. White there, white here," he said poking Eli's shirt.

"Yum yum," she grunted, reaching toward a child carrying a pink swirl of cotton candy, opening and closing her fists.

"You can have some later, but Piper pay attention," Clayton said, rolling his eyes. "Your mama has to ride around them barrels real fast. You just wait. She's gonna win."

"Cay Cay." She lunged for him, grabbing a handful of his thick mop of dark curls. He giggled and tried to pry her fingers off. "Let go you little muppet. That hurts." She pulled harder.

"Piper, let go of Clayton's hair," Eli said. She grinned and tightened her grip. After Eli finally managed to free Clayton's hair, Clay rubbed his head, grinning happily.

"Just like her mama," Silas said, chuckling.

"Right down to her wicked green eyes," Eli agreed. "I sure hope Junior takes after me," he joked.

They heard Cassie and Kiss's names announced through the loudspeakers and the crowd cheered. She was favored to win and always a crowd favorite.

"Here comes Mommy!" Eli said, pointing to direct Piper's attention.

Clayton bounced up and down, still perched on the rail, yelling for Cassie and Kiss as they raced by and into the ring at breakneck speed. "Wow!" he cried out.

Piper's eyes were wide. "Ma ma."

Kiss's chestnut coat gleamed, her thick mane a flurry of red as they flew around the barrels. Cassie had splurged on a new set of reins in purple and a matching button-down blouse for herself. She refused to retire her old lucky boots, even though Eli had bought her a brand-new pair for her birthday. The crowd roared as she executed the clover leaf pattern perfectly and exited the stadium, beating her previous record. No one would be able to top her speed. She was a shoe-in for the win.

"Let's go find Cass," Eli said to Clayton. "Now you get to go play putt-putt with Lily and Cissy. Silas, you going with them?"

"They roped me into it," he grumbled.

"Si, how 'bout we make it girls against boys?" Clay jumped up and down with excitement.

"I like them there odds. Deal."

"Piper will probably miss me," he said.

"We'll be putting her down for a nap anyway," Eli said. "She'll probably sleep the whole time you're gone."

This cheered him up considerably. "Then she won't have to miss me."

"Exactly."

Eli put Piper down for a nap and stretched out on the couch waiting for Cass. He thought about where he was now and what he'd been doing two years ago, and could hardly compare it to his present life. Married to the love of his life, one daughter, another baby on the way. In six short months, Piper would have a baby brother. For all Cassie's fears about mothering, she'd taken to it like a duck to water. She hadn't had a bad dream since Dimitri had re-appeared in her life. The human psyche was a mystery, that was for sure. He was about to doze when the screen door squeaked open and there she was. He squinted up at her...*the girl of my dreams.*

"You rode that horse like nobody's business," he said, patting the couch cushion beside him.

"Piper down for a nap?"

"Yep, and Clay and Si just left to play putt-putt. We should have at least an hour to ourselves." Her eyes flashed fire before she toed off her boots and climbed on top, straddling him.

She slid her fingers through his hair and covered his lips with her own. She kissed him hard then tongued his mouth. When she lifted her head to lock eyes, he gently brushed her hair behind her ears.

"You're so damn beautiful, Cassie."

"Tell me all about it, cowboy." She leaned back down, peppering his face with tiny kisses as she rocked her pelvis against his.

"Want to know a secret?" he asked.

"You know I do."

"I think I loved you that very first night, you know, at the bar, when we danced."

"You can say that, even with my sassy mouth?"

He chuckled. "Yes, even with that sharp tongue of yours. I knew I was a goner. When did you know?"

Her eyes looked dreamy, then she said, "The day we shared the earbuds and you listened to my song. Oh, I fought it mind you, but it was no use. I fell into them hazel eyes and it was all over for me. You are the one Elijah Cane, you're officially stuck with me."

He pulled her down into his arms and held her against his chest. She stretched out her entire length and sprawled on top of him. He nuzzled her hair as they lay there, the rise and fall of their chests like floating on a calm lake, the familiar body smells, both heady and comforting, sexy and intimate.

Cassie sighed. "You know Silas was right. When I was trying to adjust to my new life, right after we landed in Wyoming, he said something like this," she lowered her voice, making it gravelly, trying to imitate Si, "*Tater, life takes us places we never would've gone on our own*...then something like this...*So many gal darn twists and turns, but if ya stay open, I spect ya might find out that you kin fall in love with something ya never even dreamed ya wanted.*" Cassie chuckled softly. "I suppose he had it all figured out way before we did."

"There is no doubt in my mind."

Eli felt Cassie relax, her body melting into his. Soon her breathing was steady, her lips occasionally puffing out with her exhale. He closed his eyes and followed her to sleep.

The End...for now

Thanks for reading Cowboy Surprise, Book Two of The Triple C Ranch Series. I so loved these characters and hope you did too! If you haven't read my Billionaire series there's the link below for Book One. Happy Reading!

~Jill Downey

Please Consider leaving a Review on Amazon.com.

I hope you will consider leaving a review on Amazon.com. A rating or even a even a brief comment would be very much appreciated.

Facebook page: search for Author Jill Downey
Here's the universal link to **Book One, *Seduced by a Billionaire***:
mybook.to/SeducedbyaBillionaire

Here's the universal link to **The Heartland Series complete box set:**
mybook.to/BoxSetHeartlandSeries

Please join my **Facebook readers group**, where I have giveaways, teasers and pre-release excerpts:
https://www.facebook.com/groups/1791830500622278/

BOOKS BY JILL DOWNEY

The Heartland Series:

More Than A Boss

More Than A Memory

More Than A Fling

The Heartland Series Box Set

The Carolina Series:

Seduced by a Billionaire

Secret Billionaire

Playboy Billionaire

A Billionaire's Christmas

The Carolina Series Box Set

The Triple C Ranch Series

Cowboy Magic

Cowboy Surprise

Printed in Great Britain
by Amazon